M000207068

DEVILS' ISLAND

Born in 1955 in Reykjavík, EINAR KÁRASON is regarded as the leading author of his generation. *Devils' Island* is the second of his seven novels and has been translated into nine languages. It was made into an award-winning film by Friðrík Thór Friðríksson in 1998. Einar Kárason's trilogy about post-war Reykjavík, which incorporates *Devils' Island*, has sold over 30,000 copies in Iceland, a country of 280,000 inhabitants.

DAVID MACDUFF has translated many works of Russian and Scandinavian literature. His translations of Dostoyevsky's *The House of the Dead*, *Crime and Punishment*, and *The Brothers Karamazov* are published in Penguin Classics.

MAGNUS MAGNUSSON has translated several Icelandic sagas, and five novels by Halldór Laxness – *The Atom Station*, *Paradise Reclaimed*, *The Fish Can Sing*, *World Light*, and *Christianity Under Glacier*.

DEVILS' ISLAND

Translated from the Icelandic by
David MacDuff and Magnus Magnusson

Einar Kárason

CANONGATE

First published in Great Britain in 2000
by Canongate Books Ltd,
14 High Street, Edinburgh EH1 1TE.
First published in 1983
under the title *Djöflaeyjan*
by Mál og Menning, Iceland

10 9 8 7 6 5 4 3 2 1

Devils' Island was translated with the support
of the European Commission and the
Ariane Programme 1999

The publishers gratefully acknowledge general subsidy
from the Scottish Arts Council towards the
Canongate International series

British Library Cataloguing-in-Publication Data
A catalogue record for this book is available on
request from the British Library

ISBN 1 84195 9662

Typeset by Palimpsest Book Production Limited,
Polmont, Stirlingshire
Printed and bound by
Creative Print and Design, Ebbw Vale, Wales

The story is based on fact, although the events and characters are fictitious. This book is dedicated to my friend Þórarin Óskar Þórarinsson:

'Here is another fine mess you've gotten me into, Aggi boy.'

Contents

Foreword

At dawn on 10 May 1940 – the very day on which Germany launched its blitzkrieg assault on the Low Countries and Winston Churchill replaced Neville Chamberlain as the wartime Prime Minister of Britain – a large force of British troops landed at Reykjavík, the capital of the neutral country of Iceland. Warships and troopships filled the outer harbour. Soldiers in khaki and steel helmets poured ashore, unopposed, and took over the main buildings in the town: the Second World War had caught up with Iceland in a big way.

The British occupation of Iceland came about soon after the German invasion of Denmark in April of that year: Iceland, after centuries of being a colony of Denmark, now had Home Rule under a Treaty of Union with the Danish crown, but Germany had laid claim to it nonetheless. Because of the country's immense strategic importance in the middle of the North Atlantic, Britain was desperate to ensure that Iceland should not be occupied by Germany.

The British 'invasion' of Iceland must have been the least hostile invasion ever. In Iceland, although the government lodged a formal protest (of course), most people realised that their country was bound to be drawn into the war, one way or another, and they would rather be occupied by troops from Britain than from Germany. The Icelandic government asked all Icelanders to welcome the soldiers as guests and to treat them accordingly; the British army of occupation promised not to interfere in any way in the governance of the country. There was not much friction, although a left-wing newspaper was closed down and its editors were arrested and shipped off for internment in England (they were released after vigorous protests).

After a few weeks alcohol was rationed (two bottles of spirits or four bottles of wine per month for men, but only half of that for women). Before long the Icelandic authorities were condemning the moral effect of what was delicately called 'the occupation business': in the summer of 1941 the Chief Medical Officer issued a report claiming that no fewer than 500 women (and probably many, many more) in Reykjavík, aged from twelve to sixty-one, were engaged in regular promiscuous conduct (perhaps even prostitution, which had not been known in Iceland before then), resulting in 225 illegitimate births. Icelandic girls who hobnobbed with the occupation troops were ostracised, as girls were in so many other European countries. There was a saying that the only words in Icelandic most of the troops ever learned were *Ekki núna, mamma heima* – 'Not now, mummy home'!

The war bit much more savagely in other ways, however, as Icelandic fishing-boats were targeted by German U-boats: Iceland lost more shipping, and more lives per head of population, than any of the combatant nations.

The arrival of the British troops in 1940 had a major effect on the Icelandic economy: it spelled the abrupt end of the Great Depression of the 1930s which had affected Iceland as severely as any other country in Europe. The army of occupation provided jobs – civilian employment for people who had been out of work for years on end. Commerce and industry of all kinds boomed, money started circulating freely; the cautious husbandry of earlier years gave way to widespread entrepreneurialism. There was work for anyone and everyone, but particularly for manual labourers who could wield a shovel – building roads, airfields and, especially, barracks. Reykjavík was still a relatively small town in those days. Several barracks (*braggar*), or camps (*kampar*), consisting of prefabricated Nissen huts, were constructed on the outskirts of the town.

A year later the American government, still officially neutral but providing Britain with as much behind-the-scenes help as possible, took over the defence of Iceland, in July 1941, and began to replace the British troops. The Americans were better funded and better equipped than the British forces; they started building a major air-base at Keflavík (which has now been transformed into Iceland's magnificent International Airport), 48 kilometres to the south-west of Reykjavík; they brought jeeps and bulldozers and other heavy machinery which few Icelanders had used before, and they provided even more and even better-paid civilian jobs. They also brought their own insistent culture of pop-music, flashy cars, easy money, nylons, Coca-Cola and American slang. A black market in luxuries from the States flourished exuberantly.

The sudden bonanza in Reykjavík created a severe housing shortage as people came pouring in from the country areas to share in the employment boom. Gradually, as the remaining units of the British army were withdrawn, the huge barracks such as 'Camp Thule' were taken over by homeless people in Reykjavík. The barracks districts became near-ghettoes which caused great concern and often dismay among the 'respectable' citizens of bourgeois Reykjavík: to them, the 'barracks people' were no better than feckless riff-raff. Like the pre-fabs of post-war Britain, however, the barracks-huts provided much more than temporary accommodation – they developed a robust community life of their own which lasted until well into the 1950s.

After the war the American troops did not leave, as had been agreed. On the contrary they stayed on to run a massive NATO air-base at Keflavík. By this time, Iceland had revoked the Treaty of Union with Denmark (in 1944) and declared itself an independent republic. Many Icelanders saw the continuing American military presence as an affront to their newly won independence; they were also uneasy about the insidious effect of Americanisation on their ancient language, their culture and their identity.

Such is the historical and geographical context for this novel by Einar Kárason, one of Iceland's outstanding authors. *Devils' Island*, first published in Iceland in 1983 as *Þar sem djöflaeyjan rís* ('Where the Devils' Island Rises'), was his second novel; it sold 30,000 copies – a staggering figure in a country with a population of little more than a quarter of a million. *Devils'*

Island was the first of a trilogy which further chronicled the 'barracks story' – the others were *Gulleyjan* ('Treasure Island', 1985) and *Fyrirheitna landið* ('The Promised Land', 1989). The first two novels formed the basis of a full-length feature film, *Devils' Island*, directed by Friðrík Thór Friðríksson, which won the Best Nordic Film Award in 1997 and has been shown at film festivals in Britain to considerable critical acclaim.

Devils' Island is a roistering, sprawling saga of this seamier side of post-war life on the outskirts of Reykjavík just after the Second World War, when Reykjavík was fast growing into a miniature metropolis. The story chronicles the riotous lives and tribulations, the aspirations and heartaches, of the fecund family circle of Karolina (Lína), the matriarchal fortune-teller, her long-suffering, quietly wise husband Tómas (Tommi) and their grandchildren – Baddi, the young man who visits America and comes back to the Camp as a hard-drinking Elvis Presley worshipper, and his younger brother Danni. A host of other characters, each one different, each one observed and portrayed with verve and irony, fills the pages with energetic life. Many Icelandic readers saw in Lína a thinly disguised portrait of a well-known and colourful Reykjavík woman who lived in the vicinity of the Camp and who grew rich from telling the fortunes of young girls and boys with yearnings for the future.

Devils' Island evokes a vivid picture of an urban subculture living on the periphery of accepted social values. It is very funny and very wise at the same time. Its humour is based on character and situation, wry, ironic and understated, written in a sinuous, idiomatic style which catches perfectly the cadences of everyday speech. A remarkable novel, by a remarkable novelist.

Magnus Magnusson KBE
June 2000

Characters (and nicknames)

Ásmundur (Mundi) — son of Dollí
Baddi (Bjarni Heinrich Kreutzhage) — son of Gógó, and foster-grandson of Tommi

Barði Högnason — son of Sæunn the cat-woman
Bjarni 'Tómasson' (Baddi) — son of Gógó, and foster-grandson of Tommi

Buddy (Böðvar) Billó — dance-hall vocalist
Bóbó (Halldór Halldórsson) — son of Dollí and Dóri
Bony Morony (Jakob Tryggvason) — a friend of Baddi
Charlie Brown — Gógó's American husband
Danni (Frank Daniel Levine) — son of Gógó
Diddi (Víkingur) Traustason — son of Thórgunnur
Dollí (Doróthea Giuccardini) — daughter of Gógó
Dóri (Halldór) — a joiner, Dollí's lover
Éggvan — A Faroese businessman
Fía (Snæfríður) — married to Tóti (Thorgnýr)
Gerða (HveraGerður) — Baddi's girl-friend
Gillí (Gíslína) — twin daughter of Dollí
Gíslína — sister of Lína (Karolína), and mother of Snjólfur

Gógó — daughter of Lína (Karolína)
Gosi — son of Fía and Tóti
Gréta — wife of Hreggi (Hreggviður)
Grétar — Dollí's ex-boyfriend
Grettir — husband of Dollí
Grjóni (Sigurjón) Traustason — son of Thórgunnur
Guðlaugur — police inspector, cousin of Lína
Gummi — son of Fía and Tóti
Halldór (Dóri) — a joiner, Dollí's lover
Halldór Halldórsson (Bóbó) — son of Dollí and Dóri
Hlynur Ólafsson — a mechanic, husband of Lauga
Högni — husband of Sæunn
Höski (Höskuldur) — a taxi-driver
Höskuldur (Höski) — a taxi-driver
Hreggi (Hreggviður) — a champion shot-putter

Hreggviður Barðason (Hreggi)	a champion shot-putter
Hugrún	sister of Lína (Karolína)
HveraGerður (Gerða)	Baddi's girl-friend
Jakob Tryggvason (Bony Morony)	a friend of Baddi
Kári	the camp Football Club
Karolína (Lína)	a fortune-teller, the matriarch of the family
Lauga (Lopsided Lauga)	wife of Hlynur
Lína (Karolína)	a fortune-teller, the matriarch of the family
Louie Louie (Lúddi)	friend of Baddi
Lúddi (Ludwig Hansson), aka Louie Louie	footballer and friend of Baddi
Maggi Beauty	a trawlerman rowdy
Manni	son of Fía and Tóti
Maríanna	daughter of Hreggi and Gréta
Mási	Tommi's dead brother
Mundi (Ásmundur)	son of Dollí
Ólafur (Óli) Hlynsson	son of Hlynur and Lauga
Ottó Hlynsson	son of Hlynur and Lauga
Sæunn the cat-woman	a neighbour
Sigurjón (Old Sigurjón)	father of Thórgunnur and grand-father of Gjróni
Sigurjón Traustason (Deaf Grjóni)	son of Thórgunnur
Sigurlaug (Lopsided Lauga)	wife of Hlynur
Silla	niece of Lína
Snæfríður (Fía)	wife of Tóti
Snjólfur	nephew of Lína, and son of Gíslína
Stína Begga	mother of Lúddi
Súsanna	daughter of Hreggi and Gréta
Thorgnýr (Tóti)	husband of Fía
Thórgunnur	mother of Grjóni and Diddi
Thórir	a dance-hall rowdy
Toggi (Thorgeir)	a trawlerman
Tómas Tómasson (Tommi)	husband of Lína (Karolína)
Tommi (Tómas Tómasson)	husband of Lína (Karolína)
Tóti (Thorgnýr)	Lína's nephew, husband of Fía
Tóti the Ponce	a dance-hall rowdy
Tryggvi	a dance-hall rowdy
Úlla	baby daughter of Gógó
Viðar	a dance-hall rowdy
Víkingur (Diddi)	son of Thórgunnur

Note on pronunciation

The only extra consonant in Icelandic used in this translation is ð, the so-called 'crossed d' or 'eth', which is pronounced like the voiced *th* in *breathe*.

The pronunciation of the vowels is conditioned by the accents:

á as in *owl*
é as *ye*, in *yet*
í as in *seen*
ó as in *note*
ö as in French *fleur*
ú as in *moon*
ý as in *seen*
æ as in *life*
au as in French *œil*
ei, ey as in *tray*

1

Light in the darkness

That first Christmas in the Old House the family really let itself go. Until then, Christmas had meant at most a candle and a pack of cards and an extra pickle or two with supper in a turf hut or dank den somewhere; that was how it had been for as long as anyone could remember, century after century for more than a thousand years, from the time the first settler had lost his bearings and ended up being shipwrecked on this island. The matriarch of the house, Karolína the fortune-teller, could thank her own wiles and dealings with the worldly powers (both greater and lesser) for the fact that she had neither frozen to death nor died of hunger in one of the arctic winters the Lord gave this country: if Christmas was meant to be a celebration of what life gives us, it was just a joke as far as Karolína was concerned – ha ha ha!

Take Tómas, who was supposed to be the family's breadwinner – he had always got dead drunk at Christmas. It had something to do with his wanderings in his youth and sailing the seven seas, but also because, at Christmas, loneliness is felt most keenly by people who have no other company than some poor devil the trawler-owner has put in the same berth. For all the years since Tómas had given up the sea and Lína had given up trudging through the slush of the city's streets and they had got married, Christmas had been a bit difficult, because both of them were excessively proud. It had to be all or nothing, and there was never anything in that small dark cottage except the noise of children, not all of whom were even theirs – the children were Lína's inheritance from her sister, who was not quite so good at her dealings with the worldly powers and had said farewell to this vale of tears and her fatherless toddlers. Only one of the children was Lína's

– that was Gógó, who had been born long before Tommi came along.

But these were no longer children. The children in the family now were the ones Gógó had been having by various foreigners for the last sixteen years; the three surviving ones lived with Lína and Tommi, whom they called Grandma and Dad. Dollí was the eldest, already a young lady with a sweetheart on her arm. Then there were the two boys: Baddi, who was the apple of everyone's eye, eleven years old, dark-haired, bright-eyed and lively – all the women said he was going to be a real charmer, that one. Then there was Danni: he was nine, with big feet and unsociable as well. A misery, many people said. Danni was often referred to simply as 'the other one'. 'What a lovely child that Baddi is,' people said; and after a pause the ones who liked children would add, 'The other one's more inside himself, sort of.'

Lína and Tommi never had children together, and didn't mind bringing up Gógó's blessed kids so that she could go on enjoying herself with the foreigners. Now she had even gone and married a foreigner, one of the sons of the richest nation in the world, no less. God obviously had a soft spot for Americans, because everything went well for them; and so great was the Lord's mercy that when Gógó married the American, the sun began to shine on Lína's and Tommi's life, too – so much so that they were now celebrating Christmas in a new house which they themselves actually owned.

They were all in their Sunday best. On the Christmas table there was an American turkey and in the parlour stood the prettiest artificial Christmas tree in the land, all silvery and laden with baubles and tinsel. The Christmas decorations had arrived by the crate-load, and there were presents in every nook and cranny. In Tommi's eyes the acme of earthly happiness was to be able to sit in one's own house on festive occasions, wearing one's best clothes and smoking a good cigar. That was how the bosses lived, but Tommi wasn't one of them and never would be, as far as he could tell. But that evening the old warrior sat in an armchair in the parlour in a new brown serge suit, opening a present from his stepdaughter Gógó – a whole box of large, black cigars. As Tommi lit up the first one he felt the tingling of a strange contentment, and had to concentrate on what was happening. For the rest of the evening he sat silently with a silly grin on his face, half suffocating in smoke; so thick was the smoke that you could hardly see from one wall of the room to the other. But the boss went on stoking the blaze; he swallowed the smoke and even swallowed the cigars too. When he stood up at midnight everything went dark before his eyes and it was as much as he could do to stumble off to his bed, where he lay for the next few hours in the cold sweat of nicotine poisoning. Dollí, too, went to bed ill that Christmas night, with a terrible stomach ache. The doctor said she had become constipated from all the excitement, and prescribed castor oil for the young lady – and was she embarrassed!

Old Lína had always been a bit vain and had a weakness for flashy clothes, even though she had never been able to afford anything but ordinary sheep's wool. Now she had been given a floral dress by Gógó, and a pearl necklace and bracelet to go with it, and this worldly woman vanished into the realm of daydreams – she just stood there in front of the mirror, seeing only Queen Victoria in all her regalia. She tried on more bits of finery; she hung Christmas glass beads from her ears, wound tinsel about her head and pinned stars of Bethlehem and coloured birds all over herself. When the doctor who had come to attend to Dollí saw the fortune-teller, he thought she was a madwoman and hardly dared to enter the house.

The boys had been given boxing gloves, and fought one another with increasing violence as the night wore on. Everyone forgot about the candles which burned here and there in the parlour, and when the house was asleep the side table caught fire, as did a box with the discarded Christmas wrappings. The parlour was thick with smoke and flames when, fortunately, Baddi woke up because he needed to go the toilet and was able to wake Grandma and Dad. Tommi grabbed the half-full rubbish bin under the kitchen sink, filled it at the cold tap and threw the lot over the conflagration, then ran back to the kitchen to fill the bin again. Meanwhile Lína rushed through to the scullery where some aprons were soaking in a large tub of water. Without a second's hesitation she hauled the tub into the parlour and emptied it over the fire, which immediately went out with a great hissing of steam. The boys were later to fill that tub in the scullery many a time and try to lift it, but it was too heavy – filled with water it weighed more than a hundred kilos, and it seemed absolutely superhuman that Lína could have moved it. They asked the old woman to repeat this feat of strength, but she swore to Jesus and would not hear of it. So they asked Tommi if it were true, and he put on a distant look and rubbed his temple and said: 'Yes, she saved us that time, all right. The house would have burned to ashes.' But usually Tommi said he didn't want to think about it: it gave him nightmares.

After that there was never so much as a candle-stub lit in that house; candles were banned and condemned as devices from hell. Later on, when people came to the door selling candles in aid of widows and orphans and offered Lína their wares, she called the charity workers 'pyromaniacs' and drove them from the neighbourhood with stones and pebbles.

That first Christmas was completely ruined. There was rubbish and soot all over the best room and the sodden remains of the things which had burned. The family had a bit of a hangover for days. Later, no one was allowed to mention the incident; from that time onwards, Christmas was always the quietest time of the year, real heavenly peace and joy. Light in the darkness.

Light in the darkness.

All around the Old House there were the old Nissen huts of the barracks.

Light . . .

Light shone in the darkness which lay like a pitch-black shroud over that time and the cold ground. The cold wind came blowing from the glacier-peaks. The ocean billows crashed over the shore.

And there was light in the windows of the grey house which was called the Old House from the day it rose from the gravel.

The Old House teemed with life. There was a smell of cooking from the kitchen. There was blazing warmth from the stove. Nothing was beyond the reach of this family, for it saw the whole world as its home; it drove huge chrome-plated limousines which were reckoned to be the finest products of western industry. And the people from the Old House took passage on aeroplanes, roaring, gleaming steel birds which clove the darkness above the seas and managed to find their way to other pinpricks of light which bore witness to life somewhere else on the flat land of the continents. But all roads led back to the Old House, of course, which was always full of clamour and noise. In the kitchen, fortunes were told and magic spells were mumbled. In one of the rooms, over steaming coffee, an accordion played a lively waltz. Someone told anecdotes in a hesitant voice. Children sang, cried and laughed, and tough guys with water-combed hair and sunglasses snapped their fingers in time to loud rock and roll.

'Is the world coming to an end?' people asked.

Some people died, at any rate, and one dark day the Old House itself was obliterated. Yet someone managed to save the light and carry it out of the ruins . . .

Strange.

What was so strange about this family? Was it perhaps the queen herself, Karolína the fortune-teller, who had acquired the reputation of being a bit crazy in those years when she trudged through the slush of the streets of the capital and scared the life out of people in their homes?

Then there was her Gógó, the only child she ever bore – Gógó, who laid the foundations for the whole great family, the whole empire. Gógó might resemble her mother in appearance but she differed from most of the other people in that melancholy town because she was forever smiling, with a gleam of joy in her eyes which spread light everywhere she went. It was odd, because Karolína the fortune-teller was a truly hard-bitten soul who was never seen to smile; she was loud of voice and sharp of tongue and was also thought to be an out-and-out witch. It was nothing short of magical and miraculous that she was able to keep body and soul together, a single mother with a child after she lost her family – her mother and the sisters who had left her nothing but the children. She had to wander about, alone, with Gógó and all those pale-faced orphaned children, and it was common knowledge that she often went without food, money or shelter when pestilence and deadly storms stalked the land and the universe was on fire in the Great World War.

So when, then, did the family's history begin? Perhaps with the birth of Karolína herself, for she was the eldest – if, indeed, it is possible to say that someone is the eldest in a family, because Lína's parents had their history, of course, and so did their parents, and so on, and so on. No, it is probably best to begin the story at the point when Lína married Tommi, who was also alone in the world but who rode the waves lightly, as people do when they have sailed the seven seas for many years and have no other aim in life than to make the best of the day at hand. When Tommi came home he made a certain impression on the town, for he was a good dancer and an agile wrestler. They found one another, he and the woman who had such a dubious reputation that when they got married he was fired from the fine job he had as a sales assistant in a shoeshop.

After that he began to sell goods for various merchants; he became a pedlar, plodding around the town with a horse and cart, which was considered odd, even bizarre. To begin with, Tommi himself considered it bizarre, but there was nothing else for it, and so he just got drunk. Tommi's drinking bouts were long and spectacular, and he always gathered a crowd of happy people around him. They would all come home with him, where Lína would meet them with curses, for she thought that people who drank were possessed by evil spirits; there would then be shouting and fighting in the hovel where they lived in those days. After breaking up the party, Lína would lay a curse on the drinking companions; this curse was said to be highly effective, and people tried to run from it, but Lína pursued them with oaths and incantations, until finally no one dared to drink with Tommi, let alone go home with him, and he was left to stagger about the town on his own, drunk and despairing. This solitary drinking went on until the years of the Great Depression; but it is said that it was not because of the Depression that folk began to go on the town with Tommi again, but rather because the girl children in his home had grown into ladies – nubile, pretty young ladies who were considered free with their favours. Perhaps Tommi's drinking companions hoped for a young girl in their beds as a bonus to their merry-making. Perhaps they got what they wanted, too. The gossip-mongers said that Lína now let the merry-making continue unhindered to a much greater extent than she had done before, because the presence of scantily clad young women made the gentlemen more free with their money and with other items of value which her home sorely needed in those lean years.

Yes, they were much sought after, those young ladies, Lína's nieces; but it was Gógó, Lína's daughter, who was the plum in the pudding, and many a man would have given everything he possessed for her. But Gógó was choosy, and when she had a baby it was not with any old riff-raff in wellies and a balaclava. No, she had the baby of an Italian flying ace who made a stopover in the town, and the little girl was given an Italian name: Dóróthea Giuccardini. This was Dollí, and she was perhaps more patriotic than her mother because she did not use this Italian name and never even learned how to pronounce it.

Gógó had affairs only with foreigners: one baby, a girl who died at birth, was fathered by a Finnish athlete. Then she got engaged to a Danish boy from a training ship, and a long time after the ship departed under full sail she had this very small, sickly baby girl who was given the name Úlla at a hasty home christening, but who nonetheless survived.

Gógó was full of maternal love for these little mites, but she did not allow their illnesses and deaths to unsettle her; she was always cheerful and relaxed and did not hesitate to bring more children of mixed origin into the world. A few months before the Allies occupied Iceland she was pregnant with her first son, Baddi, who she said was the son of a

German orchestral conductor, a highly educated man. The son was given his father's Germanic name: Bjarni Heinrich Kreutzhage.

In those years the Old House did not yet exist. The whole great family lived in a tumbledown shanty they later called the Old Cottage, to distinguish it from the New Cottage which they moved into after the Old House was pulled down. Later still, Baddi called the cottage 'Auschwitz', and Tommi said it had originally been an outhouse belonging to Little Farm, which bore the name with justification.

Then one fine day Tommi took the pledge, and stopped drinking away what little money the household managed to scrape together. Even so, life there was sunk in poverty, as it was in the hovels around it. It was like a village of its own out there in the marshland beyond the city proper. Slowly and steadily the capital crept towards this cluster of houses, which were given names and numbers like other districts in the city, and Lína's and Tommi's family were deemed to live at Little Farm 7c. When the city finally reached all the way to Little Farm district, it brought the great world with it: the Allied troops settled in the neighbourhood, and built military camps they called 'barracks'. These resembled barrels lying on their sides, half-buried in the ground. The Allied troops drove about in jeeps and spoke languages which few people understood apart from one or two globe-trotters like Tommi, the earl of 7c. Tommi would stroll off in the evening to Camp Thule with his hands in his pockets to talk to the 'Charlies', the British soldiers, about the great commercial centres and seaports of Cardiff and Aberdeen, where he knew every seaman's pub from the time around the First World War. Lína was less taken with the Allies: 'What are they doing there sitting on their backsides talking?' she would say. 'The Germans have the Polish Corridor!' The ladies of the Cottage must have liked the Brits, for they visited the barracks often, no doubt to discuss international affairs; the soldiers came visiting the Cottage and in no time at all a tent had been pitched on the grass outside. Later Dollí said that Tommi could not have suffered much from insomnia: throughout the war years he lay there snoring, even though the fires of love were raging in every bed.

Then the Americans arrived, with their pockets stuffed with dollars, and Gógó had her fifth child by one of them. This was Danni, who was given his father's name: Frank Daniel Levine, later changed to Tómasson.

But Gógó did not leave it at that. Only twenty-six, and a mother of five, at the end of the war she had yet another daughter. That ended in tragedy, for when the baby was about a month old an infectious disease broke out in the Cottage, and the child died, and so did little Úlla, who had always been sickly.

Some seeds fall on stony ground . . .

The barracks were remarkable houses; some people even say they were the result of the tireless labours of Europe's finest architects. They were dirt cheap and easy to put up. The gables consisted of two semi-circles of timber, with corrugated iron cladding in between. Inside, a wooden floor sat directly on top of Reykjavík's glacier-raked soil. There was a coal stove with a chimney flue, or smoke-hole, in the ceiling.

In the war years people streamed into the capital, for anyone could get work with the Occupation forces – among other things, putting up barracks. Whole districts spread out across the gravel plains. From a distance they looked like the marquees at the millennial celebrations of the Icelandic Parliament.* The largest districts were much more than a few temporary tents; they were enormous military installations with arsenals and supply dumps, air-raid shelters and underground passages. There were also prisons, canteens, cinemas, clubs and shops.

Only soldiers lived in the barracks. The native labourers had endless problems, moving from one basement to another, their families sleeping in turf huts and tents. Children were born in sheep sheds.

Those who were well-off could afford to pay the sky-high rents; others had to live out in the mud and mire – workers

* In 1930, in the open air at Thingvellir.

with young children and sick wives. Single mothers were not in a good position, especially if their children had foreign fathers. A popular and progressive-minded newspaper reported proudly that Icelandic men had begun to form associations with the aim of ostracising young women who were suspected of having liaisons with soldiers: when there was a hop they were not to be asked to dance to the strains of the accordion. Many workers went to the dogs, spending their weekly wages, everything they owned even, on drink. Others became incapacitated through workplace accidents or fell ill with pneumonia, tuberculosis and other hardship-related diseases. Families broke up. Trawlermen died at sea as a result of gales and torpedo attacks, and destitute widows with children were left without means of support. Respectable citizens looked with trepidation at this army of poverty-stricken people who filled the city streets. Then, out in the wide world, it happened that Germany lost the war, and the Allies were able to lift the Occupation and say farewell. The barracks remained as housing for the poor.

Yabbadabbadoo!

Whose job is it to protect a small country in a precarious world? The Americans considered it their task and offered military protection for the next century, for eternity even, but that was politely refused. Gógó needed a husband and was looking for one among the Americans, but she would be in trouble if they were all going to leave the country. The military forces took their time, however, and were given temporary permission to make use of Keflavík airfield for another six years.

In those years after the war Gógó devoted long hours to wine and song out at the American base at Keflavík, and at last found the right man there almost six years after the fall of Berlin. A few months later the agreement concerning the base was renewed for an indefinite period, so it was just as well the Americans had put up various installations there, to prepare the ground as it were. They sent businessmen and contractors, one of whom was Gógó's future husband, a pleasant and well-to-do bulldozer driver approaching forty, whose name was Charlie Brown.

She came home and introduced her future spouse. Charlie was the kindest of men. They brought presents for everyone and after the marriage ceremony three weeks later Lína and Tommy held a reception for them at Little Farm 7c.

There was no partying room at the cottage, but the old couple did their best and tidied the place upstairs and down; the fortune-teller baked flat-bread and spread it with liver pâté, and made pot after pot of sickly-sweet milky coffee. The guests, mostly neighbours from Little Farm district, thought the Americans fascinating and they all turned up far too early. They stood around, constantly shifting from one foot to the other, but at last the men sat down on chairs and sofas and passed the snuff around. After that there was much grunting, sighing and farting. The women gathered in the kitchen corner and talked about high prices and rationing cards. Old men, young men, old women and young girls – all were dressed the same, in rubber boots, hooded anoraks and mittens.

Into this company the Americans arrived like beings from another planet. Charlie and his two best friends from the base arrived in a black Lincoln, wearing fashionable suits, white socks and shiny moccasins; they were sun-tanned and crew-cut, and reeked of Old Spice. The bride was also quite something, with make-up, a beehive hairdo and an American wedding dress, snow-white and close-fitting. She had a long white veil which Dollí and her female companions were supposed to hold up, but as they entered the house the rain poured down and the veil was covered in mud. Gógó just laughed, kissed the girls on the cheek, crumpled up the veil and threw it away in a corner.

These people brought a breath of something new. The Icelanders withdrew into their shells, standing in silence, their heads turned away as if coping with a northerly gale. The Americans had brought a carload of beer and spirits and a record-player, and soon the Cottage was filled with the voices of Bing and Frankie and the stars of the Hollywood movies. Tommi knew English, but had little to talk about with these people from the West who had never been to Cardiff, Aberdeen, or anywhere in Britain at all. Otherwise, apart from Gógó, no one knew English, and many had a feeling that the Americans were making fun of them as they sat there smiling and loud-voiced, pointing in all directions with bursts of sudden, male laughter.

Baddi was eleven years old and the only one who dared go near the foreigners; he sat down with them and watched everything. Charlie was wildly enthusiastic about the new stepson he had acquired, and introduced him to the other Americans.

'This is Baddi.'

'Baddie!' they cried, laughing. 'Hey, Baddie, you must be a bad boy, havin' that name!'

'There's nothing wrong with being a bad boy at your age, we've all been bad boys, haven't we, Charlie?'

'We sure have,' Charlie agreed, laughing.

The friend of Charlie's who sat nearest to him was called Bob, a young man of about twenty. Slightly drunk, he gave Dollí the eye. Sixteen years old, shy and blushing, she smiled at him.

Danni kept his distance and, later on, he remembered this as a black day. He squinted from a corner with a frown on his face, and when Charlie tried to talk to him, with the idea of giving the boy some sweets or money, Danni tore himself free and ran from the room. They did not find him until evening, in tears in the farmyard barn. He refused to move, defending himself with screams, until old Tommi came out, took his stepdaughter's son in his arms, stroked him on the cheek and murmured, 'My darling boy. My darling little boy.'

The party at the Cottage lasted all afternoon and, as time passed, the alcohol began to flow. It softened the Icelanders a little, though most just sat swaying from side to side. The Americans began to dance – Charlie with Gógó and Bob with Dollí, and that did not augur well, as she and Grétar, the neighbouring farm's eldest son, were almost engaged to be married. Grétar was a tall, lanky fellow, freckled, with light-red hair and a downy beard. He watched the dancing with a frown, and could see no solution but to get drunk. Dollí turned away, pretending to ignore him.

As the party drew to a close, Bob gathered everyone together on the paving in front of the farmhouse and lined them up.

He wanted to photograph the bride and bridegroom and the wedding guests. In the centre stood the newly married couple, Charlie in his brand-new American clothes and Gógó in her wedding dress, both smiling for the photo. Next to them stood the old couple, and Dollí and Baddi. Standing around them were the neighbours and relatives; it was still drizzling and they were all wearing hooded anoraks, mittens and rubber boots. The Icelanders squinted gloomily at the photographer.

At the left of the picture one can see a manure heap, a 1922 Ford van, an old-fashioned harvesting machine and a rusty corrugated-iron barn. To the right the rear end of Charlie's Lincoln is visible. Hanging from it is a placard, 'Just Married'.

Charlie had a flat out at the base, where Gógó and he planned to live temporarily. At about suppertime they and the other two Americans said goodbye. Bob petted Dollí a bit on the sly, which was more than Grétar could endure. He grabbed Bob in a wrestling hold and with a swing of his hip flung him to the ground. Dollí screamed and Bob leapt up, his fists raised, but Charlie grabbed him, whispered something to him and after much effort succeeded in getting his enraged friend into the car, which sprayed mud from the farmyard as it lurched away. Baddi stared after the old jalopy in rapture.

Grétar could be such an idiot. He probably supposed people would say he had guts, knocking the soldier flat like that. If so, he was mistaken. Most people thought it was embarrassing to behave like that with a man who was all dressed up. But this affair was soon overshadowed by another incident, a marital quarrel which began almost as soon as the Lincoln disappeared from view.

A sound of crashing and banging came from one of the cottages: Fía and Tóti were having a quarrel. They were remarkable people, Fía and Tóti: Snæfríður and Thorgnýr. Very remarkable, not least because they were the relatives who had the most contact with Lína's and Tommi's family. There was never a party nor a coffee evening to which Fía and Tóti were not invited. If there were ever talk of relatives or other families, it was Fía and Tóti who were discussed. They had always lived close to Lína and Tommi. Tóti was Lína's nephew, and perhaps because of their close association over many years, the two families sometimes despised one another.

Everyone knew the story of how Fía and Tóti had met. Lína often recounted her own version of events, but at the party Tóti, who had had a few, took it upon himself to tell his own story of this unusual marriage.

The truth of it was that Fía had once happened to be at a traditional slaughter festival which was being held in an old warehouse; she was a farmer's daughter from Suðurnes, and it was the first time she had been to the capital. She was on the plump side, unmarried and still living in her father's house. She was given a lift on the lorry which took lambs to the slaughterhouse. In the evening she tagged along to the dance; most of those present were farmers visiting the town. A musical entertainer from the east of the country took his accordion up on to the stage and there were reels and polkas. Snæfríður was not exactly famed for her beauty; farming folk did not sit preening themselves in front of a mirror at harvest time. In her mousy hair there were traces of milking-time and other traditional cowshed work; on her overalls one could see that blood had flowed in the slaughterhouse earlier in the day.

Tóti's arms were like two dead sharks swinging from his shoulders. He was shy and rather clumsy in his wellies. He drank a lot and did not carry his drink very well. He would become half-mad with rage, and if he gave the girls the eye they thought he was out to rape them; he often had his shins kicked by dance-floor cavaliers intent on protecting the honour of the women. Eventually they met one another, Tóti and Fía. She had never been exposed to the attentions of a man before, and soon they were rolling about among some barrels out in the yard. In the end it was all too much for Tóti, and Fía left him snoring on the gravel.

The upshot of all this was that Fía became pregnant, and as far as she was concerned it was perfectly obvious who the child's father was. She had made enquiries at the dance as to who the young man was who lay there snoring behind the barrels, and now she arrived in Reykjavík with her farmer father to have a word with Tóti.

Tóti totally denied everything. To be sure, through the mist of alcohol he had a vague memory of some sort of hanky-panky out in the yard, but he reckoned that the lady had been nice to all the farmhands day and night out in the barn, and that one of them might just as easily be the father. He was not to be moved. 'Tóti can be as stiff and stubborn as his idiot of a father,' Lína would often say, and when the child was born – a healthy, good-looking boy – he was given for adoption to a childless married couple in Reykjavík.

Three months after the child came into the world, a year after Fía and Tóti had met one another that first time, she was back in Reykjavík again. There was a dance that evening, in the same place, and the same entertainer played. Tóti was there, too, and in his cups. He and Fía got talking again, and ended up in the yard. And an odd thing happened: she got pregnant again.

So that was that.

'And then you got married?' someone asked at the wedding party, and Tóti barely managed to say yes before Fía herself came over to him and gave him a severe look and signalled to him to come inside. He had probably not had enough to drink, because he obeyed her meekly. Tóti was increasingly under Fía's thumb these days. This he had not been at the outset, after he acknowledged the second child, gave up going to sea and set up house with her in town. In those early years he was often drunk, and then he was sometimes cruel to Fía, and beat her. But she was tough and strong-willed and gradually managed to get the upper hand. At home he became shy and submissive towards her, except on two or three days of the year when he got tanked up on booze and waxed eloquent, brave and bold. Fía would get a black eye or two and the furniture would suffer. While he was boss he would lay down the law, but eventually he fell asleep and subsided after a couple of days of martial law. When he woke up his soul and body were like the 'little flower of eternity with trembling tear' in the National Anthem* as tanks and bulldozers approached from every side; he did not even pray to God but begged for mercy as Fía stood by his bedside, hitting him over and over again with a wet floor-mop and reminding him of everything he had on his conscience. And in the end they agreed that it must never happen again.

Tóti could not have had too much to drink at the wedding party, for the quarrel subsided without ending in fisticuffs, and after crossing herself and invoking Jesus several times, Fía took Tóti by the arm and led him back into the house.

The reason for Tóti's circumspection might also have been that Fía now had a new hold on him: she was well on the way to becoming the family's main breadwinner. Fía's childhood home in Suðurnes had long ago been abandoned. Her parents had moved out and died soon after she went to the capital, and there was no one to take over the property; she had only one brother, Gosi, who was an invalid and could not endure the harshness of country life. Gosi lived in Njarðvík, a village near Keflavík; and the old family property, which consisted mostly of worthless lava, lay there deserted and of no benefit to anyone.

But miracles still happen, and somehow or other it came to light that the army and NATO had for a long time had various projects under way. One of them, which was just starting up, might make Fía and her brother Gosi a lot of money, an incredible amount of money – astronomical sums by the standards of Little Farm.

As they said goodbye after the party and all the hullabaloo, Tommi stood and watched them go: Fía, small and plump in a man's old anorak, leading Tóti, who had once been a tall young man but had now become bent and stooped with the passage of time.

'There go the millionaires,' muttered Tommi, and shook his head.

---

* The Icelandic National Anthem, Ó Guð vors lands (O God of our land), was written by Matthías Jochumsson and set to music by Sveinbjörn Sveinbjörnsson in 1930.

2

Is that my sou'wester or yours?

Tower blocks are always built directly opposite barracks
(Tómas Jónsson)

Gógó showed the old couple every kindness. They no longer had to pay for anything. Everything flowed into the house from the military base. Karolína the fortune-teller now had a Mixmaster, an electric can-opener, a cream-whipper, a potato-peeler, an egg-boiler and an orange-squeezer on the table beside the cooking stove. One day a vacuum-cleaner the size of an oil-drum arrived in the Cottage, which had always had an earthen floor. Then came a radio and a load of furniture: enormous corner-sofas, couches, armchairs, a chrome dining-room suite and twin beds separated by a bedside table. Gógó even ordered garden tools from a catalogue – shears, hoses and a lawnmower – and gave them to the family, even though there was no garden. Twice a week she brought a carload of tinned food, biscuits, packet soups and goodies. Little Farm 7c was bursting at the seams with all this stuff.

Those were wonderful days. And it seemed there would be no end to the world's bounty, for one day, at the end of his sales round, some momentous news awaited Tommi.

It was three weeks after the wedding, and Tommi had begun his sales tour at Camp Thule, which was one of the biggest barracks districts. He arrived there in the morning with his horse-drawn cart laden with goods and provisions from Gúndi and Gísli's Colonial Store – foodstuffs, mittens, boots, sweets, kerosene, light bulbs, lamp oil and a cash-box for change. The weather was fine and Tommi was whistling cheerfully, even though business was not quite as good as it had been in the

well-to-do districts before they got their own shops. Tommi had
been coming to Camp Thule every day for so long that he didn't
need to bother shouting and hollering among the barracks in
order to attract attention, but would quietly set up his pitch in
the centre of the camp, lay out his goods and wait for customers.
He lived so close at hand that he knew almost everyone. Some
of them were famous men, like Hreggviður, the shot-putter, who
was often in the sports pages of the newspapers, and was one of
the country's leading field athletes. Shot, discus or hammer, no
matter which, he could throw them all huge distances. Only the
javelin gave him trouble: it wasn't manageable enough.

   Hreggi had a reputation for being fond of a drink; on his sales
rounds, Tommi had seen the athlete standing there with a bottle
in his hand, singing and shouting at the barracks doors:

> Is that my sou'wester or yours?
> Is that my sou'wester or yours?
> It's mine, not yours.
> Yes it's my sou'wester not your
> sou'wester
> sou'wester
> sou'wester
> sou'we-e-e-ster!

Meanwhile his little wife Gréta would stand at the cart with her
two pale and sickly daughters, and always took so long to make
up her mind what she wanted to buy that the troll had fallen
asleep or gone off somewhere before the mother and daughters
returned home with a loaf of rye bread and a reel of thread.
But it gave her a chance to have a chat with Tommi, the mobile
grocer, to gossip about the other residents in the district and
exchange news.

   Along came a long-faced, middle-aged tough guy with a
rubbery yellow face and a matchstick in the corner of his
mouth: this was Höski the taxi-driver, a notorious bootlegger
and wheeler-dealer. He had been arrested many times, but had
usually got off.

Then a bent, sick-looking woman came over to the cart. Her hair was going grey, and she was fishing out a few small coins from her purse with blue, arthritic fingers. She didn't have enough, and Tommi said, 'Don't worry about that just now, my dear.' She mumbled some embarrassed thanks. When she had gone, Gréta said, 'To think that Thórgunnur isn't even thirty yet!'

'Yes, it's a sorry sight,' said Tommi. He knew a few things about Thórgunnur, because her elder son, Grjóni, was Baddi's best friend.

Gréta was at least married to a nationally famous athlete, so Thórgunnur, in her eyes, was very nearly at the bottom of the social ladder. Thórgunnur was a frail widow with four children; her husband had been a trawlerman who had lost his life in a submarine attack. Thórgunnur had no one but her father, who was an old widower and thought it a disgrace that his only daughter had no more pride than to live in an army barracks. Thórgunnur had to manage alone in a cold, leaky Nissen hut, and tried to support herself and her children by working at the fish factory when there was work to be had and her health allowed. Her children were those 'barracks children' one saw on the street. In particular Diddi, the younger boy, seemed rather strange. He was a bit of an oddity and never went around with anyone; he never talked to a soul and sometimes had fits of rage.

'Those poor kids,' Gréta said. 'Thórgunnur is never particularly well, but she does her best to sew clothes for them and so on. I remember when the boys were to go to school for the first time in the autumn, she didn't want to send them to the school here; she sent them to the other one, which is supposed to be more refined. Poor lads, they left so clean and brushed, she'd mended their best clothes for them. You should have seen the look on her face as they left with their satchels, which she had also made herself – she was so pleased and proud of her boys. They were going to school! To a proper school! But she had a different look on her face later that day when they came home long before time, all ragged and torn and bloodied. They had been bullied so dreadfully. Little Diddi was sobbing and howling. And I can tell you he's never wanted to go to school since. But then he's always been a bit strange, everyone says he has problems. I think he's putting it on . . .'

'But Grjóni can usually stand up for himself,' said Tommi.

'Yes,' Gréta said, 'but he's also always fighting and up to some mischief or other. The police have even been making enquiries about him!'

'Yes . . . the police,' said Tommi, scratching his head and looking troubled. 'I know . . .'

When Tommi arrived with his half-empty cart at Gúndi and Gísli's Colonial Store that afternoon, both of the merchants were waiting for him down in the storeroom. Tommi conscientiously began to tot up the takings and return the unsold items. Gúndi was a short, stout man; he had thrust his hands deep into his trouser pockets and was pulling faces as he tried to hold an enormous fat cigar between his teeth.

'How was business today, Tommi?'

'Oh, so-so, you know . . .'

'That cart is becoming a bit of a waste of time, although the devil himself couldn't peddle as much stuff to people as you do, I know.'

'Well, thank . . .'

'The sales are only a drop in the ocean, there's no getting away from that, compared with the war years, for example. Since then it's all gone downhill. It's hardly worth the effort any more, either for you or for us. It only needs some devil to open a shop in the barracks district, and that will be curtains for us. Finito. Frozen out, my friend.'

'Yes, it would be . . .'

'What are we going to do about it, Tommi? What the devil can we do?'

'What can we do, yes, quite . . .'

'If you can't think of anything, we're all going to have to put our heads together before we end up in the street with our backsides in the gutter!'

Tommi was completely at a loss. For years he had trudged

around the town with his horse and cart, sold all kinds of things and provided his enormous family with salt for its porridge; but when he was bombarded with this kind of talk and questions about the future, he had nothing to offer. Gúndi said nothing. In the silence which followed he inhaled the cigar smoke, his face dark as thunder, scowling and swollen, his eyes moist with tears. He had one buttock on the edge of the table and was waggling his foot at 78 revs per minute.

His partner, Gísli, had stuck his feet on a shelf and tilted back his chair, with a grey Tyrolean hat pulled down over his eyes. He was toying with a pencil as though he were about to shoot it at a target: 'We are thinking of getting in first, Tommi, and opening a shop ourselves up at Camp Thule. It's to be called Tommi's Shop.'

'Tommi's Shop?'

'That's right, my friend. Tommi's Shop. And you will be the manager. You've been selling for us for ages. What do you think of it? Tommi's Shop, see – the rabble like to think they're dealing directly with the grocer himself, you see. And you live nearby and know your way around. What do you say? And I ask you now, Tommi, do we dare let this rabble have things on credit? How do we answer that?'

'I think that . . .'

'You must decide that for yourself, but as shop manager you are of course answerable to us, and all that sort of thing.'

Tommi's Shop! Good Lord, the old fellow was to be boss in his own shop! Bye-bye, horse and cart. He stood there facing the merchants' searching eyes, in his baggy overalls, old for his years and rummaging in a rustling packet of cotton wool as if he were trying to decide whether it was nine carat or twenty-four.

'The barracks folk need to do their shopping the same as everyone else, of course,' he said at last. This was his way of saying yes.

The next day, he and Gúndi the merchant went up to the Camp to have a look at the lie of the land. Baddi came along with them to see some old friends in the district. He and Grjóni,

Thórgunnur's son, circled around Tommi, who was curious to learn about this and that.

'Whose son are you, Sigurjón, my boy?' asked Tommi.

'Trausti's son – Traustason.'

'And what is your brother's name?'

'Víkingur, but we call him Diddi.'

'How old is he?'

'He'll soon be ten.'

'Why don't you all let him play with you?'

'He's just a baby.'

'But he's only a year younger than the rest of you!'

'Yes, but he never wants to play with other boys.'

With that the boys were off and disappeared among the barracks which lay broad-bellied on the gravel. Coal-smoke curled from their chimneys. It occurred to Tommi that it must be easy to get lost in large barracks districts, for they were like labyrinths and all the barracks-huts were the same.

After the war many of the buildings were used for different purposes. Most of the residential barracks continued to be residential, while other buildings were given new roles. The former officers' club was turned into a primary school. The prison became a dairy. The canteen for other ranks became a car workshop. These were all timber shacks. But a solid stone house still stood empty. There they got permission to open Tommi's Shop. The walls were almost a metre thick. People thought it had probably been a military depot, or perhaps even an ammunition dump. The building had a concrete cellar, with an underground passage leading out of it.

Before they left the district that day, Tommi paid a visit to Thórgunnur. He said he was looking for Baddi. They chatted for a while, and Tommi glanced round at the dark barracks-hut; it was not wind- and water-tight, and Thórgunnur had stuffed rags in the cracks, or paper bags in some places. It was late winter, with frost in the air; even the rotting floor looked half-frozen, except around the stove. Tommi asked about various things as if at random. 'Where do your folks come from?' 'Oh, are you his daughter?' 'Yes, I know who that is, more or less.' She was not very forthcoming, but answered his questions; she did some sewing, she wasn't always well enough to work at the fish factory, but life was quite different now that the kids were old enough for her to be able to go out to work and leave them if necessary. Her father had gone into an old folks' home; he had lived with them to begin with after her husband Trausti died, but when they lost their flat at Norðurmýri he hadn't wanted to come with them here: 'This isn't really ideal accommodation for folk who are old and ailing, anyway,' she said, and Tommi was glad to take the chance to leave this uncomfortable subject; they both smiled and nodded and said goodbye, in cordial agreement that this was not really ideal accommodation for folk who were old and ailing, without considering more carefully for whom the accommodation really was ideal. With the farewell smile stiffening and fading from Tommi's lips as he made his way home, he had a slight attack of conscience for not having offered the woman any help, for not being able to help a family like that. And when he came across Grjóni out there in the darkness, he was glad of the opportunity to chat to the boy while he tried to think of something he could do to help him. Before they parted, old Tommi had taught the boy to walk like Charlie Chaplin.

When Tommi came home to the Little Cottage at Little Farm 7c, Lína was sitting there, telling the fortune of the mayor's daughter, no less. Lína had once dreamt that an American would turn up; she had seen the wedding and the favourable days in the cards, and since it had all come true she had taken it as a clear sign that she ought to develop her gifts of prophecy. She put an advertisement in the newspaper: 'I tell people's fortunes . . .' There was no shortage of clients; they came flocking to the cottage to see the sybil; they had their future set out in the cards, along with detailed information about life's cruelty and the jungle where you're on your own against the rest of the world. The name of this mystical woman was on everyone's lips and there were all kinds of stories about her magic powers; a journalist and a photographer once came to talk to the fortune-teller, but she refused to show her face and said there were nothing but 'character-assassins' in the newspapers.

Character-assassins and envy-mongers also spread lies about Karolína. Many said, for example, that she was fabulously wealthy and owned properties all over town and had coffers crammed with the money she had raked in with her black arts and tax-free fortune-telling.

This was pure nonsense, of course, but it could not be denied that the family had never had its hands on so much money. Tommi's income shot up as soon as the shop got going, and on top of it came the fortune-telling fees. Moreover, there were far fewer mouths to feed than there had been in the past.

To be sure, a new character had joined the household in place of all those who had either left the nest or died: Dollí's fiancé. After the wedding party for Gógó and Charlie, Dollí had had nothing but contempt for Grétar, the farmer's son; on a hike with the Ramblers' Association she had met a short man from out of town who was apprenticed in the capital as a plumber. His name was Grettir, and Lína had little time for him: 'That damned little twerp!' She pretended not to notice Grettir, and called him Grétar if she ever had to mention him by name. This obviously got on Dollí's nerves and she kept correcting Lína, who only yielded grudgingly. 'Well, Gretir, then!' she would say, and that was far as she would go.

Grettir at once moved into the Cottage with all his belongings: a rifle, a shotgun and an old Nimbus motorbike. 'He seems a reliable fellow,' said Tommi, who liked people who didn't get excited. Grettir never got excited; he always had something to keep him busy, polishing and adjusting his guns, or tinkering with his motorbike. In fact, he had nothing to get excited about; everyone could be happy, and no one needed to work, for Tommi was earning well and Grettir didn't even need to do his plumber's apprenticeship. He just pottered about and didn't say much, but he seemed to like listening to people, and said 'Huh!' whenever his interlocutor took a pause for breath. Nothing ever seemed to ruffle Grettir. Baddi noticed that Lína was not all that keen on Grettir and that she kept trying to catch him out. 'That'll do. Enough!' Grettir would mutter. Only once did he try shouting, but it didn't work: instead of a thunderous voice only a few

squeaks came out, and everyone began to laugh. So Grettir stuck
to keeping himself to himself.

'Have you given up the plumbing?' Tommi asked one day.

'Dunno,' Grettir replied. 'I'd learned it all anyway!'

'Could you lay pipes in a house?' Tommi asked. This was the
first time that building work had been mentioned in the home.
The whole family sat in American armchairs which filled the
Cottage to the point where it was almost impossible to find room
for one's feet. They all started imagining the great mansions they
would build, and next day the old couple set off to look into the
necessary formalities.

They knew so many people. People who were now smiths,
bricklayers, electricians or timber merchants had at one time or
another got something on tick from Tommi's cart. Lína had told
the fortune of a bank manager, who wanted to know if his wife
was being unfaithful; the bank manager's wife had also come to
have her fortune told, in order to find out how much her husband
knew. Through such respectable people it was not hard to obtain
a loan. Everything worked out well, and the house went up in
record time. Only two months after the subject of building work
was first mentioned, the family moved in. Minor problems were
given no chance of becoming major ones.

For example, it could have taken an age and much bureaucracy
and hassle to find an acceptable building site. Some people built
without permission; they simply picked an empty lot outside the
planning system and got on with it – mostly poor folk who
perhaps had a few planks of wood, some packing cases or a
mobile summer home. In searching for a building site their
choice usually fell on empty spaces in the barracks districts. At
the town hall it was thought that this was because there were
various facilities in the area already, such as running water and a
sewage system. The sewage installations in most of the barracks
districts were such that the run-off water flowed in open ditches
between the buildings.

In the middle of Camp Thule there was an uninhabited area,
a kind of town square. Some people thought it had been a lorry
park during the war. Höskuldur the taxi-driver claimed that the

British had had a flogging post with stands for spectators in the square.

The square was where Tommi had usually parked his cart, and he thought it a splendid site to build on. But he was a law-abiding man and would possibly have given up the whole idea had not Lína, through her connections with the mayor's family, managed to extract from that good man a rather special document which was later to prove a headache for officialdom: in his own hand the mayor wrote that, as far as he was concerned, there was no bar to their building a house there.

After that the house had to be designed, and Tommi got an artisan he knew to do that. He was a bit of a drinker who had exhibited some paintings and published some poems in the newspapers. He agreed to go on the wagon for a few days and make the drawings for the house in exchange for a few groceries from Tommi's Shop.

Perhaps he was ill or a bit hungover, for the house did not turn out quite as intended. It was a box, with no outbuildings, and a steep roof with no eaves. The windows were small and did not match. The entrance was a door with one corner of the frame missing: the door had no glass panes, and opened outwards.

But the house was wonderfully large, and that was what mattered most. Downstairs there was a kitchen big enough for a hotel, three rooms and also a big room which, after much family discussion, was to be the telephone room. Upstairs there was a passage and four bedrooms, one for the old couple, one for Dollí and Grettir, the third for Baddi and finally a guest room, for instance if Gógó and Charlie came to town. Everywhere there were enormous cupboards: the largest was a windowless closet under the roof-beams, where Danni was lodged.

Charlie came to town in a lorry with tools and doors and windows and a mechanical cement-mixer in the back. The workmen brought spirit-levels, trowels, hammers and crowbars, and set to work. The foundations were no problem, for they were building on top of rock which in former times had borne the weight of a whole ice-age glacier.

As the loud churning of the cement-mixer mingled with the

sound of the workmen's hammers, the men of the neighbourhood came to lend a hand. Hreggviður the shot-putter emerged
from the barracks on the other side of the road and heaved heavy
beams and posts around: he was both crane and tackle. Hreggi
no doubt saw the advantage of keeping in with the local grocer,
but he was also the hero of the hour. One after another the men
took a break from their work to admire the giant's strength.

When the cement-mixer broke down, Hlynur the car-mechanic
was sent for. He was black with oil and so small and thin that he
could squeeze himself into the innards of engines, something of
which he was very proud. Nonetheless he was a man with all
his wits about him; he worked all day in a shed which adjoined
his barracks-hut and was called Hlynur Ólafsson's Garage.

Höskuldur the taxi-driver could always lay his hands on any
anything: he got hold of cut-price *brennivín** for the party to
celebrate the roof going up. The dark and rainy day when the Old
House was considered weatherproof was one of the brightest in
the history of the district. At roof-raisings it is customary to
adorn the house with the national flag, and of course Tommi
did not want to miss out on that. But it was hard to get hold
of a flag, for only the rich owned such treasures. He had more
or less given up on the idea when the situation was rescued at
the last moment: Charlie managed to borrow an Icelandic flag
out at the American NATO base.

All the workmen were invited, of course, as well as the neighbours, both from the Camp and from Little Farm district. Tommi
went round thanking people for their help and offering them
cigarettes, biscuits and tinned food. Everyone could drink as
much as they liked. And when the party was in full swing, Grettir
and Dollí announced their engagement; to general rejoicing he
gave her a ring. Gógó posed them by the Icelandic flag so she
could take a photograph of them with her new box camera.
Dollí was grinning from ear to ear, while Grettir tried not to
look too proud, standing on tiptoe to make himself as tall as

---

* *Brennivín* is the Icelandic form of schnapps, flavoured with caraway
seeds. It is familiarly known as 'Black Death'.

his fiancée. He was twenty-five while she was only sixteen, and it took eleven years for the marriage to bear fruit.

Fía and Tóti were at the roof-raising, of course. They were now rolling in money, having received a contract and payment for the use of the property at Suðurnes. That helped to tighten Fía's grip on Tóti; he had become so submissive that the first thing he did after getting to his feet after each drubbing with a floor-mop was to stagger down to the shop and buy a new floor-mop. He toiled and laboured at the Electricity Works, mainly digging ditches – even after becoming a millionaire. He would stand with his pick and shovel, up to his knees in ditch-water, hacking and scraping at the half-frozen turf for the lowest hourly wage in the land. No one supposed it was possible to support an entire family on that kind of income; yet they managed to survive on his wages alone, eking out the cash. Not one farthing of the Suðurnes money was to be touched. That money was put into stocks and shares and property, and even into foreign bank accounts; they had millions of *krónur* in foreign banks, these ordinary Icelandic folk, secret bank accounts just like the poshest people in the world. This had been arranged through a lawyer, for they never went abroad themselves – they never even travelled beyond the county border, those two. There was no shortage of money, but it was not to be *squandered*.

Tóti and Fía talked with contempt mixed with apprehension of people who made lots of money quickly and unexpectedly, got above themselves, lost their heads and spent, spent and spent until after a short time they woke up as if in a bad dream, stony broke and ridiculed.

The thought of wasting money on luxuries lay heavy on Fía. She would come to Lína to talk about nightmares; she was often in terror, dreaming of seeing her banknotes fluttering away into the blue, or of hairy fists grabbing at the money, and she often woke up in the night screaming and with palpitations.

'I advised her to talk to a doctor,' said Lína. 'But she's too stingy for that!'

Sometimes Fía said in great agitation that she had grounds for suspecting Tóti and their sons of secretly spending the money.

('Munnnny', Fía called it.) Just recently she had found in Tóti's pocket a five-*króna* note he was unable to account for. Most of all, she feared that the boys would start throwing money around on loose women!

The boys went with them to the roof-raising, all except for the eldest, of course, who had been given away for adoption and whom they never saw. The one who was a year younger was called Gummi, and he took after Fía.

One might have supposed that they were an exceptionally fertile couple, because a child had resulted from each of their two first encounters. But it was fifteen years before they had the third child, who was also a boy; he was christened Gosi, and was the same age as Danni. He not only took after Fía, but was reckoned quite simply to be a male clone of her.

There seemed to be an air of ill-omen about these brothers, Gummi and Gosi. From an early age they kept themselves to themselves; they were outsiders, they did badly at school, they stayed indoors and listened sullenly to their mother's scolding. In due course they both got married and their wives were frequent visitors to the casualty department with facial injuries.

The eldest son, on the other hand, the one whom Tóti had refused to acknowledge, was very different. He looked like Tóti, but was nonetheless considered handsome. As a young man he became a famous athlete, well-mannered and decent, captain of the national team and later a national hero as a commander of a coastguard vessel. In time Tóti began to acknowledge the boy; he boasted about him and tried to establish contact, but the son did not want to see or hear anything of him.

Fía and Tóti were naturally the centre of the roof-raising party. They sat on a short bench in the parlour which later became the telephone room, telling the inhabitants of the Camp what a burden it was to have money. When they were in the middle of describing their troubles there were sounds of rumbling, crashing and shouting; people rushed out into the passage and saw Hreggviður the shot-putter, all twenty-two stone of him, tumbling down the staircase. He landed on the floor with such force that there were cracks in the floorboards.

Luckily he was not harmed; he just sat up, shook himself like a bear and asked for another drink.

'That staircase is a death-trap,' someone said, as the menfolk stood discussing the reasons for the accident. The staircase was almost vertical, and even the cat had difficulty in climbing it later. In fact, it was hardly a staircase at all; it had very small steps, almost like the gangplank of a ship. After Hreggviður's fall the staircase was never the same again, but groaned and creaked every time anyone used it.

Another major flaw in the house's construction came to light at the roof-raising party: the lack of a toilet. The only sanitary provision in the entire house was the kitchen sink. That was all. In the rejoicing at the creation of a house for the whole family there was no time to bother about things like that; people simply went and used Hreggviður's outside privy when they needed to. After the family moved in, however, this lack was felt rather keenly, and Tommi had to get one of the artisans to come back and equip the largest of the downstairs cupboards with a WC and wash-hand basin. At the same time an extension was built on the east side of the house. This was to be the scullery, and there they installed the bathtub which Gógó had acquired from the base.

The artisan who did the job said he was astounded that such vital and obvious fittings could have been overlooked: 'Was it a professional who designed the house?'

'Well, he's a craftsman,' said Tommi.

'A craftsman? A house-builder, or . . . ?'

'Nooo, I don't think so. I think he's a wallpaperer.'

No sooner had the family moved in than they began to call this grey, plaster-covered wooden house The Old House. In reality it never became old in terms of age – that was just its name.

The Old House reared above the low barracks buildings like a fortress in the midst of a medieval settlement. All that was lacking was a city wall, a moat and a drawbridge to go with it. There were, however, the makings of a moat right from the start. A deep and long muddy pond lay in a semi-circle along the eastern bounds of the district. It was more or less a lake. Rumour had it that the pond had formed on an old army quarry.

The pond was a playground, creche, swimming-pool and even a kindergarten for the children of Camp Thule. They built cabins on its shores, with a little jetty out into the pond. They played on it with little toy boats, and the bigger boys later built a wooden raft, rowing it and punting it with sticks and planks between the shores. Baddi and Grjóni managed to get hold of some empty oil-drums which were closed at both ends and floated like corks; they would jump on to the drums and cross the deeps on them. The drums turned and rolled in the water, and it required great skill to keep one's balance on them. If ballet-steps and foot-running on floating oil-drums had been an Olympic sport, the youngsters of Camp Thule would have filled the winners' rostrum. But the pond was deep in many places, the water was cold and most of the youngsters could not swim. It was a dangerous sport; so the oil-drums were much more exciting than the rafts, which were solid and slow like river barges. When the bigger boys had got so good at oil-drum sailing that they were no longer in imminent danger of drowning, it became a popular sport to do battle with sticks, each on his own drum, out in the middle of the pond until someone fell into the dark brown depths. Then only strength and endurance could save them. The children were always plummeting into the pond; but no one from Camp Thule ever drowned. Even one-year-old infants were invariably rescued.

The most perilous dives took place from the drums, because they were in the middle of the pond, but even then the sea-warriors always made it to land, even though they were some-times near death from lack of oxygen and all the water they had swallowed, and were turning blue by the time they were hauled ashore.

Tommi called the pond the Pacific Ocean. The grown-ups were in mortal fear of this death-trap. Lína organised a petition to the municipal authorities, asking for the pond to be filled in. An opposition newspaper sent a man to take a look at this children's playground, just before the municipal elections. His article began:

> There were children everywhere. They ran to and fro through the narrow alleyways between the barracks, jumping over dustbins and chasing one another. Young toddlers were splashing in puddles out in the street. These were large puddles, for no one has thought it worth the bother to fill in the holes in the streets for ages. On the other hand, the road grader comes round once in a while and stirs up the mud. It really serves no more useful a purpose than that. The sewer passes along the edge of the play area. For a long time it was open at one place, and the boys would sneak down there to play with their boats. The sewer was always full to the brim . . .

From the pond the road led down to the primary school, which was a very peculiar building: a two-storey barracks-hut. This giant hut had been the officers' club during the war, but had now acquired the new and noble function of housing the education of the district's children. Baddi and Danni both went to this school, and Dollí had taken her final exam there two years earlier with excellent marks for handwriting but below average for deportment. It was in many ways a unique educational institution: for example, the floors and walls were crawling with cockroaches, those foreign insects which flourish only in a very few houses in Iceland.

A new school was on the way, and it was planned to build it just outside the Little Farm district. The designs were published in the newspapers at the same time as a new plan for the city was announced, only three weeks after the family moved into the Old House.

The plans provided this little medieval settlement with town walls in the form of some four-storey tower blocks which began to rise from the ground that very summer.

The new city plan did not take account of the Camp Thule barracks district, but it was there nonetheless, and perhaps this was why the main street, Aðalgata, was laid in a handsome curve around the district to the north and west. Beside it stood the tower blocks, ranked in such a way that they did not engulf the barracks; the barracks, however, lay where the planners envisaged parks and playgrounds for the new blocks.

The sites on which the blocks were to be constructed were allocated to the wage-earners' associations. The Bank Staff Housing Society built a block which was, of course, named the Bank Block. Then there were blocks like the Shop Assistants' Block and the Electricity Workers' Block.

The block closest to the barracks district, half protruding into it, was built by the Union of Professional Artists; it was occupied almost exclusively by staff of the National Theatre and the Symphony Orchestra. These were people with a cultural background quite different from that of the people at Camp Thule, as was later to become apparent.

Fía and Tóti bought a flat in the Electricity Workers' Block. As an Electricity Board employee, Tóti acquired it at a good discount. They had little choice but to move into this flat, for the Little Farm district was to be demolished in accordance with the building work for the new town plan. In fact, their shack was pulled down before they could move into the tower block. So Fía put an advertisement in the newspaper: 'SOS! Married couple with two children on the street!' They got replies from some good-hearted people, but all of them wanted rent, 'munnny', and Fía and Tóti talked about money-grubbers and usurers and misers and in the end Tommi and Lína gave the poor couple a roof over their heads for a few weeks until they could move into their flat.

Their flat was weatherproof, and it was large. But there the luxury had to stop for a while. It was much too expensive to put down wall-to-wall carpeting; not even the bathroom and kitchen got a proper floor-covering for a long time – they made do with the bare cement, which had at least been painted grey. Tóti himself made the kitchen table and benches out of lumber which he collected from building sites; the timber was coarse and full of splinters, but one got used to it in time – the wood became shiny and their bottoms hardened. In those early years the rest of the inventory in this 130-square-metre flat consisted mainly of various shabby and ill-matched items of kitchen furniture. No curtains. No radio. The heating was hardly ever turned on, except at Christmas.

Many years later, Fía seemed to develop an obsession with furniture, and they invested in all the most expensive items to be had in the land. They had only to hear of some Chesterfield sofa which was expensive enough, or a table made of some rare hardwood or a cupboard made of ebony, and the couple would rush out to buy it, irrespective of whether the new furniture would go with what they had already; so their parlour soon came to resemble the repository of a furniture store where everything was jumbled together.

The furniture became Fía's pride and joy; she opened the parlour to any guest who arrived and showed off her costly treasures. But no one was allowed to sit down. Oh no, don't touch the exhibits; and to be on the safe side Fía never removed the plastic covering in which the shops delivered the treasures. The parlour was like a dead person's apartment in which there is no sign of life other than an old, hollow-sounding grandfather clock.

3

Long live Kári's heroes!

A meeting at the Old House: the main men of the barracks district, along with cousin Tóti, were wallowing in memories of old times. They were wondering what could be done for the youth of today, but the past kept assailing them.

Tommi was in the middle of a long soliloquy, while the others were sipping coffee and looking thoughtful. 'Boys will be boys,' said Tommi. 'They always need something to fight over, they are tireless, and there's not a damned thing they don't get up to. When we were young, life was nothing but toil and trouble, as we all remember; at sea and on land, children had to slave away more or less from the time they could walk, and had to put up with all kinds of hardship.'

'Yes, I'm afraid so,' the men murmured in a tuneless chorus, with their fists on their knees, twiddling their thumbs. Then they pursed their lips in soundless whistling and buried their heads on their chests: 'There's no getting away from tha-a-at . . .'

Tommi suddenly lost the thread and forgot what he was going to say next, and went on with the same old line about child slavery in the old days, in its various different guises. The old men were happy with this theme and felt proud of themselves for having worked so hard when they were children. Shyness and embarrassment melted away and, a-glow with coffee and bittersweet memories, they began to tell stories of their boyhood, one after the other. At the age of ten, Höskuldur the taxi-driver had had to stay up every night and keep watch for his father who was making moonshine liquor in a potato shed: 'If anyone approached I had to blow on a bird whistle which was used when shooting ducks, and if I fell asleep I was locked in my room on bread and water for a whole week.' Hreggviður told them about the time when, as an orphaned eight-year-old, he was sent to work as an assistant to the local blacksmith, to pump the bellows or to stand at the anvil with hammer and tongs and red-hot iron.

Tóti's childhood memories made quite an impression on most of his listeners: as a baby in nappies he had learned how to bait a hook, and his boyhood had been spent standing up to the knees in slush in unheated bait sheds, threading frozen cuttlefish on to hooks with numb, bloodstained fingers. As soon as he could handle an oar he went to the fishing with his father; they would row out in an open boat every evening, no matter how terrible the weather, and no one asked if he had been standing in the bait shed all day, not to mention all the other jobs connected with that. It was all sweat-of-the-brow toil, I can tell you. Us lads had become real men by getting to know the realities of life.

Tóti was quickly off on the same subject again. He sat there on the kitchen stool, twisted and crippled with rheumatism and sciatica, chewing on a half-burned pipe-stem, and seemed almost drunk with the thought of all that joyous work; he told about the time he lost his father when he was only eleven years old and got a berth for the winter season on a boat from Sandgerði. He would not be the man he was today if he hadn't learned more in his boyhood than sitting on his arse over a pile of books day in and day out.

Old Tommi tried to strike a different note: he and Karolína didn't want their children to have to undergo what they had had to endure in their youth – 'although you may well be right, Thorgnýr, to say that it isn't good for youngsters to be idle and mollycoddled'. But Tommi also thought that times had changed, thank goodness. Children had been treated very badly in the old days: he remembered the merciless cruelty of his home village – the paupers had tied children of two to four years old to bedposts or door-handles in their homes and left them alone all day while they were out at work. Perhaps there was nothing else they could have done, but of course the children were terrified out of their wits, and cried to the point of exhaustion and fell asleep, only to wake up again even more terrified, and so it went on, over and over again. As a youngster, Tommi had seen children turned into imbeciles by the harsh treatment they received. And the child slavery! Five- and six-year-old children were worked so hard that they were worn-out old men before they were adults.

Höskuldur the taxi-driver was of the opinion that the child slavery was not the worst of it, it was the damned beatings and thrashings: in the year he was born, a boy from the neighbouring farm in Skaptárdalur had died as a result of the ill treatment he had received.

Tommi recalled this, too: perhaps it had not been caused just by wickedness, for people believed that it did children good, though it was not ordinary smacking: fists and sticks rained down until the blood flowed; one father he knew beat his son so much that when the boy grew up he was all bent and twisted and walked, like, like . . . and now Tommi blushed and glanced across at Hlynur the mechanic . . . 'like . . . like I don't know what!'

The Kári Football Club was the pride of the neighbourhood. It was at this meeting that the old men had founded the club. Old Tommi was later chosen to be its first honorary member.

Right from the start the children of the district more or less brought themselves up. They arrived like the seasons for the barracks-parents, the first smiles of the babies seemed a ray of spring sunshine. Some of the children died, but life is stronger than death and so, slowly but surely, the little creatures multiplied, and soon they filled every nook and cranny in the barracks. Then the ones who could stand on their feet were put out to look at the world for themselves, first tethered to a clothes post with a piece of string (there were no flagpoles in Camp Thule), then set free when the clothes post had to be vacated to make room for the next generation. The world stood open to them.

To youthful eyes the district was full of wonders and entertainments, but it soon became too small to contain all that horde of children, who then began to overflow into the neighbouring districts.

Inside the district, life's struggle was hard but for the barracks children it was no easier when they spilled out into the better-off areas. There they were certainly not welcomed with any deference, and so the raids by the barracks children on neighbouring districts soon took on the aspect of regular guerrilla warfare. The oldest boys formed small, tough viking bands which went through the neighbouring districts like fire through brushwood. These raids often began with innocent intentions, but the warriors were prepared to defend themselves and soon learned that attack was the best defence; often they came home torn and bleeding, richer in experience and now and again also better off in terms of worldly goods from sheds and out-houses and self-service stores. And then complaints were lodged against them.

Every so often regular wars broke out between districts. Then the Camp Thulers would arm themselves with sticks and bows and arrows. They often fought against superior numbers and only their toughness and nerve prevented a rout. Sometimes two or more districts formed a league; they were always against Camp Thule, which never took part in any defence alliances.

On the other hand, the barracks boys enjoyed the military privilege of never having to fight in their own territory; like a powerful medieval fortress their district was a completely secure stronghold. If they had to resort to flight, the retreat never needed to be farther than to the district boundary – the other lads were terrified of this place, which they had been told was full of delinquents, drunkards, prostitutes and madmen. In groups of twenty or more, armed to the teeth and itching for a fight, the warriors would take up position in Aðalgata or at the Dirt-Pond, but no one dared to go farther, no one would volunteer to put his head in the lion's den.

There was something ill-starred about the lads of Camp Thule. For one thing, it was they who always got the blame. For example, Grjóni and Baddi sometimes returned injured after a fight in the neighbouring districts, their clothes in tatters, with bleeding noses and black eyes. Before they had time to blow their noses the complaints began, because their opponents had also received injuries in the same battle; furious parents telephoned and arrived on the scene, sometimes it was the police or the Society for the Prevention of Cruelty to Children. Injured, maimed and mutilated, Grjóni would perhaps be stood up against a wall and interrogated as to whether he had been fighting. Some mummy's boy or other had come home crying his eyes out, with a cut lip. 'What is the meaning of this, Sigurjón?' He had no answer. Sometimes old Tommi would try to mediate: 'Boys are boys and always will be,' he said. 'It's not always possible to say who started a fight!'

But there Tommi was wrong: the police, the SPCC and the outraged parents from the neighbouring districts knew without a shadow of doubt just who were responsible for all the fighting and goings-on. Grjóni, for his part, caught on to this at once; had he found these people's omniscience surprising to start with, he soon grasped this basic truth. It did him no good to answer questions, and so he might as well stop listening; at the same time, he stopped hearing anything. Later on, when he became a criminal and the bane of the police, he was always called Deaf Grjóni because of this ailment which afflicted him during questioning.

If there were a broken window-pane anywhere, a stolen bicycle, a vandalised lamppost, a bus with the air let out of its tyres, or a burgled garage, the barracks parents were held to account. Mothers would sometimes deny vehemently that their sons had stolen the bicycle, only for the loot to be found right next to a barracks-hut on closer investigation. Sometimes the thief was not found, but the mothers would be reminded that they had denied it the last time, and what had come to light? And if they began to grumble and object, they would simply be told that the boy would be 'sent to the country'. Many of the parents were from the country themselves, and knew what a threat of this kind meant. The boys saw in their minds endless rows of numbered youngsters in prison dress with chains clamped to their ankles, slurping soup which was slopped into tin plates from a pail, while guards in leather boots stood all around with whips at the ready.

Old Tommi was always willing to help if complaints were

made against Baddi. He just pulled his worn wallet from his back pocket, and paid up.

Complaints about Baddi had started coming in even before the family had moved to Camp Thule. Tommi had immediately begun to mutter that they would have to find something wholesome for these boys to do. During the spring in which the family moved into the Old House there was a lot of trouble between the districts: houses and buses were wrecked, the contents of dustbins were strewn all over the streets, many boys were injured, and the old women could hardly find words to describe it. On one of the Camp Thulers' commando raids the leader of the opposition alliance was taken prisoner and carted off, bound and gagged, into the heart of darkness, Hreggviður's outside privy, which was turned into a military prison by nailing the door shut. The boy, whose name was Kobbi, cried and howled, but subsided into sobs when Baddi and Grjóni, who were standing guard at the door, threatened to drown him in the Shell drum which served as the toilet bowl if he didn't shut up. Kobbi had to stay in the privy until nightfall, when his frightened brothers and sisters finally confessed that bad boys had captured him and taken him all the way into the Camp. Solid fathers from the respectable districts paid no attention to the hysterics of their spouses, but looked one another in the eye without a word, armed themselves with golf clubs and wrenches and strode to Camp Thule, determined as the Twelve Just Men, and released Kobbi, who was overcome by humiliation and sobbing. In the footsteps of these sturdy fathers in their white shirts came the police, telling everyone to behave themselves, and at that the Twelve Just Men went away; they shook their fists as they left and said God help the barracks rabble if the boy had been hurt. The guardians of the law stayed behind and told Tommi that Baddi would probably have to be sent to the country.

There had been much talk about 'being sent to the country' at the meeting to which Tommi had invited the main men of the neighbourhood for a discussion on what could be done for the youngsters in the district. When he had mentioned Baddi's problems to Lína, she had reached for her cards, which told her that Baddi had a bright future ahead of him if he were left alone. Tommi realised that this meant getting a proper job.

It was an odd sort of meeting. After all, they were not exactly experts in sociology, these old men of the district, but they arrived one after the other with solemn faces and sat down around the kitchen table. Tommi was seated at the head of the table when Hreggviður the shot-putter and Höskuldur the taxi-driver turned up, the first to arrive; they had no idea what the meeting was about. Höskuldur was relaxed, nonchalantly chewing a matchstick, but Hreggi was a little nervous, completely sober; he generally had no difficulty in talking, but he was unused to meetings with speeches, minutes and complicated discussions.

Hlynur the mechanic played the role of the educated man, since he was teetotal and lived in a painted barracks-hut. He arrived in his Sunday best and with his hair plastered down with water; he knew how handle himself on such occasions – he had been to the meetings of the Philatelic Club. He cleared his throat like a bank manager as he sat down, and fiddled with a row of pens in his breast pocket. He asked what the first item on the agenda was, and this made Hreggi even more nervous – he was regretting that he hadn't had a nip before leaving home, even wishing that he not come to such an important meeting. Hreggi had not even had the sense to dress properly for the occasion, he could see that now; he was wearing rubber boots, stained trousers and a vest, with a gaudy red handkerchief round his neck. Höskuldur paid little attention to dress either; he made no distinction between Sunday best and working clothes and was just wearing his taxi-driver's outfit, shiny at the elbows, back and bottom.

The shot-putter was relieved when cousin Tóti arrived, for Tóti was wearing his ordinary patched working clothes, though he was, of course, a man of wealth and would surely know what was right and proper. Tóti was the only man at the meeting who did not live in Camp Thule. He had not moved into the Electricity Workers' Block yet, either – indeed nothing of the tower block existed except for its foundations, which yellow bulldozers and diggers were busy excavating; but Tóti lived nearby and was an obvious delegate to this meeting because of his connection with the family in the Old House.

Lína kept going around the house like a gust of wind; she never said anything, but looked in to see them from time to time and clattered pots and pans in the sink, so that awkward pauses seldom lasted very long. Tommi had a secretive, brooding look, and refused to start the discussion until everyone had arrived. They waited for almost half an hour for Toggi the trawlerman, who had said he would come; at last he appeared, along with his father who had just been made a widower and had moved into his son's barracks-hut. He was doddery with age and hardened arteries, and was also called Toggi – Old Toggi – a white-haired and emaciated seaman from the west coast. He went all round the table, shook hands with everyone and introduced himself, even though he had met most of them several times before. The old man's name was Thormóður Marselíus, and he had variously been known as Móði or Marsi, but never as Toggi, like his son Thorgeir – never, that is, until he arrived in the district. The old man's introductions did much to lighten the atmosphere at the table; the men became more friendly and smiled cheerfully at the old man, for they had now acquired an audience for the forthcoming discussion – a man who knew nothing about them except that they might well be old hands at meetings, and men of standing.

As soon as Tommi opened his mouth to start the proceedings he realised that he had to go to the toilet – it could be a mistake to delay that any longer. The toilet was in the unventilated cupboard next to the kitchen, with only a thin partition in between.

The men waited for ages at the kitchen table while Tommi went about his business, and tried to pretend that nothing was happening as intestinal noises, groans and sour-smelling flatulence spread through the air. Old Toggi was the only one who had no manners: he pricked up his ears, wrinkled his nose and asked what was going on. At last Tommi reappeared, fastened his belt and sat down looking a bit uncomfortable, as if he hadn't really managed to finish properly.

So what did they discuss at this residents' meeting, the only one in the history of the district ever to have been held? Toggi the trawlerman had a flask of *brennivín* with him, but they all declined to have a drop in their coffee except for the shot-putter and Old Toggi. Lína stood at the stove and made pot after pot of coffee, which received high praise; she certainly didn't stint on the beans, did Lína! Toggi gulped down cup after cup of coffee stiffened with *brennivín* and became raucous and loud-mouthed, banging his cup on the table and shouting: 'More coffee, Lína!' And because the talk was of past times, he kept repeating in a doom-laden voice, 'I reme-e-ember, Dad, when you boxed me on the ear with a wet fish-glove. I didn't like it at the time, but I like the thought of it now.'

So dear to him was this memory that when the flask was empty he got up and kissed his father who just sat there, doddery and out of it all, and thanked him for that box on the ear with a wet fish-glove: 'I didn't like it then, but I like the thought of it now.'

Although Toggi was half drunk, it was he who suddenly remembered that there was some purpose to this meeting other than recalling one's childhood and bygone days. 'What are we doing here?' he asked raucously. 'Weren't we supposed to be doing something?'

Tommi came to with a start and began again on the introductory speech he had been preparing in his mind long before the meeting; but soon he was back in the old days: as a child he had lost his mother and five siblings and not had many opportunities, and then his twin brother Mási had also died, in an avalanche . . . But then Tommi came to again, and said that he wanted his children to enjoy some of the things he had missed out on, like family life, for example, an education and leisure time as well. Even sport . . . 'I'm thinking in particular about the boys here – they ought to have something to occupy them.'

Well? What could it be? Was it work they needed? Hlynur suggested potato-growing, school gardens, that kind of thing . . .'

'No, I'm thinking mainly about their leisure hours,' Tommi said, a little testily, 'to keep them away from a life of crime . . .'

'We mustn't be too soft on these brats!' shouted Tóti, as always when the subject of juvenile delinquency came up. 'They should have the pig-headedness beaten out of them! And then teach them something useful!'

Tommi had begun to sweat at the temples and he put his hands to his head, but he didn't want to argue and pretended not to hear Tóti. 'Listen,' he said. 'In every other district in town there are various places where youngsters can get together, boys' clubs, the YMCA, the Scouts, and sports clubs. But what do we have here? Practically a gangster mafia among the boys. Should we not do something about it?'

Now all was clear. Höskuldur promptly suggested a cards club for the boys; he himself was in the taxi-drivers' bridge club, but he dropped the idea when he thought of the bridge evenings down at Citicabs where they played for money in a little smoke-filled hut and drank gin out of coffee-cups.

Hreggviður now became tense with inspiration: he wanted to found a sports club! So enthusiastic was he that he gave a speech, the longest speech of his life, though it was mostly an incoherent stream of words. What it said, in essence, was that he would never have been the man he was today had he not engaged in sport and worked at it. 'Look at me!' he said, thumping the table happily. Höskuldur and Tommi looked at him and grinned. Tommi made out that Hreggi had had a brilliantly original idea. And there and then they founded the Kári Football Club.

Tommi had had his eye on an empty stretch of turf diagonally across from Tommi's Shop; he had worked out that it could make an excellent sports ground. After the meeting the men plodded over there and began to pace out a pitch and make two sets of goalposts. Tommi had got hold of some lengths of timber, large enough to make posts and crossbars. Toggi said he knew of some old bits of netting down by the fish sheds, and he and Höskuldur went off in the taxi to fetch them. Hlynur owned hammers and pliers, Hreggviður a shovel, and they managed to borrow a wheelbarrow from somewhere.

It was a bright May evening and the men were all in excellent fettle as they trudged out with their stuff to the empty field and began to clear it of rubbish and stones. Children and youngsters sensed that something was up; they followed the men and were soon hard at work together smoothing and raking and tidying. The womenfolk met between the houses to look for the children and began to talk together: most of them had looked down on all the others from the moment they moved into the district, but when harmony and solidarity began to emanate from the new sports ground, the pride and suspicion disappeared in cigarette smoke and sugary coffee at the clothes posts. Some of the women, led by Grjóni's mother, Thórgunnur, began to bake dumplings to take to the workers at the ground. Old Lína didn't take part, as she was too busy foretelling the football club's future, which apparently looked very promising. Hreggviður's wife Gréta did not join in the baking, either: she was in bed in the hut, with a bad bout of depression.

When the women turned up with hot cakes and steaming coffee out at the sports ground the men took a break from their work. Tommi sent the brothers Baddi and Danni over to Tommi's Shop for a whole case of non-alcoholic malt ale for the youngsters. He was almost in tears of happiness at the way in which this idea of his was yielding such good results right from the start.

Toggi and Höskuldur then arrived with the boot of the taxi full of rotting fishing nets which they began at once to clean and repair and disentangle; after that the men measured the goals with folding rulers and began to saw and plane suitable lengths of wood for the posts. Cousin Tóti said that nails were no problem: he had been collecting nails as a hobby for years – used nails, bent nails and rusty nails which he had straightened and polished and graded by size and shape in empty paint tins. He wanted to show Tommi his treasure and they got Höskuldur to run them home to his place. Beaming with pride, Tóti produced the tins, three two-litre paint tins full of these precious prizes, and they bent

over the cans as if they were cradles. They were loud in their
praises: 'You did all right there, Tóti!'

But when Tóti wanted to take one of the tins out of the house,
there was an outcry: Fía nearly had a fit. All those fine nails!
If they needed to use nails, why couldn't they pay through the
nose for them like everyone else? Goalposts? 'What's in it for
you, Thorgnýr?'

Gummi's large and unshaven face peered over Fía's shoulder
as she spoke. His yellow teeth gleamed in a grin as his mother
forbade Tóti to take the nails. Tommi and Höskuldur looked
away and rolled their eyes. Tóti was on the point of tears, but
then rebelled; he grabbed the tin and ran outside with it. Gummi
howled with fright and Fía fell full length on the floor, pretending
to be seriously hurt. Tóti was upset for the rest of the evening
and before he went home he got a bottle from Höskuldur. For
the next few days he was given a taste of the floor-mop.

A little later, when the pitch was ready, the football club
was officially founded. Tommi was elected managing director,
Höskuldur the taxi-driver was secretary, while Toggi and Hlynur
were committee members. Hreggviður asked to be excused any
position of responsibility, but not quite in those words.

Initially Tóti was the club's treasurer, as he was a bit of a finan-
cier. The first few coins which came into the club's coffers were
confiscated by Fía, as being no more than fair payment for the
nails. When Tommi heard about this he discreetly reassigned the
role of treasurer to the managing director's post.

The club's only asset so far was a football for which the men
of the district (mainly Tommi) forked out. Tommi was also the
team's trainer; he knew about football from the time when he
had sailed for the Charlies in the days before the war. Also,
he owned a blue uniform, a brass-band uniform he had taken
in lieu of a debt from a drunken trumpet player two years
previously. The trumpet, old and worn, had been included as
part of the deal. Three evenings a week, after supper, Tommi
put on the blue brass-band uniform complete with epaulettes
and gilt buttons, took up position in the middle of the district

and blew the trumpet; that was the signal to the boys that Kári football practice was about to begin, and they gathered around him. Then to the accompaniment of irregular trumpet-blowing they walked down to the pitch in single file; Tommi divided them into teams and they began to kick the brown leather ball around.

Sometimes there were far too many boys for two teams, but Tommi did not want to leave anyone out and so he let them all join in; there were often twenty or thirty boys in each team. They had no kit, of course, so the teams were just great hordes of boys in plimsolls and short trousers. Nor was it possible to have proper playing positions: it was just a free-for-all in which the ball was the only team-mate. Tommi refereed the games, and really excelled himself. He did not have a whistle, and at first he tried to shout the referee's decisions over the yelling of the packs of boys; this didn't work at all, as Tommi had a quiet voice, but he found a remedy: he used the trumpet, which had three valves and thus had three different sounds which Tommi could easily produce – one for a goal, another for a free kick, and a third for a penalty. It was an extremely effective system and it is truly remarkable that FIFA has never thought of using a trumpet for refereeing instead of that stupid whistle.

Not everyone thought that whistles were more stupid than trumpets, however: boys from the more respectable districts who had old and well-established sports clubs with club-houses, club colours and real referee's whistles began to make fun of the Kári lads. 'Are you a football club or a brass band?' The Kári boys had been accustomed to taunts for as long as they could remember, or at least from the time they had moved into the barracks, and were well able to answer back with tongue and fist, but the trumpet got under their skin. Late that summer when Tommi had a birthday (no one knew how old he was), Baddi and Danni gave him a real whistle, a brass one with a pea inside: Baddi had pinched it from Grettir's Boy Scout uniform.

Dollí could not join the Kári Football Club, of course: the only sport on offer was boys' football; at the very most, the girls might be allowed in when there was a tombola or a cake sale for the benefit of the club funds.

The brothers Baddi and Danni, on the other hand, were members right from the start, when they were eleven and nine years old respectively. Baddi and his friend Grjóni were born leaders and initiators. Baddi was tough, pushy and combative, and nothing could stop him once he got the ball; he would dash and dart and dribble with it until it was in the rotting fish-netting. Nothing could stop him except Grjóni, if he were in the opposing team; Grjóni was the perfect defender, a rock in a storm, and the attackers were scattered in all directions when Grjóni came charging at the ball and with his big toe hacked it away into the bushes.

Baddi was passionately keen on football. He was an instinctive solo player: concepts like team-play and making passes were completely alien to him. He didn't find it easy to accept the strict rules which Tommi insisted were part of the game. Not being allowed to pick up the ball in one's hands might be okay by Baddi, but that all those brats and whelps should be allowed to get in his way with their racket and insolence – that he could not abide. In time, however, it all worked out in such a way that the juniors learned to show Baddi and Grjóni, the uncrowned leaders of the barracks lads, the same respect on the pitch as off it.

The only person who did not follow these unwritten rules was Danni. He didn't actually shout abuse and insolence: he just charged, cold as ice, at anyone who happened to be in the way. He was just a puppy in years, but he was so big for his age that he could easily stand his ground among the ten- and eleven-year-olds. Danni was a natural football player: skilful, fast and with a powerful shot. Older football fans who came to watch the training at the new club said that the boy had the makings of another Albert Guðmundsson.*

---

* Albert Guðmundsson was Iceland's first professional footballer to play in Europe after the Second World War. He starred with Rangers, Arsenal and Racing de Paris.

Danni was full of old Tommi's *Boys' Own* wisdom and teaching about honest competition and fair play. The brothers sometimes got into fierce fights on the pitch, and Tommi usually turned a blind eye to this: nothing good had ever come of his attempts to adjudicate in the brothers' quarrels.

Gradually some order began to enter the affairs of the football club. Other sports clubs got some kind of financial support from the government, and such subvention might also be available to the Kári Club if certain formalities were completed. In order to be more than merely a disorganised boys' gang playing football under the leadership of a small-time grocer in a brass-band uniform, the club would have to be registered with the national association of clubs, play in recognised team colours and have at least the beginnings of a club-house. The spring after the club was founded saw the first Kári club-house: it was a derelict shed which lay on its side down by the shore. The men of the district, with the horde of boys at their heels, fetched it and did it up and set it up beside the pitch. Tommi saw to the team colours – in fact, it was probably Karolína who dreamed them up: dark blue shirts, dark blue shorts and dark blue socks. This was an unusual colour combination at that time, but it was thought very smart. The shirts were purchased after a collection, and the womenfolk made the shorts and knitted the socks for the team. When the money from the government began to come in, the pitch was levelled, measured out and marked with whitewash, and then proper goalposts were installed. To make it possible to train all the year round, a gravelled area was prepared nearby. Beside the main pitch running tracks, long-jump and triple-jump pits and a concrete throwing circle were laid down. Even though it was all rather primitive, the Kári sports ground was considered one of the best in town.

This club had a tremendous effect on the district. For a time, petty crime completely disappeared. Football was the only thing which meant anything to the boys. The two pitches were constantly in use for as long as it was daylight. One day, while Tommi was at work, a small select group of the oldest boys led by Baddi and Grjóni formed a team which played against a group of boys from the next district – most of whom trained and played in teams which took part in the Reykjavík Cup. The match ended in a ferocious brawl, of course, with stone-throwing and threats, but the Kári team had won an overwhelming victory: Baddi sent the goals flying in, while Grjóni made mincemeat of the opposing forwards.

There were several highly promising footballers in this Kári team. Stína Begga's Lúddi lived in the district at this time; he was a year older than Baddi and Grjóni and had begun to smoke. A dark-haired youngster with a narrow face, staring eyes and a drooping mouth, he was the goalkeeper. He was also in Kári's first championship team, until some authority or other had him sent to the country, and he wasn't seen for nearly ten years; by that time he was no longer called Stína Begga's Lúddi, but Louie Louie.

It had been agreed that Kári should take part in the Reykjavík Cup like the other teams in the city. Tommi was to select the team and manage it, and Hreggviður was to be his assistant and advisor because of his knowledge of sports training.

The championships were divided into age groups, and Kári could only take part in one of these divisions, the fourth, which at that time was the youngest group, for boys of thirteen and under. All that had to be done was to select eleven boys to make up the team. There was no shortage of suitable candidates: Tommi could have picked three or four teams. Baddi and Grjóni were automatically chosen, and Lúddi was in goal. Then Tommi selected eight other tough lads; they wore the blue team colours and spent the days in special training with Hreggviður, the evenings under the chief trainer's direction.

The men of the district were proud of their lads – they looked damned stylish in their blue strip. The men often turned out in large numbers to watch the training. They all wanted to be part of the club's life in some way, perhaps also in order to have a reason for spending all their evenings watching football down at the pitch. So Tommi arranged to have them form a kind of Old

Boys' section of the club; they could play chess and do gymnastics and discuss tactics in the club-house, which was to be enlarged at once for this purpose. Nothing came of the gymnastics, and the chess was soon put to one side, but the men continued to turn up, usually with a hip-flask; they now had a watertight excuse for having a good time, because the whole district admired the football club. The role of the Old Boys' section changed into a sort of honorary committee and support group to the club; they would put money into a collection box for whenever the club had some major project afoot.

When the box was opened, its contents were used to pay a woman who advertised that she could compose poems and songs to order. Tommi felt that the club wouldn't be a proper one until it had its own song. At nights he dreamed of annual jubilees and meetings; these would begin with him, as chairman of the management committee, delivering a light-hearted speech of exhortation and giving an account of the team's results in the championships. Then there would be films and other entertainments, interspersed with community singing, in which the crowd would sing rousing hymns, and the proceedings would end with everyone singing the 'Kári Song'.

This poet's main source of income was the writing of rhymed obituaries (signed: 'A Friend'), so she had developed a rather melancholy poetic style, and the sonnet she composed was not particularly well suited to a song of exhortation – even the least poetic of the oldsters could see that. But the two last lines did arouse enthusiasm and were kept as the team's motto; the rest was thrown away. The motto was painted on the team's emblem:

Long live Kári's heroes
In adversity, victory and every kind of endeavour

Fía's and Tóti's sons took no part in the football club. There was really not much hope for Gummi, as he was too old, and Manni, the youngest of the brothers, wasn't born until two years after the club was founded, when Fía was fifty-one.

Gummi was twenty-four, and had an office job with the Electricity Board. It was said that he was such a clumsy oaf that he was turning everyone's hair grey. Even Tóti once admitted that God had not made a very good job of his Gummi: 'Sometimes I think he has a diesel engine inside his head,' Tóti said, as he sat for a whole day chatting to Tommi down at the shop, drinking half a bottle of spirits and not daring to go home.

Gosi took no part in the football either, even though he was the same age as Danni. Gosi went to the Camp Thule primary school, and he was lucky to have got in there; at any other school he would have been teased to death because of his clothes. Fía and Tóti never spent money on clothes for the boys except what Fía could pick up at flea markets. These were mostly windcheaters which Fía piled on to her boys until they could hardly move. They waddled about like penguins. Of course, they sweated buckets under these warm clothes, but Fía adhered to the doctrine that sweaty children were more vulnerable to catching colds – and against colds there was only one sure remedy: more and thicker windcheaters.

These anoraks were the only Christmas and birthday presents they got. Toys, bicycles, sledges – those were all non-essentials. When all the children in the tower block were out on their bicycles, Gosi ran after them, crop-haired, big-bottomed and with his boots on, beside himself with laughter. He loved to play this game. Occasionally he was allowed a turn, but he didn't know how to ride a bike and fell off, and nearly died of laughter. He was so heavy and clumsy that the bikes buckled under him and were broken in the fall, and eventually he was chased away from the crowd of youngsters with shouts and curses. After that he just sat at the window and looked on. If he saw anyone with sweets he began to feel itchy until he could contain himself no longer and ran outside in the hope of getting some, too, but was chased away with yells of abuse. 'Gosi Fatty! Your granny drives a dustcart! Wipe your arse with barbed wire!' Then tears would come to Gosi's eyes, for he loved sweets, which he hardly ever got except on visits to the Old House. Nonetheless, his teeth rotted. That was another story. For more than two years he could hardly move for toothache. But dentists are the biggest profiteers and money-grubbers in town – Fía knew that! She wasn't going to support their swindling. And Gosi had to suffer at his window.

Fía never sang lullabies to her boys, but she did read to them in bed. It was supposed to teach them to handle money, to understand the value of money, and to experience the happiness which results from seeing one's bank balance grow. When the boys lost their first tooth they would be given a ten-year bank deposit book with a hundred *krónur* paid in, and Fía would then deposit another ten *krónur* each month; then there was the interest and the interest on the interest, and it was all entered in the brown bank books which Fía would read aloud when the boys were tucked up in bed: 'And what happens? Look, Gosi, there's more mun-n-n-y here!'

Tóti and his sons were involved in a perpetual struggle, all against all; they knew that if anything entered the home which could be called a luxury, the main thing was to be bold, quick and tough enough to get a share.

Luxury? Not just luxury. Sometimes the law of the jungle held sway merely to get enough to eat. Sometimes there were accidents: after little Manni was born, a small bag of caramels crept into the house, and so savagely did the brothers fight one another over them that Manni got concussion and lost consciousness, and Gummi was badly hurt in the eye from biting and scratching; perhaps it was worth it, because he got the caramels. But he did not always win, by any means; when the fights began there was little to choose between them, despite the big age difference: Manni was about ten, Gosi twenty-one, Gummi thirty-six, and the old man himself, who enjoyed a fight as much as the rest of them, was nearly seventy.

A festive crate of Coke was always bought on the night before Christmas Eve, and drunk within the space of a few minutes. Magnificent! It was a matter of being quick enough to open one bottle after the other and guzzle it down so as to get as much as possible. Gosi became a real master of this art: he invented a special drinking technique which meant that he didn't need to swallow – he just opened his gullet somehow from the pharynx and let the Coke gush down into his stomach without a break. The Christmas after he was confirmed, this was nearly his undoing: he was so incredibly quick and drank so much that his stomach filled up completely and the Coke began to flow into his lungs. He writhed and turned blue, but his life was saved when he vomited and it all came frothing out of him again. He was driven to hospital, where the doctors tried to clear most of the Coke from his lungs.

In her heart of hearts, Fía probably had nothing against these drinking contests on the night before Christmas Eve, even though she complained about their greed, for the menfolk of the family usually had such bad stomach-aches from all the Coke they'd drunk that the Christmas fare lasted well into the New Year.

'Do you know what Fía and Tóti sing when they go round the Christmas tree?' Baddi once asked. 'They sing: SAVE! SAVE! SAVE! SAVE! SAVE! SAVE! SAVE! SAVE!'

4

I sure as hell won't want to
live here

It was always said of the children in the district that they were riff-raff. Ill-brought-up louts. Breaking window-panes, stealing and fighting. A filthy rabble who poisoned everything around them, unwashed and foul-mouthed.

It was hard to find teachers for the district primary school. One or two idealists tried it but gave up after a short time, scarred all over from catapults.

There was no fun in firing catapults at the school pastor: he just wept – grown man that he was, standing there crying at the blackboard, grey-haired, with a broad face and headmaster's spectacles. It wasn't any fun, so the pastor took over more and more of the teaching; he put the curriculum aside and talked instead in a plaintive voice about divine love and the forgiveness of sin.

That autumn Danni and Gosi, Fía and Tóti's middle sons, were to enter the form for eleven-year-olds, and the pastor was trying to advise the young riff-raff to look on the bright side of life. He had been out for a stroll on the hill one sunny day: 'And what do you think I found, dear children?' he asked above the racket in the classroom. 'One of the most beautiful things which bears witness to divine love, a sight which warms our innermost hearts. What do you think I found, dear children?'

'MONEY!' Gosi answered with a howl of delight.

'No, dear children, it was not money. It was a little plover's nest.'

Could this have been the day on which Hreggviður tried to set the world record in the shot-putt? The same day on which the deputation arrived from the Artists' Block? Baddi and Grjóni were both nearly thirteen then and it was autumn and they had both skipped school, which was hardly news. Grjóni went out delivering the newspaper *Vísir*; it was his own idea, so that he could sometimes have pocket-money like the other boys, but in the end the few *krónur* he managed to earn by delivering papers were spent on food for his mother and siblings. His delivery area was the barracks district and the tower blocks, forty-three copies. He was usually given fifty; as a fringe benefit he was allowed to keep the extra papers and sell them off for a *króna* each.

It was a Monday, and everyone wanted to read the *Vísir*. The semi-finals of the All-Iceland Athletics Championships had been held that weekend, an oil-tanker had gone aground off Reykjanes, everything was just hunky-dory.

Baddi never did a delivery round – the old couple wouldn't hear of him tiring himself out with that kind of thing. And to tell the truth, it suited the dear boy just fine to sleep until noon and potter about in the afternoon, and perhaps stroll down to the Kári ground of an evening and play a little football.

When Grjóni came shooting out of the shadows of the barracks shortly after midday with the blue *Vísir* bag over his shoulder, Baddi had been carving a target on the scullery wall and was practising throwing a bowie knife from the Scout shop at it. Grjóni admired the target, ten circles set inside one another and marked with elaborately formed figures. Baddi had become quite skilled with the knife; he usually managed to throw it so that it stuck somewhere on the target or near it. Grjóni was clumsy, however; he was all thumbs, and when he was given a turn he flung the knife so that the flat of the blade or the shaft hit the wall all over the place. They were dressed the same: in rubber shoes, woollen socks, wide trousers and sweaters. Both were dirty with soot and grime, but this was less noticeable on Baddi's dark features than on Grjóni's, which were so pale.

They sat down behind the lumber which still lay in a pile beside the Old House – leftovers from the building work which had been completed two years previously. Old Tommi saw no reason to throw the timber away or to part with it, for it might come in useful in the depths of winter when there was not much coal in the district's homes. The two friends sat there with some cigarette-ends which Baddi had sneaked from an ashtray. They looked round quickly when they heard someone coming, and hid the fag-ends in their hands, but it was just brother Danni coming home from school. With ironic camaraderie they offered him a smoke, but he shook his head worriedly, since he knew very well that smoking, drinking and gambling were the direct road to perdition. Never take the first glass!

'He's not like my young brother,' said Grjóni. 'Diddi is always drunk, and he's not even twelve yet.'

'Danni's only eleven,' said Baddi.

'Danni's not such a big idiot as Diddi.'

'It doesn't matter if he's strong, he's an idiot all the same.'

'Hey, here's a picture of Hreggviður the shot-putter!' said Grjóni, who was flicking through *Vísir*.

In the picture, someone was pinning a medal to a gloomy, black-bearded and tousled Hreggi. The champion was six foot six and weighed twenty-two stones and lived on an invalid's pension. The boys knew that he was able to lift cars. He sometimes lifted cars at the Artists' Block when he was in a good mood and had had a few drinks; he would take hold of the bumper and turn a car crosswise so that it was impossible to move it backwards or forwards in the carpark and no one could understand how the car could have been manoeuvred into that position. Famous playwrights and film directors stood outside in the carpark contemplating this phenomenon, and eventually half of the Symphony Orchestra arrived to help jiggle the vehicle back into an acceptable driving position. Once when Hreggviður lost his temper in his barracks-hut he had struck the gable end so hard that it collapsed. The gable end lay on its side out on the gravel and the barracks-hut gaped like a cavern into the winter darkness. When he had slept off his anger and was growing cold he went outside, lifted the gable and put it back in the gaping hole. With his bare hands. Alone.

Invalid? He was no armless hunchback in a wheelchair. Old Tommi sometimes said that Hreggviður had a screw or two loose, but few people knew what was wrong with him, not even Gréta, his wife. In fact, it seemed more likely that there was something wrong with her: she was always either incredibly cheerful or horribly depressed. Strange. On one occasion she tried to hang herself from one of the clothes posts, but old Lína saw her from the window and ran outside and told her to stop that damned nonsense: 'You must have got out of bed on the wrong side this morning!' Lína then brought the woman into the kitchen of the Old House to calm her down. The odd thing was that when this happened, everything was going just fine. Nothing was wrong. The weather was good. The children were well. Hreggviður hadn't had a drop to drink for more than a month and had just become Reykjavík champion in hammer-throwing. But some two months later everything had gone to pot; the barracks-hut was as cold as an igloo, both daughters had bronchitis, Hreggviður was stark raving mad, smashing everything to bits and drinking like a maniac, and Gréta's cheeks had grown sunken and her face had gone grey – yet now she was as cheerful as could be. She went sailing around in a blissful rapture, and talked about the house they were going to build – a villa. And she was going to get her teeth seen to. Make a record, too – that was what she told the family at the Old House, because she had been a singer with a dance band before she had met Hreggviður. Then she did a couple of listless steps on the kitchen floor and laughed a sharp, trilling laugh. Everyone smiled. Even old Lína smiled. Gréta's laugh was so infectious and warm. Meanwhile the coughing of bronchitis could be heard from the barracks-hut, all the way into the kitchen.

The boys wanted to show Hreggviður the newspaper picture, but before they could knock on his door, the giant athlete came rushing out with his sports bag on his way to the Kári ground where, later that day, the final of a minor competition which had begun at the weekend was to be decided. Hreggi looked gloomy, but brightened up considerably when he saw the adulation on the faces of the boys who he knew were his most fervent, perhaps his only, admirers.

'Yes, I got a bronze in the discus.'

'A bronze? Who won?'

'Some ballet dancer or other. He's no good. But there's still the shot.'

'Do you think you'll win?'

'Win? Ha! Hahah! Come over a bit later and I'll show you how to set a world record!'

'Oh, wow, a world record, eh?'

'That's right, boys, now give me a copy of *Vísir*, you can chalk it up on my account, Grjóni.'

Lying by the wall of the old warehouse there were some gardeners and labourers who were working on a site next to the Electricity Board Block; Grjóni sold them four copies. Then the boys walked by the milk shop and sold a few more.

They looked in at Tommi's Shop where Old Tommi was sorting oranges; he was in an excellent mood because a Finnish accordion virtuoso was playing hot stuff on the radio. They let him have the paper and showed him the picture of Hreggviður.

'Do you think he'll win the shot-putt, Dad?'

'He shouldn't have any difficulty there, Baddi my boy, he's the only competitor! Heh heh. Well, boys, here's a five-*króna* piece for the paper.'

A five-*króna* piece for the paper! They ran back to the milk shop and bought themselves ice lollies. They hung over the counter as they ate the lollies and chatted to the shop-girls, two lipsticked teenagers with beehive hairdos and nail varnish who made insinuating remarks to the boys and talked to them as if they were inexperienced children; the boys grew big and bold and called them 'birds' and 'broads' and chanted 'breast, breast, thigh, thigh, now's your opportunity', and the girls laughed and giggled and shook their heads as if scandalised at the way boys spoke nowadays. One of the girls was from the country and asked: 'What's the matter, boys, have you caught a dose of puppy love?'

Housewives from the block who were coming in for milk bought some papers from Grjóni, who was now so laden with gilt *króna* coins that he jingled with every step. He counted the papers in the bag when he came out, and there were only thirty-six left of the forty-three he was supposed to deliver.

Hlynur the mechanic was in his garage, grimy and oil-stained, wearing an old pair of horn-rimmed spectacles which he fastened with a black rubber band over the grey hair at the nape of his neck.

Hlynur wasn't really a mechanic, and the garage wasn't a garage; he was just a nimble-fingered scrap-metal collector who had this shed at his disposal and who pottered about repairing the wrecked cars he had collected. He was an expert on East European cars, Russian Moskviches, Czech Skodas and East German Trabants. As a rule they were almost worthless after a few years, without necessarily being completely useless; in that condition Hlynur got them for a song, and hauled them home to his shed. The idea was to do them up and then sell them at a profit. He always set to work on them with enormous enthusiasm, taking them to bits, repairing, fixing and patching. One car might have a decent body but a useless gearbox; he would transfer the gearbox from another wreck which had a ruined body. He screwed, sprayed and greased, but never completed anything. He only enjoyed working on cars which were heaps of scrap metal, and lost interest in them as soon as they were on the point of turning into usable cars. Half-finished, they stood there in the shed gathering dust by the month, then gradually they got in the way and were hauled outside to decompose and turn into heaps of scrap metal again.

There were countless wrecks around the shed, and it was debatable which could be called a car. Some were only halves of cars, others nothing but a chassis with tyres; windscreens and doors lay in piles, engines and gearboxes were scattered around in between. It was impossible to count the wrecks: they could only be reckoned in terms of weight, like broken biscuits from a biscuit factory.

Hlynur was considered a good-natured man. He smiled a lot, but the smile never reached his eyes before it would fade and he would once again be the same old worried, wrinkled and sighing Hlynur.

No one could understand why he was always so worried. He wasn't that badly off, after all. He owned his own barracks-hut, Hlynur's Barracks, which was the biggest one in the district, shaped like a T, with a kind of appendix which stuck out from the main building; Hlynur called it the Calf. The hut was in good condition and stood out from the rest because it was usually freshly painted. He lived there with Sigurlaug his wife – Lopsided Lauga she was called, because she was a bit lame and limped when she walked. She did the laundry for people all over town, and earned so much money that Hlynur was able to go on with his scrap-metal collecting unconcerned, without ever finishing a job. They had two sons who were said to be short, pleasant young men in their twenties; one was a plumber's apprentice in Selfoss, and the other was married and lived in Súðavík and worked at the fish-freezing plant there. They were model sons of whom any of the families in the neighbourhood would have been proud.

A small lorry with a crane was in the middle of hauling yet another wrecked car up to the shed. Hlynur was watching worriedly, sometimes lifting his arms and shouting 'hohoho' to the driver. Baddi and Grjóni came strolling by and stopped to watch the manoeuvring. It was the remains of a Skoda Popular of the same vintage as the car which Hlynur himself drove.

When the wreck was in place near the door of the shed, the driver turned off the ignition, got out and gave the tyres a few hefty kicks. Grjóni asked: 'How many two-*króna* pieces did that cost you, Hlynur?'

Hlynur smiled amiably. 'How many two-*króna* pieces, my friend? Eh? E-e-eh?' he said, smiling even more broadly. Then he looked worriedly at the driver, who was rattling the doors of the Skoda.

'You want to know how many two-*króna* pieces it cost, Grjóni, my boy?' Hlynur murmured absently.

The crane-lorry driver bought a newspaper from the boys; meanwhile Hlynur waltzed into the open garage and began to fiddle about with an oilcan. Suddenly he seemed to awaken from a dream. He hurried straight up to Grjóni and looked him in the eye: 'It didn't even cost two *krónur*, my friend. I was given it.'

Silence. Hlynur looked searchingly at Grjóni, as if he wanted to be sure that this business of the money had sunk home.

'But what does *Vísir* cost, Grjóni? How many two-*króna* pieces does *Vísir* cost?'

'One *króna*.'

'You shall have two *krónur*! Here is a two-*króna* piece for *Vísir*,' said Hlynur, smiling so warmly that the depression wrinkles stood out on his forehead.

The boys hung around while Hlynur settled with the driver, who then got in behind the wheel and went off in the lorry. Hlynur vanished into the shed with a brooding look, while the friends went on their way with the newspapers. When they had gone about twenty metres Hlynur appeared at the doorway again with a rag in his hands, and called them back.

'Hey, Sigurjón, come here a minute . . . Listen, Grjóni, my boy, I'm a bit worried about your brother Diddi,' he said when they came over.

Grjóni scraped his rubber shoe in the gravel.

'He came round here this morning, then he went away, but came back and was so strange I even think he might have been drinking. I could make neither head nor tail of him.'

Grjóni cursed softly between clenched teeth and turned red in the face.

'What's more, he kept talking about killing someone. He went over to my house and tried to pinch a knife!'

Grjóni had stopped cursing, and was staring Hlynur straight in the eye.

'Do you know anything about it, Grjóni, my boy?'

'No.'

'It's not that I'm complaining, even though he sometimes gives me a bit of bother. I'm only telling you this because you're his brother! How is your mother, by the way, Sigurjón, my boy?'

'She's ill.'

Hlynur wiped the sweat from his brow with an oily rag,

and said with a sigh: 'I wish I could do something to help you all!'

Grjóni said nothing. After shifting from one foot to the other on the gravel for a while, Hlynur waltzed back into the shed.

Grjóni was silent and walked in zig-zags, making the *Vísir* bag swing around him.

'Where does Diddi get *brennivín* all the time?' Baddi asked.

'He's completely off his rocker. Not so long ago he drank some of that anti-freeze stuff they put in cars and was ill for several days afterwards: I had to sit with him . . . he kept howling and screaming even though he's nearly twelve . . . then Mum began to blubber, too . . .' Now Grjóni fell dead silent, and clenched his teeth. Then he said savagely: 'Hlynur's an ass and a fool!'

Throwing stones at a bus was always fun, and when the bus came rattling along pothole-strewn Aðalgata the friends threw pebbles after it, but only managed to hit the small window at the rear of the kiosk at the bus-stop. The glass shattered loudly, and when people came rushing out of the kiosk the friends took to their heels and ran past the next row of barracks and the Pacific Ocean pond to the Artists' Block, round the corner and up a flight of stairs. From a window on the fourth floor they watched their pursuers go rushing past; with that they relaxed and sat down, then set off down the polished linoleum of the staircase. On the second floor they met some youngsters who lived in the tower block.

'What are you doing here?'

'None of your business!'

'Have you farted, too? Hee-hee-hee!'

'Campers! Campers! Barracks riff-raff!'

'As if I wanted to be a miserable blockie!'

'Hee-hee-hee. You're just jealous because you don't live here! Hee-hee-hee!'

'Hah! I sure as hell woon't want to live here!'

'It's stupid to say woon't, it's wouldn't. Can't talk proper! Can't talk proper! Can't –'

Baddi ran up to the girl who was shouting loudest and kicked her in the backside with his rubber shoe. She gave a piercing wail and rushed away screaming at the top of her voice in floods of tears. The other children also began to cry, and went back into their flats. The boys went down the stairs to the street door, which they gave a good slam; but they didn't go out. They crept stealthily down some more stairs to the rubber-smelling cycle-store in the basement. They went through it and into the scullery, where they opened the window, ready to jump out on to the newly planted slope outside if anyone came.

But no one came. They sat there waiting, thirsting for revenge. Then they went into a long corridor with numbered storerooms on both sides. Each flat had its own storeroom, and they could easily have got into some of them without making a sound. On previous occasions they had often found empty soft-drink bottles to sell at the kiosk, but now they were looking for more valuable loot. In one of the storerooms they had sometimes found beer and preserved fruit, but now the door fastening had been strengthened: there was a hasp on it, and a strong padlock from Basti.

This struck the friends as brazen impertinence; what was more, these new arrangements suggested that the room was now stuffed with things of even more value. They jumped at the door with both feet, and at the fifth kick the frame gave way, and bits and pieces of wood flew about the corridor as the door fell in.

Oddly enough, the room contained nothing special, nothing but tyres and boots and a gas primus stove, along with fruit juice and jam with the year marked. The family which owned this storeroom had laid in a hoard of toilet paper, and in a fit of petulance the boys stole a large polythene bag full of rolls of the stuff, rather than leave empty-handed.

As they were on their way out along the corridor laden with these necessities of life, a door suddenly opened and two men in fighting posture appeared, looking very pleased with themselves. 'Well now, you rascals! Caught in the act!'

These were men in their prime, and one of them, a renowned cellist, seized hold of Grjóni: 'Now it's down to the station with you!'

With that, the lights in the corridor went out, and from the darkness came half-smothered shouts and the sound of scuffling; when a hand wearing a ring found the switch again and turned it on, the boys were dashing out of the door with the bag of toilet paper, and the cellist lay on the floor holding a bloody nose. The boys ran out of the flats and round the corner and across to the Electricity Board Block, where they got their breath back and rang all the doorbells and amused themselves by listening to a whole staircase engage in bewildered conversation about the alarm system. In the midst of all the gabbling, Fía's mournful cries of 'Jesus!' could be heard.

Then they discovered that they were being chased by people from the Artists' Block and ran off. They would probably have been caught had a taxi not stopped; they jumped in and disappeared in it.

'Were you taking the piss out of those idiots?' asked Höskuldur the taxi-driver. He drove around the district in his old, foul-smelling taxi, this worn middle-aged bachelor, and told the boys stories of his womanising adventures when he was their age. He thought he could not have been more than ten years old when he first got to grips with women. Then he told them jokes about *Vísir* and toilet paper: it didn't matter which one bought, but toilet paper was better, naturally, because it was softer to wipe oneself with. But he accepted a newspaper as payment for the trip and the rescue before dropping them off at the Kári sports ground.

Several athletes, supporters and enthusiasts were there, with their backs to the wind, wearing hooded anoraks and doing some exercises.

Hreggviður was dressed in his athletics gear – wide jeans which were tight round the waist, braces over a checked flannel shirt with its sleeves ripped off, and sockless in rubber shoes. He spoke more loudly than anyone else, shaking his enormous fists. A few drunks sat on a wooden bench a little apart from the main group. Now and again Hreggviður strode over to them, singing, and made some remark, and the laughter blared like a chorus of trawler foghorns on New Year's Eve. Then he took a drink, pulled a face and laughed some more. The mountain giant. The troll. Like the strongest wrestlers from *Gold Key* and *Dell* magazines.

The two boys were still lugging that damned toilet paper around. At last they found a use for it. Throwing the rolls was fun; they soared high and far like flying dragons, unrolling in flight and trailing long white tails in the air. They hurled a few rolls in all directions. The rolls flew. Not all the same distance. They began to compare who could throw the farthest, got bitten by the competitive bug just like the other athletes, and since the discus-throwing circle at the end of the ground was not in use, they ran over there with their hoard of toilet paper.

The throwing-circle was a concrete slab in the ground, a little under one and a half metres in diameter. A short distance away semi-circles had been drawn, marking the number of metres from the throwing-circle, from ten up to twenty. A little way beyond the centre of the cluster of lines a small Icelandic flag had been stuck in the soil, to mark the Icelandic record. Even further away there was a pennant with a picture of the globe cut into halves, to mark the world record; the pennant belonged to Hreggviður, from the days when he had sailed the world's oceans as an assistant engineer.

The boys took up position in the circle and began to hurl toilet rolls. One after another the rolls flew out over the semi-circles and greyish-white ribbons of paper straggled over the ground, which began to look more and more like a rubbish tip. They became completely absorbed in their throwing contest and paid no attention to anything else until the organisers of the meeting and the athletes came running towards them with shouts and curses. 'Who gave you permission to do this? Rascals! Pests!' A wrestling champion from Eyjafjörður hit Baddi so hard that he landed on his head and scraped himself, drawing blood from his cheek. Others grabbed hold of Grjóni, but he fought them off and finally managed to bite the finger of a committee chairman from the Reykjavík Athletics Board.

The hullaballoo and shouting caught the attention of Hreggviður, who was sitting on the bench with the drunks. He came striding over to the throwing-circle, and when he saw what was going on he scattered the disputants in all directions, put his hands on the boys' shoulders and asked what the devil the others thought they were doing, treating the youngsters with such violence.

Blood was pouring from the committee chairman's finger; someone picked up a crumpled skein of toilet paper from the gravel and offered to wind it round the cut. An angry man in training kit was still holding on to Grjóni, who tore himself free and jabbed his elbow in the man's face. The brawling and mauling flared up again. Hands pointed at the heaps of paper, and loud voices complained about badly brought-up barracks kids. Under the protective wing of the mountain giant the boys were ready for anything. Baddi told the wrestler from Eyjafjörður to go and screw his mother, and Grjóni knocked the hat off a little man in an overcoat who was so furious that he was going purple in the face. Above all the commotion boomed the thunderous voice of Hreggviður, making it plain that if anyone laid a finger on his young friends they would have him to deal with, and to emphasise the point he lifted the little man in the overcoat high in the air and threw him into the disorderly crowd.

As everything was boiling up, old Tommi arrived on the scene. He had heard the racket from his shop, and decided to restore calm. He walked into the crowd, looking some of the men in the eye, and talking quietly so that everyone had to pipe down in order to hear what he was saying. He merely said a few words about the purpose and value of sport and social work; some of them ought to have had the sense not to get so worked up over trivial matters: 'You'll clear up all this mess, boys, and then the whole thing will be forgotten.' Tommi had a few words in private with Hreggviður, who became as meek as a lamb; the boys quickly tidied up the litter of paper, and a moment later everything was so peaceful that no one could have raised his voice or got worked up without making a fool of himself. Tommi said goodbye and went back to his shop to sort oranges and listen to the Finnish accordion virtuoso Hakkaralainen; the sports ground was so peaceful that everyone bought copies of

Vísir from Grjóni as though nothing had happened – even the committee chairman, whose hand was hurting so much from the bite that he needed help to get a *króna* piece out of his jacket pocket.

Then Hreggviður went out into the throwing-circle, grimaced formidably and kneaded the shot in his hand. He had promised the boys a world record. He stood motionless in the circle, then planted his left foot forward and, with a heave of his right arm, propelled the shot in the direction of the flag. Hreggviður had no special style or technique – no tucking the shot under his chin or jumping and turning; he looked as if he were standing by the seashore throwing stones into the waves.

The shot landed with a thump somewhere far short of the flag. A good fifteen metres short. With a black scowl the champion stepped out of the circle in order to make the throw invalid. He nodded to the boys, and fetched the shot. Then he walked halfway round the sports ground with it in his gigantic fist; he stopped for a while beside the drunks and gave them each a cigarette from a pack of Pall Mall which he produced from his breast pocket, and as payment received a long, slow swig from a bottle of spirits.

Then he was back in the throwing-circle again. He threw a hate-filled glance at the two flags, then hurled the shot at them with a bear-like howl. But again the attempt was far short. Now he had only one throw left. The men turned their heads to one another: 'Our lad's angry now, that's when he's best, his last throw is always the longest one.'

'Hreggi could have been Nordic champion if he wasn't always drinking.'

'And the man's an invalid, of course,' someone said in an ambiguous tone of voice, and they all grinned stupidly.

Hreggviður trudged gloomily around the field, weighing the shot in his hands. He paused for a moment in front of the blue-painted shed at the end of the ground which served as a storeroom, changing-room and club-room for the members of the Kári Football Club.

'He's taking a jolt, something to strengthen his heart,' the

men said, nudging one another as Hreggviður rummaged into
something in the doorway of the shed. Then the giant walked
towards the throwing-circle with swift steps, holding the shot
in his fist. Grunting, he tensed his feet against the concrete slab,
heaved his arm, and sent the shot whistling through the air.

Hreggviður had nearly toppled out of the circle, but regained
his balance, looking with sharp, doubtful eyes at the shot, which
had dug up the gravel on the far side of the two flags. All those
present gaped in silence, and then Hreggviður gave a whoop of
triumph, and the boys thought the earth was shaking as he began
a wild dance in the circle. They all rushed over to the spot where
the shot had landed. Hreggviður picked it up and stroked it, the
judges reeled out their measuring tapes in a trice and after further
scrutiny and hurried conversation it emerged that there was no
doubt: Hreggviður had broken the world record by almost sixty
centimetres.

The drunks came over to congratulate the giant, who put
his hands on the shoulders of Grjóni and Baddi who were
jumping and cheering. Hreggviður produced his pack of Pall
Mall again, and it contained just enough cigarettes for them
all, boys, world champion and drunks, as they stood in a huddle
beside the throwing-circle while overcoated committee chairmen,
sports enthusiasts and people from the north country gaped and
examined, measured and shook their heads, until nothing but
the fact alone looked them in the eye: the drunken invalid from
the barracks had broken the world record in the most difficult
trial of strength known to athletics.

Someone ran off at once and contacted the newsrooms of the
main media. The committee chairman with the maimed hand
telephoned his superiors and there was talk of arranging a party
that very evening to celebrate the achievement.

Hreggviður continued to stroll about the field with the shot
in his hand, and looked more and more troubled as more and
more journalists, photographers, sports fans and hangers-on
appeared. It was now public knowledge and people began to
stream in from the neighbourhood. The champion was hauled
into a car where journalists with pencils and writing pads

inundated him with questions. Then it started to rain. Grjóni
sold some more papers, and then the boys found themselves
with nothing more to do; the men from the kiosk who had been
chasing them earlier in the day were approaching the scene, so
the friends quietly made themselves scarce.

Tommi was standing in the doorway of his shop when they
arrived there. He asked what was happening at the sports ground
now. Then he shook his head and laughed doubtfully.

'It's true, man, we saw it for ourselves, he threw the thing
much further than the world-record mark!'

Tommi said that he felt a bit like his namesake the apostle
when he was told of such miracles. 'But come in, boys, and
don't get wet.'

The lads were rather annoyed that Tommi didn't really want
to believe the news. They had seen it for themselves and there
were all those men with measuring tapes and whatever!

Then Grjóni began to count the newspapers in his bag, and
started looking worried. There were only thirteen left! He racked
his brains, and calculated that there were thirty copies missing
which he ought to have delivered to the subscribers.

'Well, you're clever devils, aren't you?' said Tommi. 'You'll
just have to go down to the kiosk and buy thirty copies of *Vísir*.
Eh? Buy back the papers you were supposed to end up selling!
Ha ha ha! I don't think I'd want to be in business with you!
Ha ha!'

Grjóni was weighing the possibility of going down to the
newspaper office and stealing the number of copies which
were missing, but that would be difficult and would take a
long time, and Baddi didn't like the idea. He said that Grjóni
should just phone the office and tell them he had only been given
thirteen copies.

That was the solution! It had happened before that the van
driver had given him the wrong bundle – on one occasion far
too many copies, and on another one far too few. Grjóni asked
Tommi if he could use the phone.

But, as one might expect, Tommi had some objections to this
plan. He didn't like it. Perfectly idiotic!

'But why? What am I to do, then?'

Tommi looked thoughtful, and stroked his chin with a look of sober integrity. 'It's no good telling them that you were only given thirteen copies. That kind of thing never happens. No one would make up a bundle of thirteen copies, and no van driver would make the mistake of delivering thirteen instead of fifty.'

'Damn it! What am I going to do, then?'

'My goodness, what stupid boys you are! It's obvious! You ring the office and tell them you didn't get any copies at all! It's much more likely that you were simply forgotten, or that your bundle got lost or stolen or something.'

When the driver from *Vísir* arrived in his van a good hour later, the boys were sitting at the rear of the barracks-hut eating Danish pastries from the milk shop. The driver was a fellow of about twenty and seemed to be in a filthy temper.

'I'm not giving you one single copy,' he said. 'I came here this morning just as I always do and left the bundle by the door here.'

Grjóni said he must have forgotten to leave it.

'What the devil, man, do you think I can't remember it? And then I go back there and get hell for forgetting to deliver the papers!' He lit a cigarette and pointed at Baddi. 'You were standing on the other side of the road carving something on the wall when I arrived. As though I wouldn't remember!'

The boys looked at him and grinned.

The driver heaved a sigh, hauled a bundle of newspapers from the front seat and threw it to them. 'Don't try lying to my face again like that, or I'll beat you up!' He got in behind the wheel and put the van into gear. Then he rolled down the window and asked: 'Doesn't that guy who broke the world record not live around here somewhere?'

The boys pointed to Hreggviður's hut.

'Do you know him?'

They certainly did.

'They were talking about it down at the newspaper and it was on the radio just now. That's great, isn't it? But is it true that he's an invalid?'

'An inva – what?'

'An invalid – a cripple, or something.'

Hreggviður a cripple? The strongest man in the world a cripple? They had never heard such nonsense.

'You're liars, and a man can't believe a thing you say,' said the van driver, and drove away.

Outside Hlynur's barracks-hut he met one of the drunks who had been at the athletics event. The man had a wooden leg and a limp. The *Vísir* van stopped and backed at top speed towards the man; the driver stuck out his head and asked if he knew Hreggviður the shot-putter.

The lame drunkard livened up and he replied in a loud, thick, hoarse voice: 'I-i-i-i-i am the worl-l-l-l-d shot-putt champion!'

A short time later the van driver arrived at the newspaper office in a state of exultation with a slightly tattered page from *Vísir* which he showed to everyone.

'I got the world champion's autograph!'

Some divorced, tobacco-stained, slightly alcoholic middle-aged journalists in dust-jackets smiled worldly smiles and looked at the piece of paper. On it the lame drunkard had scrawled in clumsy letters:

'HREGVIÐUR SIGURSON'

They smiled even more, and said: 'We were told that the so-called world champion's name is Hreggviður Barðason.'

'*This* man said he was the world champion,' said the van driver, piqued.

'Well, my friend,' one journalist said, yawning, 'you could have spared yourself the effort, for there isn't any world champion in this town at all.'

'What?'

'It turns out that the giant from the barracks out there set his world record with a training shot for youngsters which is much lighter than the ones which adults use in competition!'

While the boys were delivering the new bundle of *Vísir*, Lína was lighting the coal stove. She had cleaned out most of the soot earlier that day and when she kindled the fire, black smoky and sooty debris spewed out of the chimney. The wind was blowing towards the Artists' Block, and as it had been a warm day some windows and a few balcony doors were open.

The use of coal stoves in the barracks district had been annoying the block residents for a long time, but when this filthy smoke from the chimney of the Old House came blowing in through the windows, many of the artist families felt that enough was enough. People met on the staircase landings and discussed the matter, and a large group gathered for an unofficial emergency meeting in the bicycle cellar. One thing was clear to them all: this could not continue any longer. The cellist from the Symphony Orchestra was the angriest of all; he wanted unanimous agreement that the district should be razed to the ground as soon as possible. This musician's nose was swollen and bandaged after the fight down in the storerooms earlier that day.

The cellist repeated the story every five minutes; the owner of the storeroom from which the boys had stolen the toilet paper backed him up by showing what his storeroom looked like. Most of them had the same story to tell: they had been subjected to abuse by that barracks riff-raff, they had had their flats broken into, their bicycles stolen, snowballs and gravel thrown at their windows, their cars damaged.

Some mothers announced that they didn't dare let their children go out alone after dark; other women said they didn't dare to go out themselves; it also came to light that one mother had not only kept her children indoors but had hardly dared to leave the house from the time she had moved in, neither in darkness nor daylight, for fear of the barracks riff-raff's wickedness.

A supercilious actor asked people to keep a sense of proportion: the whole thing was turning into pure farce. He laughed at the mothers who wouldn't let their children go out: 'It's just plain hysteria!'

'Oh? Do you want your children to hobnob with that riff-raff?'

That was quite all right by him – in fact, one of the barracks lads had been in to have a cup of cocoa with his eldest son the other day.

Yes, it was no wonder that his children were constantly being sent home in droves from school with lice, the women said.

Actually they had not been sent home in droves – there were not that many to be sent home – although it was indeed true that one of his sons had once been infected with lice; but it had not been very serious, the lice had been washed out of his hair in ten minutes with a solution which could be bought at any pharmacy.

It was all developing into a noisy quarrel. The actor was called a traitor and a spokesman for drunken riff-raff and wretches, while he, for his part, insisted that the people in the barracks were no less important than many of those who lived in fine houses and had posh titles: for example, Karolína the fortune-teller, who had a great gift of prophecy and was a much respected woman . . .

At this point a few right-thinking men took charge and stopped the pointless quarreling. They said that it was possible to look at the question from both sides: on the one hand it was a fact which could not be disputed that living next to the folk from the barracks district was so difficult that it could be called intolerable; the residents of the block weren't left in peace with their property and valuables, and there was that constant smoke which made it impossible for people to open their windows or enjoy the sunshine on fine days. On the other hand, one ought to be careful not to condemn the inhabitants of the barracks district out of hand – many of them lived in straitened circumstances and among them there were honourable people like Tómas the grocer, a great supporter of young people, or indeed his wife Karolína.

The outcome of these discussions was that a deputation from the block was to be sent to have a talk with Karolína and Tómas. They would try to reach some kind of agreement which might improve relations between the residents of the block and this barracks. The envoys chosen for this mission were the treasurer of the National Theatre and a writer who had a good reputation for writing patriotic historical dramas.

When the boys had finished the paper round, Grjóni's trouser pockets were stuffed with coins. They decided to go down to the Co-op and celebrate.

At the Co-op a consignment of grapes was being unpacked – an immensely expensive luxury which was very seldom seen in Iceland. The boys had never tasted 'wine grapes' before, but they thought the name exciting and bought a large paper bag full of this delicacy; then they went out and sat on the pavement to feast themselves on the berries. A muddy old landrover with a trailer pulled into the courtyard. The farmer went into the shop for snuff, while out in the landrover some country children pressed their noses against the windows.

The boys didn't think much of these berries; once they had each had five, they didn't feel like eating many more. They walked over to the landrover and offered some to the kids from the country. The kids chomped and slurped on the fruit and their innocent eyes shone; they looked longingly at the bag, wanting more but not daring to ask. Grjóni gave them the grapes and said they could keep the lot.

When the farmer came out the children were beaming happily with the bag between them, all smeared with grape juice. He looked at them in surprise and asked a few questions, and they pointed enthusiastically at Grjóni. The farmer opened the door of the landrover and looked doubtfully at the boys in their patched and dirty rags.

'Was it you who gave the children those?'

'Yes, we didn't think they were very nice.'

'Where did you get all those grapes?'

'We bought them in the shop.'

'Well, I'll be . . .' The farmer told them to stay there and hurried into the shop; he exchanged a few words with the shop-girl and came out again with a bewildered expression.

'Well, that was very nice of you, boy. Where do you live?'

They pointed to the barracks district and the farmer stroked his chin thoughtfully. 'Do you sell *Vísir*?'

'I haven't any left.'

'No, I didn't mean that, my boy.' He shifted his weight from one foot to the other for a moment, then raised the tarpaulin on the trailer, heaved out a large sack of potatoes and said to Grjóni: 'Now you go home and give this to your mother, my boy.' He put some turnips in a bag for Baddi, so that he got something too.

Then he drove away and the kids were still waving to the boys out of the rear window when the landrover disappeared from view. The boys trudged off home with the heavy sack between them.

Tommi was always hitching his trousers up, especially if he were talking to someone. At regular intervals he let his wide trousers slip down to his thighs, adjusted his shirt tails carefully so that they lay smoothly on top of his long underpants, then jerked the waistband up to his middle again and fastened it. He also farted a lot, but was well mannered enough always to cough at the same time, as if to disguise the sound of the fart. Ochohoo-brr!

Some people stroke their chins or gesture with their hands when they are talking to someone, but Tommi hitched up his trousers.

When Baddi came into the kitchen with the turnips, the two members of the deputation from the Artists' Block were standing rather nervously watching Tommi hitch up his trousers. The old man was probably having trouble with his digestion, for he was also coughing the accompanying cough long and often. They were trying to discuss some problem, but as the artists used high-flown language and in slalom fashion avoided anything which touched the heart of the matter, there was no real communication being established – not, that is, until Lína took the matter in hand. She delivered a torrent of words about problems past and present which had their origins in the darkness of men's souls and the harm done by ghosts and evil spirits. This she spiced up with examples from her own experience and that of her family. The artists listened, fascinated and confused. They clean forgot the purpose of their visit and didn't know where they were before the woman had said goodbye and they had thanked the old couple with profuse handshakes, even though they had not even been offered a seat while all this was going on, let alone anything else. They didn't come to their senses until they were on their way home, when the treasurer of the National Theatre began to worry about what he was going to tell the other residents of the block about the discussions they had had. The playwright was in a more optimistic mood, however, and thought to himself that this woman could be a great source of both material and ideas: he would go back and visit her again some time, taking paper and pencil with him or, preferably, a tape recorder.

At the kitchen table the invalidated world record was being discussed. Tommi said he had always known that Hreggviður wasn't too bright, but that the man could imagine that anyone would believe that he, the scoundrel who had thrown sixteen metres at most, should suddenly have begun to hurl the shot nearly nineteen – that beat everything! The world record, which had been set by some American, was 18.12! To think of that troll! Now the fellow would be blacklisted for ever through his own stupidity!

The boys could think of nothing but this episode. At dusk they sneaked quietly through the district round to Hreggviður's barracks-hut and tried to make some contact with the electric atmosphere they thought there must be inside; but they heard nothing except a deathly silence, occasionally broken by creaks as someone walked the floor so heavily that the barracks-hut seemed about to collapse.

After that they went over and played with some other children on Hlynur's wrecked cars, but when it was dark they returned to Hreggviður's barracks-hut and put their ears to the thin walls, but could hear nothing except the same dark silence.

In the corner by the outside privy the gravel was black and crawling with life, probably because the Shell drum with the seat on top of it had a leak, and the contents were trickling down between the floorboards. As the boys crept past they stumbled over someone lying against the wall of the privy. At first they thought it might be Hreggviður, but it was only Diddi, Grjóni's brother. Grjóni pulled him to his feet and shook him, but Diddi reacted violently and grabbed hold of the bowie knife from the Scout shop which Baddi still wore at his belt. Diddi ran off brandishing the knife but didn't get far, because the friends threw themselves on him and had to thump him to get the razor-sharp weapon off him. Before they succeeded, Grjóni had cut himself on the palm of his hand, but he gritted his teeth and took it like a man. He hoisted the screaming boy on to his shoulders and took him home to the barracks-hut and their mother, who was waiting there anxiously and smelling of drink.

In the kitchen of the Old House sat Gréta, Hreggviður's wife, with their two daughters; she was chain-smoking and babbling trivialities, but did not dare to go home because she thought Hreggviður was in a very strange mood.

Baddi lay down on the sofa in the parlour and listened to old Tommi telling Danni about a dancer he had once known in Greece when he had been taken prisoner in the First World War. Baddi lost the thread somewhere down a side-street in Piraeus, when he fell asleep, grimy, tousled and still wearing his rubber shoes.

5

A frozen pool of blood, and cackling laughter in the flames

And round about there is a rabble
Of the filthy, sturdy, unkillable infants of the very poor.
They shall inherit the earth.
(Ezra Pound)

On the day little Diddi cut his throat the bigger boys must have been suffering from a fit of magnanimity, for they allowed all the younger boys to join them on a huge expedition down to the harbour. Diddi was also invited, but when Grjóni tried to get him to come he didn't reply. Grjóni had promised their mother that he would make sure that Diddi wasn't always excluded; he claimed he wasn't anyway – Diddi was just a misery.

'You're just a misery,' Grjóni said, as he and Baddi set off with brother Danni and Fía's Gosi in tow.

This was in March. Thórgunnur was working that day at the fish factory run by the Reykjavík Fish Company. Her health was not so good and the weather was cold – so cold that when she came home the pool of blood in which the body lay had frozen.

Thórgunnur didn't start to cry right away. She hurried over to the Old House; she wasn't pale or speechless or wide-eyed with terror, just excited – overwrought, as if she had been diddled out of ten *krónur* at the dairy. Lína went over to the barracks-hut and had a look round; then she sent for Tommi, who closed up his shop at once and came home.

Thórgunnur could not sit still. She thought she had to hurry up and fetch her two little girls, who stayed during the day-time with a doctor and his wife in the centre of town, where they helped to look after the children and do the shopping. They weren't paid wages, but they got plenty to eat, and it was warm in the doctor's house. An ambulance was on its way and with it the police and some officials in suits. Lína told Thórgunnur she had to wait for them, and sent Dollí to go and collect the little girls and take them to the home of Grettir's family. She was to keep an eye on them until they were fetched.

Then the ambulance men arrived and took away the boy's bluish-white, stiffened body. Meanwhile Lína brought coal and lit the stove in the barracks-hut and set about washing the floor. Tommi accompanied Thórgunnur on a tour of the neighbourhood, where she had to answer millions of questions. She answered them all quickly and rather frantically, as if she were talking about salted fish or the weather or other everyday things. At any rate she didn't shed a tear – not until an official in a hat said straight out, as if thinking aloud, that this family would have to be broken up. At that, Thórgunnur went berserk; she began to shout incoherently, she clung to Tommi like a little girl to her father and begged him, whimpering, not to let them take her children away from her.

Tommi himself had a lump in his throat; he felt he was not man enough to cope with this and carry the weight of it all. When Thórgunnur begged him to promise on his honour that she would be able to keep her children with her, he just said, 'Yes, yes, I'll do what I can, my dear.'

As soon as the opportunity arose, Lína buttonholed the official in the hat who had told Thórgunnur that the family would have to be broken up. Lína let fly at him, saying that God would take vengeance on behalf of the weak. Two policemen who were standing nearby nodded and said it was perhaps unnecessary to be quite so harsh on a woman who had just lost a child in such a manner. Lína went on blazing at the man: he was a wretched so-and-so and a worm and his wife was a whore and a right prick-hole.

The purpose of the boys' expedition down to the harbour was to help themselves to supplies from the Eimskip shipping company's warehouse. The younger boys were to keep watch and squeeze through narrow openings. Everything was going well, and they might have got away with it had the district not been chock-a-block with cops and officials when they came round the corner in the dark to Hlynur's Garage and began to hide bags and boxes under the wrecked cars. All of a sudden two bright flashlights were turned on them. Baddi and Grjóni tried to escape but were seized and forced into a car. They cursed and swore when they were asked where they had got all that stuff, but when it emerged who Grjóni was, the policemen reddened and looked embarrassed. After scratching their heads they got hold of old Tommi, who came and told Baddi, quietly and not unkindly, to go straight into the kitchen and wait there. For some unexpected reason Baddi chose to obey without protest, even though he had been prepared to be interrogated with Grjóni for days and nights without confessing to anything. It would have made no difference anyway, because Danni had spilled the beans while howling his eyes out beside the wrecked cars where they had been caught. Gosi was escorted home by the police to his tower block, where Fía greeted him with a wet floor-mop and forbade him to leave the house for the rest of the winter.

The officials in suits wanted to take Grjóni somewhere, but Lína said he was to stay where he was. They asked Thórgunnur about the daughters; she referred them to Tommi who hitched up his trousers and pointed to Lína, but the officials in suits didn't dare question her a second time.

Thórgunnur stayed at the Old House that night; when she managed to fall asleep at last, she slept uneasily and was soon awake again, sobbing until early in the morning, when Lína told her to 'stop that terrible wailing': if Tómas had said he would see to it that families were not split up, he could be relied on to stick to his word . . .

No one was allowed to talk about it. Lína said she didn't want to resurrect the ghosts of the past; and Tommi just told stories about dancing girls in foreign ports if the talk came round to his former dealings with women. After long tirades, when Lína had scolded him for not being considerate enough to Baddi, who was such a sensitive soul, Tommi clutched his head in exhaustion and asked to be left in peace; and he said, perhaps to himself or to Danni: 'Just think, I've been married to that woman for all these years, and yet I've never loved her.'

'Oh? Why'd you marry her, then?'

'That's quite another story.'

They must have thought about it sometimes, the old couple. It must have come out in sleep or in waking or in daydreams and half-spoken words about quite different matters occasionally as time passed, however confused and hard to understand . . .

It was this terrible way of life, and the house in which the sisters lived, which made some newspaper hint, in an article about immorality and drunkenness in the town, that it might be some sort of brothel – but they could not investigate the matter more closely because all kinds of respectable citizens paid visits there. It was a small town, after all, and everyone knew the sisters, that loose-living crowd, those whores versed in the magic arts with their mortally ill mother and a litter of illegitimate children which was always growing or decreasing – there wasn't always enough money for funerals! When the mother died, screaming, the corpse had to lie unburied in the Cottage for five weeks until a young and helpful shop-assistant turned up and provided the money for a grave and a priest. He was a very helpful shop-assistant, cheerful and well travelled at sea, who enjoyed drinking and sowing his wild oats and dancing and singing in those years. He began to come to the Cottage to visit these hospitable sisters, whose company was enjoyed by trawlermen and tramps. But they were also noisy, these fellows, and that caused a scandal, and complaints poured in to the city authorities about these half-crazy sisters, who were a disgrace to themselves and a nuisance to others and should not be allowed to have children. The sisters complained in turn and kicked up a fuss and picketed the door of the Town Hall with their flock of children and a bunch of sniggering spectators, shouting and shaking their fists at the officials, those thieving devils who were stealing both their welfare payments and their child benefit. They threatened the vengeance of God and the Devil – especially the eldest, the mother of little Gríma Ólína (Gógó) who was always smiling and laughing in spite of her name and the fighting which flared up around her, the crying, the screaming, the drinking, the police, and the youngest sister dying in childbirth. Then the doctor came and said this could not go on any longer, but the municipal treasury declared it was short of funds, and nothing happened until the residents who lived in the neighbourhood gathered signatures and demanded action. By then the middle sister had moved to Norway and the youngest had died and Karolína was on her own again and was determined not to give up. She answered everyone at the top of her voice; it was said that she was crazy and dangerous to those around her when she walked through the district with little Gógó and her sister's children whom she looked after, knocking on the doors of the people who had complained and hurling abuse and obscenities at them, saying that God would wreak vengeance. Finally the officials of the SPCC decided to take the children away from her and put Lína in a home and pull down the Cottage. And now all the friends and visitors let them down; they abandoned the sinking ship, all of them, all except the shop-assistant and globetrotter Tommi, who was younger than Lína but wanted to save the family. He moved between Herod and Pilate and tried to settle the matter fairly: she was not crazy, this woman, just passionate and she loved all the children and looked after them. The authorities, however, had had enough; they took no notice even when the young man offered to guarantee and provide enough money to keep the family afloat. It seemed that there was no way out – 'Except one,' said a red-haired clerk at the Town Hall: 'If you were to marry the woman, there would be nothing we could do about it . . .'

Tommi also somehow managed to see to it that Thórgunnur's family wasn't broken up. She was allowed to go on living in the barracks with her Grjóni and the two charming daughters with whom Dollí and Grettir, as happy parents, arrived on the day after Víkingur Traustason was buried in the presence of a handful of people. Workmen came and replaced the floor of the barracks-hut, sealed it and insulated it; Lína donated a woollen blanket and a subscription to *Morgunblaðið* newspaper and Dollí gave the little girls (who were nine and ten years old) clothes and sweets, took them to the pictures and tied bows in their hair; they beamed with happiness and would have liked to stay with her for ever.

Thórgunnur was never quite her old self again, although everyone tried to help, and Tommi himself paid what she owed at Tommi's Shop at the end of every month. Thórgunnur, who had always been so hard-working, couldn't be bothered doing anything any more; she just sat staring into space and sighing, unless she was drinking: she had stopped making a secret of it, and was in the habit of buying herself a bottle now and again. But it didn't make her happy and singing like Hreggi the shot-putter; it just made her wild and quick-tempered. She switched between weeping and flinging her arms round the children until they nearly choked, or else throwing them out – yes, she must have gone a bit peculiar! Grjóni found it all intolerable and went home as little as possible; he began to spend the nights in the scullery of the Old House, surrounded by cats. Tommi found him there one morning and asked if he wouldn't rather come inside. From then on Grjóni took up residence in one of the cupboards, which became known as Grjóni's Cupboard; it was almost like a secret room – the family had lived in the Old House for months before they discovered that there was a cupboard there. As the years went by and he gradually became known as Deaf Grjóni – Sigurjón Traustason, the notorious criminal – he never forgot his benefactors at the Old House, and all his life he carried out countless robberies and break-ins in order to pay back the debt.

Grjóni stayed in Grjóni's Cupboard for more than a year, until he was fifteen, when he took the bus to the north and got a berth on a herring boat. Baddi said that he, too, wanted to leave town and get a job, but of course the old fortune-teller would not hear of the boy going away to do slave labour.

Thórgunnur was in hospital by then and the two girls at boarding school. Dollí had no time to miss them, for she was pregnant; after that her health began to deteriorate, and she became anxious, nervous and insecure.

It looked as though Dollí was going to be as fertile as her mother, Gógó, because at the end of her pregnancy she brought twins into the world, a boy and a girl. Otherwise not much happened. No big news. The winters were a cold war, but it was sometimes warm in summer. That business with Diddi was quickly forgotten, for after all no one was really surprised. Not afterwards; there was no one who wondered, 'What really happened to Diddi? I just don't understand!' No one said anything like that. That's the way it goes, people murmured, and then thought about something else.

There was plenty to think about. Some people were surprised at Grjóni – he seemed to take it all so coolly. Did the boy simply not care? People in the neighbourhood tried to console him, to comfort him; but he didn't respond. Women slipped him pieces of cake and invited him in for cocoa, but he just shook his head. The cheek of him! He might accept the cakes, but then he just turned on his heel instead of starting to cry when he was tenderly asked if it weren't a terrible thing to lose his younger brother like that. They had been so close, after all: 'I remember when you and he were starting school here a few years ago!' Grjóni remembered, too; but he said nothing. He was even rude; many people heard of the time when Hlynur stopped him at the door of his garage, with the usual oily rag in his hands, and started to say: 'Listen, Sigurjón, lad, that brother of yours, Víkingur, who passed away . . .'

Grjóni hissed: 'He was just a drip!'

Yes! Just like that. If that isn't impudence, what is? Grjóni also told Tommi that Diddi had been a crybaby and a drip, but Tommi didn't pursue it.

Grjóni wasn't a drip, quite the contrary – he was a rascal. He had always been a tough fighter, but lately he had become a heartless villain. He punched and kicked – even little boys: the devil, he attacked those who were smaller than him. There was little hope that he would do well in life, so devoid of feeling was he. He was as tough as always; no one ever saw him give way, except perhaps Baddi later on when they started drinking together: when they'd had too much to drink, Grjóni's eyes would sometimes fill with tears and he would begin to stammer incoherent sentences about the past, opening the lids so that you could catch a glimpse of the dark depths of his soul.

There were other sorrows in the district: little sadnesses were always taking place. Sæunn, the cat-woman, was not always happy; in fact, she was never happy, the poor wee soul, and had never been happy since her husband Högni had abandoned her and gone off with another woman many, many years ago. It seemed to have affected her mind, for at regular intervals she would fall into a fit, shouting Högni's name and screaming for him so loudly that it pierced the ears of the district's residents: she would see Högni visiting her at the barracks, she would see him inside the barracks-hut, sitting on a stool, perched on the edge of her bed, even hanging from the ceiling light. And she screamed, sometimes for hours on end. And although she stopped shouting his name at last, that would not be the end of it, for then she would begin to laugh. She laughed like a horse, a long-drawn-out piercing laugh like that of a witch in a fairy-tale or crazy people in films – the kind of laughter which doesn't really exist except in folk-tales and horror stories. Sæunn the cat-woman should have had dishevelled jet-black hair, a chalk-white face, fire in her eyes, sitting curled up with a black cat on her shoulder and bats fluttering around. But she wasn't like that. She was just a very ordinary Icelandic housewife in appearance; people who didn't know her would have thought that she was just a mum from the Electricity Board Block who lived a steady life with an ironing-board, a washing-machine and heaps of cornflakes for her work-horse of a husband and three school-age children.

Not Sæunn. She had no large family to look after, just the cats and her only son, Barði. Barði was the same age as

Dollí, but like poor dead Diddi he never played with other boys.

It was probably true that Högni was unfaithful to Sæunn and abandoned her when she was about to give birth to Barði. Sæunn then moved to the barracks district as soon as it became available to the public, and began to take in stray cats. Barði was nearly eleven years old then.

Everyone agreed that Barði was a good boy. He was very good and patient with his mother, even though he was a loner and down in the dumps most of the time. Perhaps that was why he looked so peculiar. At the age of seventeen he went bald: not as bald as an egg, as from some illness or other, but quite ordinarily bald, like a forty-year-old bank clerk; his forehead ran up to the crown of his head, and below it was a neat collar of blond hair. At the same time he started to grow facial hair, with a well-tended blond beard round his mouth like a secondary-school teacher. In other respects the seventeen-year-old lad was not very grown-up in appearance; apart from his bald head and beard he might have been taken for a boy of around confirmation age, small and slender with soft outlines; the beard on his face grew out of pale, childlike skin. That's how he was at the age of seventeen, and that's the way he remained for decades to come. If someone had had to guess Barði's age he would have said fifteen or thirty-five: anything in between was unthinkable.

Barði was very well behaved. He was polite and intelligent, and the very soul of integrity: 'responsibility itself', as the women of the district put it. On one occasion he found a five-*króna* piece on the floor of the dairy; he politely nudged the elbow of the woman in front of him in the queue and said: 'Did you lose this, madam?'

It brought tears to the women's eyes. Yes, he truly deserved a better role in life, did Barði – something better than spending all day caring for his mother and her screaming fits in the barracks. There he sat, hunched on a chair or a stool, staring at the floorboards while he waited for the fit to pass – together with the stray cats who for years had made their home in the kitchen or bedroom or parlour or whatever you want to call this single room which was their part of the barracks-hut. The cats, too, seemed to have got used to Sæunn's screaming and laughter; like Barði, they knew it would pass.

Perhaps Sæunn the cat-woman and Barði Högnason are not really relevant, if it's possible to speak of *relevance* in the history of the family at the Old House – except, perhaps, in that Lína and Tommi often gave things to Sæunn, mainly fish and leftovers for the cats in the harsh part of the year when there weren't many rats and mice about. If the youngsters of the district were making an expedition down to the harbour with lines, hooks and sinkers, they would give Sæunn a bag of sea-scorpion and cod in the evening if the catch had been good. At Christmas, deputations would come from the Old House with door-garlands and Christmas-tree branches for Sæunn, as for other barracks residents.

It was the fourth Christmas in the history of the Old House. Barði and Sæunn pasted newspapers on the inside of the walls, both as wallpaper and as insulation. This wall-covering was in frequent need of replacement; it ripped when the wind blew through the cracks in the corrugated iron; it got wet and soft with rain and damp. Barði and his mother would then make flour paste in a bucket and paste fresh sheets of paper to the wall with brooms. Those were their Christmas preparations, and they were right in the middle of them when Sæunn suddenly became aware of Högni. She began to scream at him and chase him, but as usual he got away. She tried to hit him with the broom, but that didn't work either. Barði tried to make his mother stop her screaming and calm down, but he knew from experience that if this didn't succeed in the first minute it was hopeless – there was nothing to be done but to sit down on the stool and wait. He was sitting there motionless when Dollí and Tommi arrived with the Christmas decorations, and by now Sæunn was changing from screaming to laughing.

'Poor lad,' said Tommi, with a bit of a lump in his throat. He asked Barði quietly if he would like to come over and have Christmas dinner at the Old House – he would be welcome.

But Barði shook his head, his bald pate: he would rather stay with his mother. He sat and waited with the bucket of paste between his feet, like a wallpaperer having his tea-break. The break probably lasted until Christmas morning, because Sæunn laughed all night: all Christmas Eve her cackling laughter echoed round the district. Towards morning the laughter began to sound like something else. Then there was silence.

Sæunn lived in one half of the barracks-hut beside Tommi's Shop; Höskuldur the taxi-driver lived in the other half. Even though the hut was situated in the outskirts, it lit up the entire district the night it burned down.

Barði was thirty years old then, but still looked either fifteen or thirty-five. He wasn't at home that night; but Sæunn was, and turned to ashes together with her home. What made the fire mysterious and akin to a folk-tale was that all the cats escaped alive and unscathed. It was as if the Fates had taken the cats into their arms and carried them outside before the fire took hold of the newspapers on the walls.

Höskuldur the taxi-driver arrived home as the fire brigade was spraying the last drops of water on to the scorched corrugated iron which lay twisted on the ground where the barracks-hut had stood. Höski looked at the ruins thoughtfully for a while, then spat out a chewed match and drove away. He got himself a suite at the Salvation Army,

Barði remained standing there, clear-headed, with an old tin full of nails and cotton reels and one green hundred-*króna* note; the tin was all it had been possible to rescue from the blaze. It contained his mother's inheritance. Barði stared down into the tin as some brave fellows dug Sæunn out of the embers of the fire. He knew that it was too late now to get Mum to calm down; it had to be done in the first minute of the fit.

Hreggviður the shot-putter was first at the scene of the fire; but he was drunk, and no one believed him when he said he had heard Sæunn's laughter cackling out of the sea of flames.

6

With a gold medal
on your chest

Must I always be feeling bad, then? No, at such troubled periods in the district it was a great comfort to many that there were lighter moments, like the year when the Kári Club sent its first team to the Reykjavík Boys' Football Tournament. In its sports pages the newspaper *Alþýðublaðið* described the decisive match in the division for the youngest competitors as follows:

In the fourth division the result was no less unexpected, when Kári, the city's youngest team, scored a decisive victory over the Valur team. The Kári lads' victory is noteworthy not least because this is the first and only football tournament in which the club has taken part. It was founded in the Thule district just over a year ago by some of the residents there, under the management of grocer Tómas Tómasson and shot-putter Hreggviður Barðason.

In the final there was never any doubt as to who was going to win. In the first half the blue-clad Kári side scored three goals, and added a fourth in the second half. At the end of the match Valur got the chance of saving a little face when they were awarded a penalty, but Kári's excellent goalkeeper, Ludwig Hansson, saved it brilliantly. The young football club seems to have a great future, for there are many talented players in the team. The goalkeeper has already been mentioned, but the team's centre-back, big, red-haired Sigurjón Traustason, also caught the attention, and will do so even more in future if he learns to polish up his act on the field; nor should we overlook the inside-forward, Bjarni Tómasson, who scored a hat-trick to claim three of the game's four goals. This

Bjarni is the foster-son of Tómas Tómasson, the team's founder. *Alþýðublaðið* congratulates Kári on winning the cup.

The cup was a challenge cup: it had to be given back the following summer and handed over to the next champions, but it soon got lost, and Tommi had to pay for a new one. The cup was found many years later when Hreggviður was sorting his collection of medals.

There was a holiday atmosphere in the district the night the Kári lads won the final. Tommi had the team's badge painted on a flag which was nailed to a long pole and fluttered above Tommi's Shop. Gógó and Charlie were on a visit to the Old House and Charlie went out and photographed the team with his box camera. The rest of the youngsters from the district were allowed to be in the photo, and they were all smiling from ear to ear, even Barði Högnason. Then a second photo was taken of the team's best players together with Tommi, Hreggviður, Hlynur and Höskuldur. Hlynur's face is hidden behind Hreggviður's triumphantly waving fist; the giant is unshaven, wearing a vest and with fire in his eyes. Tommi, who is standing by his side, is looking away with the face he always pulls when the smell of stale liquor reaches his nostrils. Höskuldur is standing nonchalantly with his hands in his pockets and a matchstick between his teeth. These pictures can still be seen in an album at Kári's new and spacious club-house at the other end of town.

Toggi the trawlerman was not in the photo, as he had gone off to fetch some ship's flares, and he brought a full box of catherine wheels and sparklers which they saved until midnight, when it was dark enough for fireworks. Then they were set off, even though a strong wind was blowing and the club's Old Boys' section, Tommi and Toggi excepted, were well and truly plastered. They went on letting off flares in spite of some grumbling from the Artists' Block, where it was feared that the fireworks might come through the windows and on to the parlour carpets. The party lasted well into the night, and everyone tried to sing the Kári Song even though no one knew any of it except the last lines, which boomed out to all kinds of

tunes which pierced the sensitive musical ears of the residents of
the Artists' Block:

Long live Kári's heroes!
In adversity, victory and every kind of endeavour!
Kári's heroes! Kári's heroes!

The police were called in the middle of the night so that the artists
could get some sleep, but the men in uniform became a little more
sympathetic towards the district residents when they learned of
the reason for the celebration; in fact, the squad which arrived
was the nucleus of the team which had won the national company
and institution team tournament in water polo earlier that year.
'Maybe you should keep it down a bit,' they said, half-seriously,
and they could be seen blushing, caps in their hands, taking a few
minutes off from their duties and accepting a cup of coffee and a
slice of cake in the kitchen. 'Yes, we know Inspector Guðlaugur,
the desk officer,' they said, nodding their heads, 'he's a great chap!'
And for that remark they received praise and a pat on the head
from Lína (whose cousin Guðlaugur was), and then they departed
with a salute and with sunshine in their hearts.

They were no small fry, the lads who strode through the city streets
eleven abreast during the next few days, each one of them with a
gold medal on his chest. They were the Reykjavík fourth-division
champions, and their skill with the ball was becoming legendary.
If they entered other districts of the town they were met, not with
stone-throwing or threats, but with a challenge to play against
the best of the neighbourhood teams. The Kári lads never lost a
game. They were even invited to make training and playing tours
in Scandinavia, and returned without having lost a single match.
    Oh yes!

For the previous two years the Reykjavík champion team had
received financial support from the municipal authorities for a
tour abroad (the managers of both winning clubs were members of
the city council). The demand from the members of the opposition

parties that the Kári Club should now also receive this kind of support was acknowledged as reasonable, although during the council debate someone said that it seemed to him 'rather stupid to give money for a luxury tour abroad to residents of a district in which the majority of people live on public welfare . . .'

The grant covered about half the travel expenses for a team of boys and some group leaders; the rest had to be found by the club. Kári could never have managed this, but it could just work, at a pinch, if Tommi were to go alone with the eleven players.

Lína didn't want Tommi to go, however: she would not hear of him leaving – there were bad omens in the cards. This was the speech she made at the supper table:

'I remember when we lived at Lagsteinn on Urðarstigur and Mother and Gíslína died, poof, just like that. I wanted to move from there, but Tómas didn't rent the place here at Little Farm 7 until Dollí was eight months old. Well, enough of that. Tómas then worked for Kristgeir – you remember Kristgeir the trawler owner? – Kristgeir wanted to have a word with him, and he went down there to see him, but I felt I really had to get on with something, even go and do some washing, so I said to Silla, Gíslína's daughter, that I really had to go and do some washing. All right, she said. I'm not going down to the basement yet, I said, I'll stay in the passage, but if you want to help me just be in the kitchen. I'm not going down yet, I said. Then Tómas came home, and of course he had to come through the passage where I was standing, and I said, what did Kristgeir want? He wanted me to join the motor trawler *Loftur*, he said. I don't believe you, I said, not a word of it. But when he had gone inside, I heard this voice, such a mi-i-ld and ge-nt-le voice, saying: *"Ye-e-es – now I'll tell you what Kristgeir wanted with him. He wasn't asking him to join the motor trawler* Loftur, *he was asking him to be foreman over in Thorlákshöfn!"* That was a bit different, ehhh?

'So when the voice fell silent I went inside and said, Where is Tómas? He's in the kitchen, making coffee, said Silla. Then I said to him, What did you say Kristgeir wanted with you? He didn't say anything. Ohh, I'd better tell you what he wanted, hadn't I, I said, and I told him. And if you won't admit the truth then as sure

as I stand here I'll go down to Tryggvagata and get the truth out
of him. Then he said, What's this about? Are you trying to ruin a
good job for me? I replied, I don't give a damn about good jobs,
but you won't be going there with my blessing. Or my permission.
But by God, off he went next day all the same, but I-I-I'm not going
to take my revenge on the mo-o-otor trawler, that I'm not; but on
the other hand I'm going to see to it that you won't get so much as
a fish-scale out of the sea and it won't be much of a trip for you,
this one. So I kept the radio on all the time and he wasn't gone for
more than a fortnight and they didn't land a single herring, but
he got an inflammation of the throat and was very ill and then
came home and that was the end of the story. Yes, indeed. Isn't
that strange?'

'The devil!' said Grettir. 'The devil!'

'Yes and he's not getting my permission to go and visit Éggvan
the Faroese and a bunch of whores, do you hear, Tómas, a bunch
of Norwegian whor –'

'Ahem! There are children at the table,' said Tommi.

The woman kept on going. She was up to high doh now
and began to do a war-dance round the kitchen, and Dollí
joined in, but Tommi was growing angry and in the end he
made a scene; he banged the table and said he was going with
the lads no matter how much fuss she made: 'So shut up for
once, Lína.'

Lína stopped talking and Tommi made a rapid exit, closing the
door behind him. He went to the front door and had a smoke,
leaning against the door frame and looking out. His hands shook
a little as he raised the cigarette to his lips.

Then Grettir came out to him, furtive and low-voiced; he made
sure that no one was listening, and began to praise Tommi: 'You
bloody well gave it to the old woman! The fist on the table, man!
Nothing else works with these women, you should just have given
her one on the chops while you were at it! The devil! That's the
only thing they understand!'

Tommi's hands were no longer shaking. He exhaled smoke and
gave Grettir a searching look with a resigned expression. Then he
went inside and heard Lína starting to jabber in the kitchen again.

He shook his head and murmured, 'To think I've been married to that woman for thirty years . . .'

They made the trip nonetheless. Youngsters' trips of this kind were usually arranged in co-operation with sister organisations in the rest of Scandinavia: KR visited KB in Copenhagen, Fram went to Frem in Valby and Víkingur to Viking in Stavanger.

Kári didn't have a sister organisation, not even a friendly association. But Lína's middle sister still lived in Tromsø in Norway and was both fortune-teller and missionary to a small religious community there. Tommi got in touch with her because he, too, had a desire to meet Norwegians whom, along with the British, he considered to be the most remarkable people in the world. Hugrún said she could arrange the whole thing, footballs and whatever else, and Tommi had a word with someone from the Faroese Society in Reykjavík who said that there would be no difficulty in arranging a match against the boys' team of Havnar Boltklubb in Tórshavn; it was all cut and dried, they should just go and knock on the door of a man called Napoleon from Dseggvi.

And so off they sailed on a Danish passenger ship, Tommi in his blazer with the Kári Club insignia sewn on the breast pocket, and the lads, Baddi and Grjóni and Lúddi and all the others, looking like motley-coloured sheep in anoraks and plimsolls and woollen sweaters and rubber boots and each with his blue sea-bag from Ellingsen's which Toggi had got at wholesale prices. Tommi hardly slept a wink all the way; he was so delighted to be at sea, he sat in the smoking saloon and was even a bit drunk, the old temperance warrior.

Most of the boys had no appetite. They felt a bit lost in the ship's elegant saloons and stayed below decks in a quiet and taciturn group, looking apprehensive like people in an air-raid shelter hearing the bombs go off above their heads. Baddi gaped open-mouthed at all the foreigners on board and felt disappointed.

Over Tórshavn in the Faroes there was a dense, milky-white mist. The ship put in at the pier and the Faroese on board quickly disembarked to happy cries of welcome. Tommi called the boys up on deck and then they all stood together there, waiting

for something to happen; Tommi didn't know what – he had
somehow reckoned that someone would be there to meet them.
But as they stood waiting in the mist and watching the last cars
with people to pick up driving away from the quayside, he realised
that this was not exactly an official state visit. Tommi was dead
tired, it was drawing towards the close of day and he was afraid
they would all get lost if they began to walk up to the town in the
pitch darkness. So they just went below decks again and slept until
the following morning.

Next day they succeeded in finding the house of this Napoleon
with whom the man from the Faroese Society said he had in been
in touch by phone; but there was no one at home. However,
they managed to get a football match arranged nonetheless. In
an interview Tommi later gave to one of the newspapers he
described it in the following terms under the headline: 'Good
result on foreign ground':

> In Tórshavn it had been planned to play against the town's
> boys' team. Because of a mix-up over dates this did not
> happen, but when word of our arrival spread we were
> challenged by a picked team from the staff of the Baccalao
> fish factory, which I understand is one of the country's
> largest employers. Suffice it to say that even though most
> of the Faroese were older than the Kári lads they couldn't
> match my men, who won 6–5 after a very exciting game.

When the battle-hardened Kári team arrived in Tromsø, in
Norway, the reception was markedly more imposing. A whole
congregation was waiting for them, headed by Lína's sister Hugrún, and the Reykjavík champions from the Thule
Camp spent three days there at religious meetings, prayers
and hymn-singing. Tommi quickly gave up asking the zealots
about the football activities in the town; they scarcely knew
what football was. Even so, with his smattering of Norwegian,
Tommi managed to arrange a match with a team picked from
the young men of the town; and what a match it was! It was a
real fireworks display, the biggest win an Icelandic football team

had ever achieved abroad: the Kári side won 17–0. Baddi was the game's top goal-scorer, of course, but in fact nearly all of them managed to score – even the goalkeeper, Lúddi, who joined the attack until he too got a ball into the net from point-blank range. In the evening the heroes sat in the community hall and listened with happy faces to sermons in Norwegian about the emissaries of the Devil.

Next day they travelled by train to Bergen, from where there was a scheduled flight to Iceland. There they experienced the only mishap of this whole splendid tour, a mishap which made the trip memorable for the other residents of the Old House: as the result of some misunderstanding the plane was over-booked, and old Tommi was unable to get a seat on it.

Lína very nearly went off her head when the Icelandair Skymaster landed at Reykjavík Airport without the tour leader, who had been left behind in *Norway*, the very place he had just come from when they got married. She would not listen to reason and went rampaging around the house in a fury, and even though he arrived on the next flight two days later it took her a long time to calm down, and she always got worked up if this episode were ever mentioned.

Danni had been put in charge of the shop while its manager was away, and it took Tommi many weeks to sort out the book-keeping after he came home. He sat scratching his head and puffing cigarettes and muttering to himself that he must have been crazy to leave an eleven-year-old boy in charge of a whole shop for more than a week.

The invincible Kári team continued training in the autumn; if the weather was bad, there were film shows in the club-house. The cartoons flickered on the wall and the rain drummed on the roof. In the semi-darkness steam rose from the lads' wet jerseys; the boys had pulled the bench out on to the floor and were eating the doughnuts Lína had donated to the club. Old Tommi sat right at the back, proud and pleased that he had managed to learn to work the film projector which hissed and clattered on the table at his side. The beam of light from its lens gathered dust and steam in a cone which was projected on to the wall. A blue-clad mariner with a pipe like a block of wood and a tin of spinach appeared.

'Tommi! That's Popeye, isn't it?'

'Hrm! Quite right, my lad,' Tommi replied in fatherly fashion. 'That's Popeye, all right.'

7

Lonesome in the Old House?

If you're looking for trouble, you came to the right place!
(Elvis Presley)

And the days went by in humdrum calm. The Old House gathered the years as they eroded the timber floors and the scrawled children's drawings on the walls. Not much happened in the district, and there was peaceful prosperity in Lína's and Tommi's home.

During the day Tommi stood in the shop whistling to the accompaniment of the state radio programmes from the dusty old valve set which stood on the shelf; he was in a good mood as usual and sometimes had to pinch himself in order to realise that he had every reason to feel so relaxed. He wasn't even running away from unpleasant problems, for fortune smiled on him. He had never expected that life would be free of care; for all his forefathers, relatives, neighbours and colleagues, life had been full of toil and misery. That was just the way it was: life's a vale of tears. But now, all of a sudden, Tommi had acquired almost everything: his own house, a shop of which he was manager, dollars and luxuries from America. Important people greeted him in the street, there were even interviews with him in the newspapers, where he was referred to as the well-known youth benefactor and sports promoter.

All this must be a warning of something worse to come, thought Tommi with his hands in his pockets, clicking his new false teeth. False teeth? Yes, they were another sign of the times, shining white and entire.

Lína missed Baddi, who had flown out west, yet she seemed to take to the unchanging routine which accompanied his absence.

For the most part she predicted a promising future, and even advised dejected souls to look on the bright side of life.

Even the weather chimed in; the seasons were no longer noteworthy, like old times: no more Great Frozen-Sea Winters, no more Hard Frost Winters, no more Endless Rainy Summers – they all coalesced into the greyness of the sky. For the most part, any bad news could be expected from the Government: some false prophets and pharisees had taken over, who threatened to chuck the soldiers out of the country, those fine upstanding young lads. Some of the soldiers even had wives and children – were they going to be torn up by the roots? Didn't they have a right to live in peace like everyone else?

But nothing came of the plan to get rid of the army, which was just as well, because then Grettir would have been out of work. Grettir, you see, had got this great job with the Americans, as a kind of factotum. It suited him very well; he made deliveries and carried messages and did various jobs in town, or up in Hvalfjörður, but mostly down at Keflavík Airport, and then he sometimes didn't come home for weeks on end. During the day he ran small errands, and at night he talked via an interpreter with the soldiers about firearms. When they called on Grettir they didn't come to a mindless house; those cowboys from Texas and triumphant officers from the Pacific War admired and marvelled at the knowledge which this shy, small denizen of the Arctic regions showed about the trends in the history of the western rifle.

Grettir thought this a splendid way of making a living; although he was proud of his family, it was bliss to be able to take a break from them and be away for a week from time to time. The only shadow on his happiness was that English was such a difficult and complicated language. He scarcely understood a word, no matter how hard he tried.

He earned so much with the Americans that Dollí always had plenty of money. Also, they lived in the Old House with Lína and Tommi for nothing, free board and lodging, everything as it should be.

And yet Dollí wasn't satisfied.

It was strange. She was bored. Perhaps it was something more than that. 'Alienation' did not exist then; phrases like 'empty life' and 'purposelessness' were unknown to her. And she was often ill; she suffered from tiredness, headaches, fainting fits, insomnia, loss of appetite. She slopped around the house with her two children, the twins who had been given names after a great deal of bother. Dollí, who was to decide on the girl's name, wanted her to be called Karolína, but the old woman would not hear of it – she had always hated the name; a man called Karl who had died through sorcery and hauntings* had visited the name upon her mother in his time, and there was a curse associated with the name, Lína said. She had therefore seen to it that the girl was christened Gíslína after her dead sister, while the boy was given the name Ásmundur, on Grettir's suggestion.** So Dollí trudged around the house with Gillí and Mundi, who she thought must be the most difficult children in the world: 'They're giving me grey hair!' she said – she who had always been so fond of children. 'I can't sta-a-a-nd it!' she had also begun to wail, like the old fortune-teller.

Poor Dollí – only just twenty and yet in such bad health. Lína tried to make things a little easier for her; it was certainly needed. She got the twins dressed in the mornings and fed them, and Dollí came downstairs about midday, grey from smoking and lack of sleep, so listless that she didn't even have the energy to get dressed; she just wore a dressing gown and smoked cigarettes in a holder, so as not to get shreds of tobacco in her mouth.

Why was it so lonely and uneventful in the Old House, which had always teemed with life? Where had the flower of youth gone? Most of the children Lína had brought up had flown the nest or died. Gógó's two little daughters had died in the same influenza epidemic. Gógó herself had moved all the way

---

* In Icelandic folklore, people could be driven to death by apparitions and corpses which would not stay in their graves.

** Grettir the Outlaw, the eponymous hero of *Grettir's Saga*, was 'Asmundarson – the son of Ásmundur.

to Kansas in America with Charlie Brown. There she had had a daughter, but there seemed to be something wrong with the little girl. Rumour had it that Gógó was expecting another, although she was no spring chicken, the lady – she was well into her forties. Baddi had gone out west to be with her, to Mamma Gógó; he had been there for almost a year; he had become very restless and unsettled after Grjóni and others of his closest friends had left the district.

He seemed to be doing well out there in the west. He spoke with an American accent on the telephone, sounding very manly now. Lína missed her beloved boy and asked him if he weren't coming home soon. But it didn't sound like it. 'Devils' Island!' he said on the phone. 'You come over here, woman!'

'Yes, you can hardly move here for pharisees and character-assassins,' she said. Then Danni went to America as well. He said he wanted to see his mother; Tommi quite understood, and had bought him a ticket a few months earlier.

But Danni didn't sound so up-beat the one time he was able to say hello to his grandmother and grandfather on the phone to Iceland. He sounded rather low. He just wanted to come home. So Tommi said he would buy him another ticket. But Lína asked what kind of nonsense was that? There was no point in encouraging the boy's fecklessness; he had cried for his mother before he left, and most probably he'd just start up again as soon as he got back!

Yes, the group had dispersed. There were also the orphaned penniless nieces and nephews whom Lína had adopted – that ungrateful rabble, she never heard anything from them. What peculiar people – they could at least have looked in! The two girls had settled down as wives with families; both had married penniless manual labourers, one of whom began to earn money later on, after he got a job with the Customs and Excise. This was Silla's husband; she herself was also astute at earning money – she had inherited psychic talents, like several of the women in the family, and went in for spiritual healing in a big way.

And then there was the boy, Gíslína's youngest child. What

was he doing all this time? He was a mysterious and odd person, cousin Snjólfur. No one ever knew where he was; now and again you heard something of him, one month in the west at Snæfellsnes, the next in the east at Melrakkaslétta. Then perhaps two or three years would go by until some far-flung traveller who came into Tommi's Shop would say he had met Snjólfur in the Vestmann Islands.

There wasn't really any reason to be worried about him: Snjólfur seemed to be able to get by anywhere. Lína just couldn't understand him – did he have quicksilver on his tail, that Snjólfur? Why was he always travelling around in the sticks? Lína had never been farther up-country than Gufunes, when she was young, and that had been more than enough for her.

Tommi found it easier to understand Snjólfur; sometimes it occurred to him that his might be the truly happy life, wandering the country roads, alone and without ties. Then one wouldn't get that feeling of claustrophobia which came over him in the barracks district now and again.

In fact, Snjólfur couldn't be accused of neglecting his foster-parents; he never failed to look in when he was in the capital. It was just that it was such a rare occurrence.

But they were all delighted, one of those uneventful days, when this cousin popped up out of the dust of the country roads and without a word made himself at home in one of the cupboards.

Where had he been?

They should rather have asked where had he *not* been. Snjólfur had ploughed his own furrow for the last ten years. He had been a fireman, a customs official, a policeman, a foreman, a lorry driver, a warehouse manager, a chief gravedigger, a chief watchman at a herring processing plant, a chief this, a chief that, a man of the world with a whispering, fugitive voice.

Those ten years were a whole life, the way he told it, and it was amazing that nothing had appeared about him in the newspapers, in spite of everything he had achieved; it was amazing that he had not acquired a special place in Icelandic history, like Skúli Magnússon* and Jón Sigurðsson.** Snjólfur had laid roads, built bridges, erected whole villages and fathered children who had grown up to be men of standing, all in those ten years. No one thought it remarkable – that was just how cousin Snjólfur was, and now he was tired. He needed a fire in the hearth and a good rocking-chair – what a pity there was no hearth in the Old House. Snjólfur didn't do much work, either, he had already done enough. He had also become an abstainer, from spirits, tobacco and women.

That pleased Lína: you knew where you were with Snjólfur, he could do anything, even stop drinking completely, at least for two days. Two evenings after his return he slipped out for a constitutional and came back the next morning, noisy and happy, with a bottle in his belt and in the company of Hreggviður the shot-putter. They sat together in the kitchen all day; Snjólfur told stories and Hreggviður listened. His tally of achievements had not diminished in the course of that drunken night. Snjólfur had even begun to get his voice back and had stopped whispering; he had been a director, a ship's captain, even a local council director, a town clerk, a co-op director. Hreggi listened with one ear and enjoyed the contents of the bottle with all his senses. Lína also listened to the stories as she stood at the stove and the sink, and during lulls in the stories she kept up a constant refrain of 'what a load of rubbish', 'drunken blethers' and 'the demon drink'.

'It's about as true as saying you had given up drinking!'

But Snjólfur *had* given up, he was insistent on that; it was simply that he must not stop too suddenly – for health reasons.

---

* Skúli Magnússon (1711–94) is known as the 'Father of Reykjavík'. He was the first Icelander to be appointed High Sheriff of Iceland by the Danes. He founded several workshops in Reykjavík (a tiny village at the time) and broke the Danish trade monopoly in Iceland.

** Jón Sigurðsson (1811–79) is revered as the 'Father of the Nation'. Born in the Westfjords, he spent much of his life in Denmark, where he be- came leader of the Independence movement of the nineteenth century.

You see, he suffered from a very rare illness; now and again the blood suddenly stopped flowing in his veins, and he would go completely cold and stiff. Also, his limbs would lock up in the most peculiar positions: one day Lína found him locked stiff on the corner sofa; he sat there rigid with his legs hooked behind his neck and his hands gripping his thighs. He might have been sitting there to this day had he not managed to gasp that he needed a drink, something to strengthen his heart. After Lína gave him coffee laced with white spirit, his limbs unlocked and he was free again. Great are the curative powers of coffee laced with white spirit! But Lína was resourceful, too, for when Snjólfur locked up again a few days later, she said she hadn't any spirit left and poured cold water over him instead, and Snjólfur threw off his fetters, gasping for air and yelling.

All the same he was never angry with Lína; on the contrary, he liked it best when she was shouting at him, especially if he were on the bottle. He would splutter and crow with laughter to the accompaniment of her stream of curses. When she tried to exorcise the evil spirit in him, the demon drink, with her bible in one hand and the Passion Hymns in the other, he nearly choked with laughter. He went blue in the face and there was a rasping sound as he drew breath.

'You're a pearl, Lína!' he cackled when he recovered the power of speech. 'A di-i-i-amond!'

Dollí livened up a lot after Snjólfur arrived; she liked Snjólfur – she had always thought him funny. The colour began to come back to her cheeks and she laughed a trilling laugh as she sat listening to the cousin's stories of his feats. She liked doing things for him; she washed, ironed and mended his clothes, bought him a nice pair of shoes and made him a present of a new Tyrolean hat with a feather in it. Snjólfur tried to persuade her that he also needed a cane, preferably a white one, a dandy's cane, like the ones in Hollywood musicals; but Dollí thought canes were rubbish – only old men carried walking-sticks; in the end they agreed she would buy him an umbrella, a long black umbrella which he twirled around him in the streets or carried under his arm. Then he got himself white gloves and grew a moustache, a grey-tinged Hitler moustache; he looked every inch a gent with the green feather hat and black umbrella, just like an English bank manager.

With that sort of appearance, the ladies didn't half notice him. 'Who is that young man?' asked women whose bottom drawers were crammed with wedding trousseaux after decades of collecting items for a home they had not yet established. It wasn't long before Snjólfur hit it off with one of them, a very substantial widow by the name of Karitas; she had a house in Hafnarfjörður, and Snjólfur moved in with her.

Things quietened down in the Old House once again – not least for poor Dollí who, on top of all her other problems, began to worry a lot about Grettir. Not for his life, or his health – she was just worried, even convinced, that he was chasing after women: 'What's the man doing up in Hvalfjörður all the time if he isn't screwing around?' There she sat, ill, tired and alone in the misery of the barracks district, tied hand and foot by children who were no less his than hers. There weren't even any people of her own age in the district, or any she liked. She didn't feel like hanging out with Hreggviður's little Gréta, Lopsided Lauga, Stína Begga or Sæunn the cat-woman. Now and again she talked to poor Barði; they were the same age, in years at least, even if he didn't show it, and although he was a man one couldn't call him male company. He felt sorry for himself and she felt sorry for him, but of course she couldn't go around feeling sorry for everyone for ever, not with the life she herself led. Other men in the district? Emaciated drunkards, cripples and trouble-makers.

It was a great relief for Dollí when new people moved into one of the barracks-huts, a young couple from the west with two children. They had come to the city because the wife needed medical treatment for a kidney complaint. They were not planning to stay long; they weren't happy with having ended up in a camp like down-and-outs, but they could not find anywhere else to live, so the husband began to do up a barracks-hut. He was a skilled and hard-working joiner, and he repaired and fixed and painted everything. In the end they were really quite pleased with life.

During the day Dollí and the wife sat and drank coffee together; they talked about illness and fashion, and in the evenings they popped out to the cinema. Dollí had now acquired a female friend and, what was more, the friend had this rather stylish husband – a big blond work-horse with eyes the colour of blue sky.

The work-horse's name was Halldór. He had a job in a carpenter's shop during the day and was indispensable in a neighbourhood where skilled and obliging workmen were few and far between. He was always ready to lend a hand, and people were not slow to ask him for help – not least in the Old House where there was always something which needed fixing: the windows didn't fit, the roof leaked, the cupboard doors were hanging off their hinges, the banisters were loose. If anything was broken, Dóri the joiner arrived with his bag of tricks and fixed it.

This was quite a change for Dollí, who often lacked a pair of male hands around the house, since Grettir was always away on his travels. Dóri helped to carry her shopping when she went to the store, and gave her advice when she bought clothes, because men know best what suits a woman. He polished and lacquered her writing-desk, and mended the floor in the bedroom. He also repaired her double bed, which had begun to creak. Maybe they also used various methods of finding out if it had stopped creaking; at any rate he spent more and more of his spare time in Dollí's bedroom, and even whole nights there.

The colour had returned to Dollí's cheeks, and there was a healthy glow in her eyes; she looked quite a new person. She enjoyed life and was in good health, she was patient with the children and sang the 'Telephone Song' as she did her kitchen chores: 'Hallo / Haaaallo / Hallo / can you come and see me tonight?'

How delighted Grettir was with these changes! He had become despondent over Dollí's depression; he had even been on the point of giving up working for the Americans, which would have been very regrettable, but was now quite unnecessary. Dollí was so cheerful. She received him with open arms when he came home at weekends, they kissed and hugged and went for Sunday

walks with the children, she trilled and laughed at everything
he said. On Monday mornings he went back to his job again,
brimming with happiness at the world and his work and his wife
and the beauty of the sky. Of course, the rumours in the district
finally reached his ears: something about Dóri the joiner's visits
and remarkably long sojourns in Dollí's bedroom. But Grettir
didn't listen to such gossip. He wouldn't hear a word of it!

But Dóri's wife heard it. Dóri's wife also knew that he
sometimes didn't come home at night, and then she sat alone
in the darkness of the barracks-hut listening to the children's
breathing, apprehensive but reluctant to believe that there could
be anything bad in the behaviour of her big, solid husband. In
despair, and ill with kidney trouble, she sat looking out through
the window; outside, the grey and brown barracks-huts stood
there like worn-out buses, each with a light glowing on the gable.
Among them stood the Old House, dark, asleep and peaceful
until early morning, when the door would be cautiously pushed
open and, with a quick look round, Dóri the joiner would sneak
out on to the gravel.

Old Lína had never thought that poor little squirt Grettir much of
a man, thin and wretched as he was; Dóri the joiner, on the other
hand, was a man after her own heart. In that respect she could
well understand Dollí. All the same, she agreed with Tommi
that Dóri was behaving like a thorough swine towards his sick
wife. Fancy the bloody fellow taking such liberties! Eventually
Lína told Dollí that she would no longer tolerate such damned
whoring in her house.

That was how badly Dollí was treated, even by her closest
kin. She rushed up to her room and locked herself in, deeply
offended; she refused to answer when they called her and would
not open the door for a whole day and night, not even to her
children. In the end she came out and looked disdainfully at
the old couple. It was all very theatrical: without a word she
threw back her head, making her hair swirl behind her. She
was clearly trying to face the fortune-teller down, but Lína was
not to be intimidated; when Dollí spoke up and tried to defend

herself, the old woman launched a counter-attack: 'Shut your mouth and stop carrying on like this!' Dollí rushed back up to her room, slammed the door, and then rushed out again to the telephone. She rang Grettir hysterically and said she was being persecuted. She gabbled a story about this one and that one and a secret affair, and Grettir could make neither head nor tail of it; she might as well have been speaking English. However, as usual he agreed, said 'The devil . . . !' seven times and 'The very devil! . . .' once, but that was all.

There was nothing more Dollí could do. She had found it so nice having two men, one for weekdays and another for the weekends. But now it looked as if her luck had turned: she had to take a *decision*, and that's what ruins all romance. Dóri the joiner was also demanding an answer; his wife had started threatening divorce, you see. That was all right with Dóri, as long as he got Dollí instead. Otherwise not. So he kept nagging at Dollí about how she ought to give Grettir the boot so that the two of them could live happily ever after.

Grettir refused either to hear or to see for a very long time: he couldn't cope with such a complex riddle. Besides, he didn't really have anything to complain about. The couple's relationship had not been so good since their courting days. But then, one day, Dóri's sick wife accosted Grettir while he was out walking, and told him the whole sorry story, sobbing hysterically: how his witch whore of a wife had seduced her Halldór. How can you be married to such a cow? On the same day Lína shouted abuse at him in a Delphic style (though not too Delphic), so that even Grettir got the point: if you were any sort of a man, you'd try to keep order in your own marriage bed!

What was Grettir to do? He moped – not necessarily because he was hurt by the news; he simply disliked all this endless chatter. Why couldn't he be left in peace, a man with work to do? He sat hunched all day, poking around in the brimming ashtray with a cigarette stub, muttering to himself, so softly that only the s's could be heard. Dollí had a suspicion of what was wrong; she was on tenterhooks, not mentally prepared for a showdown at this moment. She fluttered around him, chattering enthusiastically about this and that – the film she had just seen with Marlon Brando in it: 'Ga-a-wd, he's so handsome,' she let slip, clapping her hand over her mouth and falling silent, then frantically continuing to talk about the gre-e-eat motorcycle he had in the film: 'But it wasn't as good as yours!' Honestly, she was bored stiff at the pictures when he didn't go with her, they went out far too little, the two of them, she enjoyed it so much better if he came too – they really ought to go to the pictures that weekend, she suggested. Grettir blushed with pride and satisfaction and found it hard to keep looking miserable. The corners of his mouth twitched. 'Ye-e-s, perhaps go to the pictures?' he muttered, even though they both knew that the cinema only made him uncomfortable – he was much too restless to sit still watching a full-length feature film, and was only too happy when the lights went up and he could drag himself on numbed feet out into the cold, half asleep, his mind a blank.

They talked no more of going to the pictures, but Dollí continued to rack her brains for a way of pleasing him. At last she had a good idea: the motorbike was in the scullery, broken down, and looked unlikely ever to work again. 'You should just buy yourself a car!' she said.

With that, the lights came on again. It was true that Grettir had the use of an army car for his work, but he rarely had a limousine which could be used in his free time when all true family men took their wives and children out for a drive. Besides, he had to commute to work and was tired of standing in bus queues in town, and then having to rely on buses or colleagues for the journey to Keflavík. He had never dared so much as mention buying a car to Dollí; but since she was now proposing it, he cheered up and at once began to look around for a place where he could buy a used car at a reasonable price. Hlynur the mechanic said he could fix him up with a newly overhauled Skoda, but Grettir had his sights set higher – he wanted a decent car, a big saloon, preferably American.

A cheap American car? Was the man mad? When worn-out

wrecks sold for extortionate sums? Mad or not, Grettir got hold
of an American car at a ridiculous price – and what a car! Ten
years old but as good as new, little used, no rust, everything in
tip-top condition. All the instruments, switches, lights, handles
– everything like new. And yet there was no competition for it.
The car was parked in a municipal garage, and Grettir was able
to examine it at his leisure. He thought it was a pity that there
was only room for two or three, on the banquette in front; but as
the gnarled old fellow who showed him the car pointed out, there
would be no problem in making another banquette in the back,
or even two, and then it would be a six- or nine-seater car.

It was a custom-built station-wagon with doors at the rear,
jet black and with gold crosses on the sides. It had been used
for taking coffins from the cathedral to the cemetery for many
years, but the funeral director had acquired another custom-built
carriage which stood beside the old one.

How proud and pleased Grettir was when he returned home
to the district in his new car! Hlynur let him bring the carriage
into his garage and there they worked together to bolt a new
banquette in the coffin space and to paint over the crosses with
black paint. The car was a Plymouth, and Grettir called it the
'Black Plymount'. During the evenings which followed he was
busy inviting people for a drive. The folk at the Old House took
a few trial runs around the town – all except old Lína; she threw
up her hands and said she hoped it would be some time yet before
she had to be transported in such a vehicle.

That was how the days passed at the Old House. Elsewhere
in the neighbourhood there was always something happening,
more than one could keep up with. Hlynur the mechanic and
his Lopsided Lauga suffered a setback when it emerged that their
model sons in Selfoss and Súðavík were not so model as had been
thought. Now they were in town, living in their parents' large
barracks-hut.

One of them, the one from Selfoss, seemed to be quite properly
married and had become a plumber. His name was Ottó, and
he had an enormous wife and two noisy sons. But he was also

damned fond of the bottle, blast him, and rumour had it that
he had drunk his good name away in Selfoss, even though he
said he had only come to the capital on a short visit.

On a visit? To whom? He spent the whole time drinking and
was free with his fists; he went around threatening people,
especially women and children, and yet claimed to be afraid
of no one. He pissed against the front door of Hreggviður's
barracks-hut, and when the shot-putter came at him with murder
in his eyes, Ottó the plumber was not at all scared, and invited
him to a punch-up or even a fight to the death. Hreggviður had
never been spoken to like that by anyone; he was so taken aback
that he nearly collapsed. He went back inside the barracks-hut
again, and people thought he was afraid of Ottó Hlynsson the
plumber, who only came up to his waist. But that is the way
it goes, as Tommi used to say: for example, Hreggi was more
afraid of mice than any woman in the district.

Ottó had plenty of faults, but the other brother was much
worse – he was counterfeit goods, through and through. This
model son, Ólafur, who was supposed to be married in Súðavík
and well on the way to working his way up to the position of
manager at the freezing plant, now seemed to have come to town
for good – with no wife. He had probably never had one.

No one had ever seen anything quite so effeminate. He
wiggled his hips as he walked and simpered like a young girl.
'Súúú ðavík?' he would say, affectedly, when people asked if he
had moved from there; he had not been in Súðavík for many
years. He had been in Ísafjörður where he had been a model
for some painter or other. 'But then he cheated on me,' he said,
and put on a stricken expression.

What had he been cheated of? Money? No. Nor of a job either.
It was all a bit fishy. Did respectable folk have to listen to such
infernal rubbish? The menfolk clenched their fists and said that
people like him should be given a good hiding. Many of the
women had nothing against Ólafur; he hung around in Tommi's
Shop and chatted to the housewives about how dreadfully bad
this or that type of soap was for the skin. Such a very pleasant
and easy-going man!

Lína had nothing against Ólafur, but no one doubted her superior knowledge of human nature, and when she was asked she pronounced the verdict: 'He is clearly a sodomist!' This judgement of Solomon spread like wildfire, and stuck to him: after this he was called Óli the Sodomist, or simply Óli Sódó. What this meant, precisely, no one really knew, but the man was at least very mixed-up and therefore rather dangerous. Parents began to keep a close watch on their children, or kept them in the barracks-huts all day long until they either pined away or went mad.

Good God! And the infernal fellow appeared to have no sense of shame. Youngsters with their noses pressed to the windowpane said they had seen Óli trying on his mother's nightdresses; and one evening he had arrived at Sæunn the cat-woman's house wearing lipstick and wanting to borrow some shampoo, and Sæunn had been so taken aback that she laughed all night.

Jerks like him should be taught a lesson, said the fathers, and the youngsters took them at their word and followed Óli around in large groups: 'Óli turd! Óli shit-stink! Óli sódó!' – even 'Óli tight-wad!' (which he could not for the life of him understand). Shit-pails were emptied outside the door of Hlynur's barracks-hut, arses were drawn on the gable wall and the youngsters urinated through the windows. The grown-ups turned a blind eye and didn't interfere, but some of them talked to Tommi and asked him to throw Óli out of the shop; it was intolerable for the regular customers to be served with that queer hanging around the counter all the time. Tommi promised to look into the matter, but never did anything about it.

They were quite a pair, those brothers. Some model sons! Lopsided Lauga had become almost doubled up by this time – though not from work, because no one wanted her to do their laundry now, with such goings-on in her home. Poor Hlynur would creep along the side of the street, overcome with shame – and serve him right, for he had been so stuck-up, setting himself high above the rest, not least because of those sons of his.

There was one person who was more ashamed of Óli the

Sodomist than anyone else, and that was his brother Ottó. He would yell at his brother like a madman and hit him so hard that the blows could be heard all over the district. The brothers were as alike as two pins in appearance, but it was as if Ottó were trying to convince people that they were very different on the inside. His aggressiveness redoubled, the bloody man became like a bull in a rage. Drunkenness and violence were not exactly unknown in the district, but Ottó broke all records. He got worse and worse every day; he threatened to rape housewives and even grandmothers wherever he met them, and he was always ready for a fight. He even tried to beat up old Tommi, but was fortunately so drunk that Tommi managed to fell him with a simple wrestling throw.

What had people done to deserve this scourge? While they were all in despair over the misfortune the brothers had brought upon the district, the problem quickly and happily solved itself: Óli-Sódó landed in hospital, Ottó in prison. It so happened that Óli complained, one suppertime, about the terrible stink of Ottó's sweaty feet. Ottó was quick to retaliate; he pulled off his socks, stuffed one of them down his brother's throat and wound the other one round his neck and pulled it tight. The doctors doubted if Óli would ever fully recover, and Ottó got four years.

But things didn't always work out that well. The daughters of Hreggviður and Gréta were ill most of the time – at least they were always very pale and coughed a lot. At around this time they both contracted severe pneumonia and were bedridden for ages. The younger one, Súsanna, eventually began to recover, but Maríanna, the elder one, never got better and died in hospital.

This seemed to be a great shock to Hreggviður; and people found this surprising, as he had never been particularly fond of children. He became as thin as a rake, his hair began to turn grey and it was difficult to get so much as a word out of him. Gréta, on the other hand, seemed to brighten up when Maríanna died; at any rate, she showed no more grief than at other times when something went wrong – except at the funeral, when she suddenly threw herself screaming on the coffin and they had to put a cotton-reel between her teeth and carry her out.

The residents of the district were much preoccupied with such events, but not Dollí. She had more than enough on her plate as it was, the poor woman, torn apart with desperation and headaches. As always when she was beginning to feel good, she found no peace. She had to choose between Grettir and Dóri, but did not want to lose either of them. But then she got pregnant with her third child, and knew there could be no more messing about. On a Monday evening when Grettir had left on a long journey for the US army, all the way east to Stokksnes, she finally succumbed to Dóri's pleas: he was the father of the child she was carrying, and Grettir would have to sail his own sea.

The honeymoon began. Halldór the joiner thought he had won a great victory. When he thought about it, he realised that his marriage had been on its last legs. They were so different, he and his wife. Of course he had to speak to his wife when he went to the barracks-hut for the last time to fetch his toothbrush and electric razor, and then he explained it all: he had been unhappy with the marriage for a long time and knew that she had been, too – it was just that they had never been able to talk about it; now they could each start a new life, and so on. Halldór was a smooth talker and he managed the whole thing well; from the way he put his cards on the table he really deserved to be thanked for packing his bags and going. But some women can't listen to reason, and Halldór's wife was one of them. She began to cry. Dóri said that she was only making things difficult, for herself as well as for him, by carrying on like this. But consideration didn't seem to be one of her virtues, for she was still crying when Halldór said goodbye.

'How did it go?' Dollí asked.

'Just a lot of damned whining,' Halldór replied.

Dóri took a few days off so that they could enjoy their happiness together. Those first days were pure heaven. Then one thing and another began to cast shadows.

For example, his former wife had a nervous breakdown and moved away from the capital, that cruel city which was the root of all her unhappiness. It was a mistake, because the city had all the technology she needed for her kidney complaint, but like a fool she went back with her children to her home village in the western fjords. She had parents and siblings there, but there was no doctor and none of the equipment which could save her health. So of course things went badly for her – so badly that there were fears for her life.

Everyone thought it was Halldór's fault. His parents-in-law called him on the phone in the Old House – they had refused to believe that he could have behaved so badly. Her brothers, trawlermen of elephantine strength, announced that they were on their way – someone was due a hiding.

It was all so stupid! It wasn't Halldór's fault. He wrote a letter to the western fjords in which he protested his innocence. She could have gone on living in the barracks-hut and he promised her money while she needed medical attention. In no way had he forced her to go west; on the contrary, it had been entirely her own idea. In the letter he attempted a counter-attack: he had lost out over the children; if she had stayed on in the barracks, as he had hoped, he would have been able to see them, even had them over to stay with him every other weekend, and in that way the divorce would have been easier to bear. Instead, the children had lost their father when *she* took them west with her.

The people in the west refused to look facts in the face, however. His parents wrote saying they no longer regarded him as their son. He met some old friends from the west, who advised him not to show his face there for the next ten years. On top of it all, both Lína and Tommi were cold and aloof towards him in the Old House.

But that was not the worst of it. What worried Dóri most was that it looked as though Dollí had not yet decided which one she wanted, him or Grettir. Sometimes she pushed Halldór away and buried her face in the pillow and said she was so apprehensive about seeing Grettir.

'But you have to!' said Halldór. For her sake he had given up everything – wife, children, parents, friends and even the village of his childhood where he had grown up; it was surely not too much to ask that she break from that little guy. Did Grettir deserve any better, with all his whoring up in Hvalfjörður?

But women's emotional storms are always the same. Dóri was furious – he had had enough of this fickleness, and Dollí began to cry. Dóri had gone to his job in town when Grettir, completely unsuspecting, arrived from the east, and went straight to the Old House, where Dollí threw herself into his arms. When Dóri came home from work, he was politely asked to remove his toothbrush and electric razor for a second time; it was all over between him and Dollí.

It now emerged that Dollí had every reason to be delighted to be rid of this man. He broke down at the least pressure, and just began to drink. They heard terrible stories about him; he had even been seen in drunken squalor with the city's winos and down-and-outs – he who had always been such a fine upstanding man. Someone had spotted him in an overcoat outside Ingólfur's Pharmacy. Hreggviður, who had been on the wagon since the death of his little Maríanna, shook his head in a worldly wise way and said he couldn't understand the fellow – why didn't he pull himself out of the mire again? But it was as if Dóri was unable to face facts, or to understand when he was spoken to; he just continued to make phone calls and come to the Old House, either with tearful pleas or with threats, and always drunk. Dollí could not be bothered to attend to his babbling, and Tommi would answer him in monosyllables: 'No, no, yes thanks, no, bye.' Usually it was Lína who replied on behalf of the family; she if anyone knew how to make herself understood, but even that did not help. It was not until Dollí herself came to the door and mocked him for his wretched and pathetic appearance that he finally gave in.

It was a lost cause.

He packed his bags and went west, bringing a doctor with him to try to improve his welcome.

His wife had survived and was getting her strength back after the shock. In floods of tears, Dóri told her that he had come back, his conscience had been troubling him so much; when she left he had realised that he loved only her and that it had all been a bad dream.

He was met with disbelief and suspicion, but tried to overcome it in every possible way. He worked like a maniac, he was all kindness and good nature, he paid the doctor's air-fare from Ísafjörður, he spent a lot on expensive medicines and said he was putting money aside for an operation in America if she needed it. Slowly but surely he was thawing the ice; he felt it should work – he wanted to forget Dollí and all that dreadful business in Reykjavík.

And the earth went round, and the pages were torn from the American calendar in Lína's kitchen. Dollí sat with her during the daytime, drinking coffee from a chipped cup. If she had ever had reason to be fed up and depressed it was now; the longer the pregnancy went on, the more ill Dollí became. Her first pregnancy had not exactly gone smoothly, but this one was infinitely worse. For the first two months she could not keep anything down, and she wasted away; when that phase passed she ballooned with water and fat. She was always having fits, and grew dizzy and fainted, and had dreadful palpitations and panic attacks. She would wake up screaming and crying, so that Lína had to sit with her every night when Grettir was away. Twice she was admitted to hospital with stomach cramps, and on both occasions the doctors reckoned that she would lose the baby. But Dollí was tough and got through it, in spite of all the difficulties.

At the end of the nine months she was beginning to feel a bit better, but had problems walking because of swollen legs and back pains; so she sat chalk-white but calm in a chair, counting knitting-stitches and counting minutes and seconds and waiting for the labour pains to start.

But it was as though the Fates had thought that not enough burdens had been placed on the young woman's shoulders. Days passed, weeks passed, a whole month went by and still the child showed no sign of making an appearance. Poor Dollí grew weaker and weaker, and even though she no longer had fits, Lína and Tommi were worried about her. She just sat there silently in the rocking-chair, chalk-white, her eyes bloodshot, bloated and misshapen. She only felt all right if she had plenty of sweets to munch.

Grettir was away more than usual during those last weeks; he hardly ever came home. Lína and Tommi tried to cheer her up as best they could; Dollí could barely speak, so the best thing was to tell her stories. Tommi's favourite stories were about his own affairs with women and fights with Turks and Arabs in the years before the First World War; but when he tried to remember comic and humorous episodes from those days, he realised that they were men's stories and not really suitable for pregnant women.

Lína had the bright idea of sending for cousin Snjólfur – Dollí always brightened up when he appeared with his umbrella, moustache and Tyrolean hat.

Cousin Snjólfur did splendidly; he talked of how pretty Dollí was now that she was so plump, and even though she knew it wasn't true, it warmed her heart. Snjólfur kept showing off all the time, of course, and Dollí liked that. Since they got along so well he began to open up to her and told her of his dreams: he was always painting and drawing a bit, and wanted to become famous in that field, like his half-brothers who had established themselves in the city as artists.

He had never really got to know these half-brothers; he had never really known his father, either – his father had had these sons with some woman or other in town after Gíslína died. When Snjólfur had been living in the house he sometimes used to boast about the brothers, but now he confided to Dollí with a tragic expression on his face that he was probably not good enough for such famous men, for whenever he rang or paid a visit to talk about the family and discuss painting they cut him off and didn't want to know.

Dollí loved stories of this kind, especially if there were a love interest involved. Snjólfur could serve up such stories by the barrow-load, for he had felt the scourge of love many times in his life; once, for example, he had been engaged to a girl in Kopaskeri with whom he had a child, but just before the wedding she jilted him for his best friend. Snjólfur had gone to the next county and sat up night after night with a smoky oil-lamp, writing a love letter to his girlfriend, a long and ardent letter, written in red ink, red as his heart's blood. Did he receive an answer? No, he never got any response, because he never sent the letter, he just put it in his wallet, and there it was still, a quarter of a century later. He fished it out, all crushed and yellowed, and read it to Dollí – this letter which beat all the love letters in the weekly magazines. Dollí was moved to tears, and Snjólfur had to come back day after day and read the letter again.

Six weeks had now passed since the nine months were up, and Snjólfur was in the middle of reading the letter when the baby arrived. It arrived so quickly that there was no time for a doctor or a midwife to arrive, and Lína and Snjólfur had to deliver the child. Snjólfur took charge and immediately ordered water to be boiled, which was always done in books and films; but when Lína arrived with a full kettle of scalding hot water it turned out that neither of them had any idea what the water was supposed to be for. At any rate it was there to hand, just in case, but it was never used, for the baby was born without any fuss, right there in the telephone room of the Old House.

'Without any fuss' is perhaps putting it a bit strongly, but they worked a miracle, Snjólfur and Lína.

The baby had hardly uttered its first cry before the doctor arrived and rushed it straight to hospital, so quickly that Dollí didn't even have time to see it. She gazed at Lína and Snjólfur when she realised that it was over; then she began to ask them about the baby and at once discovered that there was something they did not want to tell her. It was a boy, they said, really big and bonny – indeed, it emerged that he weighed more than ten pounds and was the biggest baby who had ever been born in the family. But Snjólfur and Lína seemed depressed about something, whispering agitatedly together, and Dollí went rigid with fear and began to cry, thinking that the same thing had happened to her as had happened to her mother, Gógó, who had recently had a child who was retarded or worse.

But it was not quite as bad as that; it was simply that the child's right leg was so crippled and withered that the surgeons had to amputate it just below the knee.

Dollí recovered physically within a short time; she shed the extra pounds and got her strength back, but for a long time she was depressed and taciturn. Grettir didn't really know how he should behave; he didn't dare to be cheerful, so he tried instead to play it tough – he looked at the child in an embarrassed sort of way and peeped at him as if out of duty. He seemed to be shy. Dollí no longer received him as warmly as she had done in the days when her affair with Dóri the joiner was in full swing. So Grettir continued to take on all sorts of jobs for the army, which meant that he was away for long periods at a time.

Lína at once lavished all her love on the little boy even though he was so maimed. She kept the cradle with her in the kitchen while she did her fortune-telling and housework. She talked to the cradle, muttering away about the evils of the world as she studied the cards, admiring the chubby, sleeping infant. 'He doesn't look a bit like Grettir!' she declared.

Dollí fully agreed. 'It's no wonder the boy doesn't look like Grettir – he's Dóri's son,' she said.

So Dóri got a message telling him he had a new-born son in the capital. Dollí made an ice-cold phone call to the west. Dóri's wife took the call. She probably recognised Dollí's voice because her own became frightened; she kept asking over and over again who it was and whether it was something important – should she give him a message about something? 'No, nothing in particular,' Dollí said, and told the woman she would ring again in the evening.

Poor Dóri! He had begun to lead a normal family life in the west, he had struggled to overcome his in-laws' suspicions, and now like a bolt from the blue he got this news from Dollí.

'What nonsense is this?' he whispered desperately.

'I can't hear you!' Dollí shouted down the crackling phone line.

'What non –'

'Nonsense? You've just had a son!'

Poor Dóri. His wife was probably sitting with her ears pricked behind the newspaper as Dóri tried to whisper all the way south across the sky-high mountains and moorlands, while Dollí shouted back so loudly that he was afraid it would be heard all over the house.

'Leave me alone,' he hissed into the receiver. 'I've got my family and you've got yours!' Then he slammed the phone down. But Dollí rang back immediately and gave him a thorough scolding: trying to pretend that having a son was none of his business, indeed!

'What do you want from me?' Dóri asked.

'You've got to accept responsibility!'

'Eh?'

'You have to pay maintenance for your child!'

Dóri hung up again. It was the last straw. This was what that rabble in the capital was like – lying about paternity, just to swindle money out of him. She herself had admitted it on the telephone!

The joiner from the western fjords was not off the hook yet, even though he had slammed down the phone on Dollí. A few days later he got a short but pointed letter telling him that if he didn't come to Reykjavík to settle his business he would be hearing from a lawyer. He showed the letter to everyone in the village. What lies and insolence! It just shows what that riff-raff in the south was like – there should be a law against people like that who stab honourable folk in the back. He persuaded everyone in the village to believe him. The letter also said that there was something wrong with the child; people could not believe that a strong, healthy man from the western fjords could father a deformed child. That was more typical of the barracks rabble on the gravel heap!

The only people in the village who were not convinced of Dóri's innocence were Dóri himself and his wife, each in their own way. But they did not talk about it. They just kept silent about it – a silence so aching that it made the walls creak. Dóri got another letter and realised that he had to go south, in the unlikely hope that he would manage to clear himself of this smear, once and for all.

The letters from the capital were signed by both Dóróthea and Grettir; it could not be said that Grettir failed to stand by his wife in these difficult times. Some husbands might perhaps have been angry if their wives began to have children with other men in the town, deformed children at that. But not Grettir. He beamed triumphantly when it turned out that he could not have been the child's father; it was proved by blood tests – he and Dollí belonged to the same common blood group, while the child belonged to a very rare one.

Dóri came south at last and took a blood test, and it turned out that he had the same blood group as the crippled boy. He realised that the case was lost. Although he continued to deny it, he knew that no one was prepared to believe him. A broken man, he signed the certificate and child maintenance order in the judge's chambers.

Dollí and Grettir were grinning from ear to ear when they brought the news home to the Old House. They had won the case! Yabbadabbadoo! Grettir offered everyone a cigar, yes! He strutted to and fro and muttered 'The devil!' to himself. He even lifted the boy out of his cradle and told him the news: 'Waddya think of that?' In the evening Tóti and Fía and some of the other neighbours from the Camp were invited to the Old House for coffee, to celebrate the outcome of the case. Fía snorted indignantly about the man's incredible cheek, trying to get away without paying all that mun-n-ny! The impudence of it! Words failed her.

'Yes! But he didn't get away with it!' said Grettir; he was still puffing at his cigar, red-eyed and swollen from the tobacco fumes which wreathed his face. He was trying to calculate for Tóti and Tommi how much money was actually involved – a good four hundred a month, eh, that would be, er, about five thousand a year, and over . . . over . . . sixteen years that would come to, how much, eh? Ninety thousand!

'Ninety thousand?' Ha ha ha, even cousin Tóti thought that a lot of money. Ninety thousand – two or three new cars!

Grettir racked his brains for the rest of the evening. When the guests had gone he fetched paper and pencil and did sums. Then he shouted for Tommi, and showed him the calculations. Tommi had gone to bed and was a bit irritated when he came to the table where Grettir was sitting.

'Look, I made a bit of a mistake there, it only comes to eighty thousand, not ninety.'

'Really.'

'Perhaps I ought to ring Tóti,' said Grettir, looking at his wristwatch. 'Just to correct this!'

Tommi leaned over towards Grettir and gave him a measured look. 'You know something, Grettir? I don't think it matters all that much.'

'We-ell, maybe not. Yes, perhaps you're right,' Grettir muttered, annoyed with himself for having done his sums wrong.

There had been another topic of discussion at the coffee evening which threatened to overshadow the victory in the paternity suit: under the headline 'Boy of 18 suspected of murder', Deaf Grjóni's name was in the newspapers. Sigurjón Traustason, seaman aboard the trawler MS *Hvanngeir*, was under arrest in Siglufjörður. After an epic bout of drinking and violence which shook the gold-rush town of Herring City for several days when the weather was too bad for fishing, a middle-aged cook from one of the boats from the western fjords had been found beaten to death in the town's main street. Grjóni and three others were on remand because of this; according to witnesses they had been in a violent fight with the crew of the boat from the western fjords the previous night – a crew which had included the dead cook. All the accused flatly denied having caused the man's death, except Sigurjón, who was both deaf and dumb throughout the interrogation and was therefore the prime suspect.

This case was discussed in all its aspects over the rattle of
coffee cups and plates of cakes; it proved that cousin Tóti had
been right when he said that one shouldn't be too soft on boys
like that – they needed to have the obstinacy thrashed out of them
right away, before they began to put their own and others' lives
in danger, as had now happened. 'We worked like dogs to make
a football club for lads like him,' cousin Tóti felt like saying, but
couldn't because Tommi was there. Fía wrung her hands, and
thought it a miracle that she was still alive; that criminal had
visited her home only a few years ago, twice indeed; and what
about her dear Gosi, good God! Sigurjón had almost succeeded
in dragging Gosi down into a life of crime, like that time he had
taken Gosi and some other innocent youngsters with him on the
break-in down at the harbour a few years ago. She could hardly
bear to think of what might have happened if she had not given
the reins a sharp tug at the time!

Just as Tóti had avoided mentioning the football club because
of Tommi, for Lína's sake Fía avoided mentioning Baddi in this
connection. But Lína knew what was what, and felt that in
all of this there were sly digs at her beloved ray of sunshine
who had now been away for so long in America that she saw
him in her dreams with dimples in his cheeks and playing on
a little golden harp. That his boyhood chum Sigurjón could do
anything as dreadful as this was quite unthinkable; it was just
these pharisees and character-assassins on the rampage again,
she had known for a long time how they worked. Of course
Lína won the battle of words with Fía and Tóti; they left the
party in a huff after Lína had proved Grjóni's innocence with
countless examples of how kind the two friends had been both
to animals and people over the years.

Grettir made no contribution to the debate; he sat there doing
his mental arithmetic and felt that the matter had nothing to do
with him. Tommi was silent, too, not because it had nothing to
do with him but because he was too immersed in thoughts about
Grjóni and his boys to want to argue about them with Fía and
Tóti. He hoped deeply and fervently that it was not true, and
prayed silently to God; he had always been afraid that it might

turn out like this. His dream and ambition had been to help the boys and set them on the right road – that was why the Kári Football Club had been founded. But it would all have been in vain if Sigurjón, that red-haired rogue, whom he had even taken into his home for a time, had committed such a crime. It couldn't be true! Or could it? No.

Lína was so convinced of Grjóni's innocence that she began to try to secure his unconditional release from detention and have him cleared of the charge. Next day she set about cultivating her family ties with a distant cousin of hers named Guðlaugur, who had done well for himself and worked his way up to the rank of inspector in the Reykjavík police. Lína went to see him and ordered her 'cousin Laugi' to see to it straight away that Grjóni was released as soon as possible. She said that she looked upon Sigurjón as one of her own children, but otherwise made no attempt to confuse the issue with digressions. Guðlaugur knew this overpowering cousin of his mostly by reputation; he sat up straight and nodded his head so hard that his neck muscles were aching when she left. Then this conscientious guardian of the law realised to his horror and dismay that he had promised to secure the release of a suspected murderer in another part of the country; if word of this were to reach the ears of his superiors, he would be lucky to be allowed to start again as a traffic warden.

This also gave the old woman a pretext for making a phone call west across the sea to tell Baddi the news. He seemed to be listening, for there was silence on the line as Lína talked; then Baddi was heard to whistle and utter a short 'Wow!'. He probably also shook his head and gave Gógó the receiver, for she came on the line and said that Baddi was getting bored with them and that she would be sending him home as soon as possible.

A few days later the fortune-teller made another phone call, this time to Inspector Guðlaugur, to thank him for attending so promptly to Sigurjón's case. Laugi mopped the sweat from his forehead, enjoyed the praise, and so did not correct the misunderstanding.

It created something of a scandal, in fact, that when the court case began in the north, and the judge examined the documents in the case, it emerged that the police and the prosecution had overlooked the fact that Sigurjón had been arrested and locked up for break-ins at both the Co-op and the post office at 2 a.m. on the night of the murder, and that the dead man had been seen alive and well in the town at least an hour later. The murder charge against Sigurjón was promptly dropped, but he was charged with the two break-ins, petty theft and grievous bodily harm; other lesser offences were added on, so that in the end there was quite an impressive list of charges. He was given eighteen months in jail, but because of his age one year was transmuted to a suspended sentence.

Since the new-born disabled child was the son of Halldór the joiner, Dollí thought it right that he should be given his patronymic in full: Halldór Halldórsson. That was all they had in common: Dóri the joiner was fair-haired and cheerful, while his son was dark and melancholy.

Lína didn't like the name Dóri, and called the boy Bóbó. Little Bóbó soon began to crawl on all threes – his hands and his left leg. Like this he was able to race round the house, and soon the whole district too. He was taciturn and aloof, especially if he were teased; he would then keep so silent that the family felt they were walking on eggshells for days. When little Bóbó was five he had a special shoe made for him. It was a ten-centimetre-long block of wood which was strapped to his right leg. He soon learned to walk on it, and there was a gleam of happiness and triumph in his eyes when he was able to start moving around upright like other people; he would thunder across the wooden floor like Admiral Nelson, making the whole house shake.

Halldór the joiner stayed in the city and never went back west again. Within a few weeks his hair had turned grey; then he got a job in a furniture workshop and rented a basement room in the Bank Block.

Father and son, Dóri and Bóbó, were to live there next door to one another for the next twenty years. They met each day, but never said hello.

8

Strong and steady stand your ground

Out west in America, where the sun was setting several hours after sending a few rays through the overcast skies above the Old House and Iceland's frozen soil, were Gógó and Baddi and Danni.

Now and again Gógó would send photographs; they looked like old postcards which had got wet. There was, for example, a picture of a whole street, a row of big white houses which stood half-hidden behind ornamental gardens and well-kept hedges which fathers in white shirts trimmed and watered. On the back of the photo Gógó had written 'Our House' – and that set them wondering in the Old House. Did Gógó own all those houses? All those palaces which looked like the mansions in the illustrated love stories in Danish magazines? Did she also own all those husbands in white shirts who were either tending the gardens or polishing the cars which stood in rows in front of the houses and were so stately that Grettir's swanky hearse looked like a horse-cart in comparison? That would be just like Gógó. There was also a photo of Baddi in a policeman's cap, and that caused much head-scratching. Tommi said it was impossible that the boy could have joined the police; he thought it was more likely to be a skipper's cap.

'Yes, but do you think it's any more likely that he's become a skipper?' Dollí asked scornfully, and Tommi said no more; his opinion carried little weight, anyway. Although he was the working head of the family and earned a little money for the daily white loaf, somehow he was like a tenant or a lodger who worked for his keep, not really one of the family. It was Gógó who provided everything which gave life and colour to their existence during those times of prosperity.

As for Baddi, he gave meaning to all the struggles of this world: that clever and handsome lad of promise, that blessed scion of the family, the granny's boy of the prayers which the queen of the Old House repeated to herself aloud as she did the dishes at the sink, or in silence as she brooded over the cards and the future of strangers – the boy with the bright eyes and the smile, always helpful and generous to everything which drew breath.

Now he was expected home.

The Americans were lucky to have enjoyed his presence all these years, thought Karolína, that steely woman who had not allowed her feelings free rein for decades. Nowadays she talked of her Baddi with such tearful longing that even Tommi was moved and began to imagine that everything would be bright and beautiful when the angel came home. But Tommi had always been much more attached to Danni; they had so much in common, he and the younger brother whom few missed and whose memory meant no more to the family than a raven landing on a gable-head and cawing.

Tommi came to think, when he looked back, that Baddi had not been such a bad lot after all – that was just exaggeration and a lack of understanding of young people. Boys would be boys, wouldn't they? Before Baddi left he had become a bit of a burden to Tommi, to be sure, because of the fines and damages he had had to pay for all kinds of minor mischief Baddi had got involved in, but youngsters grew out of that sort of thing. Tommi was far more worried about the boys when they began to tinker with *brennivín* and steal bottles and get drunk and go into sheds and shacks with girls who screamed and bawled and came rushing out with fire and frenzy in their eyes, but who always allowed themselves to be lured into the sheds again. But why should Tommi worry about that? They were young and enjoying themselves. Tommi had come to the view that it was merely from envy that grown-ups always got so scandalised about young people who were able to take life lightly. Tommi himself – well, half a century earlier he had been just like Baddi, that was how history repeated itself. People often said that they were very alike, the grandfather and son, and Tommi would be touched but somewhat embarrassed and would change the subject. Although it was hard to understand, Tommi himself knew there was a grain of truth in it, for he could often see himself in Baddi: both of them were inordinately sensitive to cold, for instance, and before Baddi went abroad he always went around in long johns under his trousers and woollen stockings which came far up his legs – that fifteen-year-old ladies' darling. And if there was no tobacco, the boys would just take a pinch of snuff like any other healthy young Icelanders.

Then again, Tommi did not forget how good the boy had become at football. It was too bad he had given up training. It happened just after the trip to the Faroes and Norway – that was when Grjóni and Lúddi and most of the old hard-core players had also dropped it, and a new generation had taken over, led by Danni and other young brats. It was an unforgettable day when Baddi came to training for the last time and said he couldn't be bothered with all that kids' stuff. Then off he stalked in his rubber shoes, lighting a cigarette stub with practised hands as he went and throwing the matchstick up in the air and back-heeling it as it fell.

That was the end of his football training.

Baddi was nearly sixteen when he set off into the world in the big aeroplane – the dear granny's boy, she remembered it so well, the day he said goodbye to them at the airport, quiet but determined.

'When things go wrong in life's daily round,
Strong and steady stand your ground.'

Of course he must have been anxious; he was constantly asking which plane he should board, just to make sure. He tripped and stumbled in his brand-new canvas shoes, with his patterned sweater and pudding-bowl haircut. In his luggage there was an extra set of woollen underwear plus dried fish and blood-sausage, so he would certainly not go hungry. His belongings were packed in a large coffin-shaped trunk which had been Tommi's from his seagoing days.

Then the announcement came for the passengers to embark,

and the boy jumped up and rushed out to the plane, without a word of goodbye to anyone.

Granny's prayers were chanted a great deal in the Old House during those last days before Baddi came home, so much so that it infected the rest of the district; at all the kitchen sinks the women carolled:

> May all good spirits bring you joy,
> Protect and bless my darling boy;
> Bring him strength and life anew,
> And luck and friends will be his due.

If anyone's memory of Baddi had grown hazy, Lína was quick to revive it with a few biblical tales. It wasn't really necessary, for Baddi had always been the kind of boy whom grown-ups liked: a lively lad with an open face and a friendly smile. He knew how to press all the right buttons, and as a little boy he sang Lenten hymns and Christmas carols to the housewives, who were moved to tears and stuffed his pockets full of cakes.

The boy was expected home at the start of winter, and the dark days had settled on the houses with suffocating weight. Even so, the hero's return was the cause of the only spring-cleaning which had ever been done in the history of the district. Tommi and Grettir tarred the roof of the Old House, Dollí raked the gravel around the house, the rubbish around the barracks was cleared up and the occasional broken window was replaced; Hlynur even had to tidy up his scrap-heap of cars. 'You'd think that rascal Baddi had become president of America,' Hlynur muttered to Lopsided Lauga, but outside his house he said nothing – it didn't pay to stick one's neck out in these last, anxious moments.

The day Baddi was due to arrive Grettir revved up the hearse, and they all drove south to the air-base at Keflavík. Dollí and the children went with them, of course, as well as Lína and Tommi and cousin Snjólfur, and Barði Högnason joined them with two women from the Baddi fan club, so the car was packed; not everyone who wanted to go could be squeezed in. The same thing happened when they were about to return to the city: the hero had so much luggage that it almost filled the car. They tried to pack it tight and jam it all in, but it was no use – some people had to be left behind at the airport. Barði Högnason had to get out, but even that was not enough; Tommi also had to give up his seat, as did Snjólfur and the two women, and Dollí's eldest children; she was even thinking of dumping little Bóbó, barely a year old, in the arms of Tommi as he stood there shuffling his feet outside the airport in the Suðurnes rain. But Baddi would not hear of it. 'No way!' He said he would rather walk than leave a handicapped infant behind. The matter was resolved with Tommi being given one of the suitcases to carry instead; but even that was not enough, the only space was on the banquette in front and there was no room for the four grown-ups who all seemed indispensable: Grettir, Dollí, Lína and the guest of honour.

Grettir sat small and hunched behind the large steering-wheel with his hand on the gear stick and said they had to sort things out. He had never before been so important and indispensable, a chauffeur personified: 'Nothing can happen without me,' as the condemned man said. Baddi was completely relaxed; he just shrugged his shoulders, hard-eyed and sharp, and walked around studying the American military aircraft. Dollí and Lína were really worked up now, shouting, pointing and giving contradictory orders. Tommi was scolded for being a mutton-head, as if it were all his fault. Dollí and Lína each had the same idea, that the other should give way, which was impossible. The solution was as simple as it was obvious: Baddi knew his way around cars like these, of course, newly arrived as he was from the country in which they were made. Grettir instantly became a nobody again, and had to squeeze out from behind the wheel. He really was put out!

It turned out that Baddi did indeed know his way around cars like these; he drove off airily with one hand on the wheel and little Bóbó on his lap. Those who didn't get seats drifted away down the slip-road from the airport, and Grettir watched, appalled, as his beautiful black hearse lurched over the pot-holes in the road.

Fortunately, the group which had been left behind at Keflavík did not have to walk the entire thirty miles back to the city; they were lucky enough to get a lift in the back of a lorry all the way back from the airport. When they finally arrived at Camp Thule, tired and chilled, the Old House was crammed with neighbours and relatives who were trampling one another underfoot to get a glimpse of the new arrival.

Baddi took it in his stride, as if all the attention were an everyday occurrence. He could not be persuaded into the parlour, where there was more room; he just sat in the kitchen. He chose a corner by the window, and from then on no one was allowed to sit there except Snjólfur once or twice, and similar guests of honour.

Some people tried to pluck up the courage to ask him for news, but for that one needed to be brave, for sometimes Baddi didn't reply; he just whistled instead, snapped his fingers or made faces at little Bóbó, who smiled from ear to ear – a rare sight. 'Cosy guy,' Baddi decided, and played 'ride-a-cock-horse' with him, in time to 'Shave and a haircut, two bits!', which two Icelandic comics, Baldur and Konni, translated in memorable fashion: 'Salt meat and beans, two kicks!' The little cosy guy gurgled with laughter. Then Uncle Baddi hoisted him high in the air, looked him sternly in the eye and asked:

'*Hey Joe!*
What do you know,
Do you come from Mexico?'

The house was agog! Hark at how the champion speaks American, the world's main foreign language! They all pressed him to say more, to say something, anything! The hero wrinkled his brow and thought for a moment, and then said: 'Wipe the windows, check the oil, dollar gas!'

How the lad had changed! He was a boy no longer, his voice was deep, cosmopolitan and manly; and not just his voice, but also his language. He didn't tell stories; he passed verdicts in a lofty oracular manner. The moss-grown mother-tongue of his ancestors was not good enough for him; he had to resort to American words and rock'n'roll lyrics. When a clamour of voices had explained to him all about Dollí's situation and the origin of little Bóbó, the hero drummed his fingers thoughtfully on the table, shook his head, and said: 'Too much monkey business.'

Everything about him had changed. The spirited lad had become so calm and sensible, like a soldier returned home from a bloody war. And the style of the guy! The slicked-back glossy hair with all its waves was just made for him, the cowboy boots, the leather jacket, the jeans and the shirt with its turned-up collar; he could have been born in them. The worldly wise, GI style suited his dark complexion and strong features perfectly. Fans of Marlon Brando and James Dean at the pictures were speechless when Baddi showed up.

Baddi also knew Elvis Presley, or so it seemed from the way he talked about this world-famous man as though he were a brother – in fact, he talked about Elvis much more than he did about his own brother; when he was asked for news of America he never said a word about Danni, it was always Elvis, whose raunchy photo was always in the papers and whose records Radio Iceland scarcely dared to play because he sang, shouted and moaned like a sex-mad, criminal lunatic.

'Elvis is the only man in the world I respect,' Baddi would often say later. He would sometimes say this of others besides Elvis, but only if they were stars of similar magnitude. It was little wonder that people shrank from asking about Gógó's little daughter who was apparently not all there, or Charlie Brown's cars or other such mundane matters.

'So what's the news of Elvis, then?' Grettir enquired at last after a long and awkward silence. The hero became downcast: things were not going well with Elvis, but what the matter was had to be dragged out of Baddi, punctuated by long dramatic pauses. Of course they wouldn't leave Elvis alone, *they* had to put him down, of course, and now they had dragged this messiah out of the concert halls and studios and sent him to an army camp in Germany. So there was nothing left for Baddi to do in the Big Country; he, too, had gone into exile in an army camp here in Camp Thule, Reykjavík, Iceland. They had left America on the same day: Elvis was to due to fly to Germany that morning, and they only just missed one another at the airport.

Then the suitcases were opened. In Reykjavík at that time Baddi could have become a millionaire if he had sold the contents of his luggage – all the clothes, the shoes, the toys for the children of the house, the pictures and the rock'n'roll records, not to mention the enormous, deafening record-player which popped out of one of the boxes. And yet the biggest thing was yet to come: a new custom-made Ford sports car which arrived in the country by ship a few days later. Swankier than the president's car, it must have cost a few bob even in the States. But that wasn't all; the freight costs to Iceland had to be paid, as well as all sorts of taxes and duty, and it added up to a huge sum. It was just as well that Tommi had been saving for the lean years; he had secretly put aside a five-*króna* note here and a ten-*króna* note there in a bank account no one knew anything about; you see, he sometimes thought that people treated money with too little respect, spending it all right away. Tommi now took out his savings and even though these were not the lean years, he was quickly made to understand that it was his duty to redeem the car for the blessed boy. In his heart of hearts, Tommi was glad to be rid of the money, for this hoard of petty cash was like poison in his bones. Tommi the grocer wanted to be generous with it – not tight-fisted like Fía and Tóti.

The car also had a record-player, an unusual sight – a gramophone with a slot for the records. The world's latest rock'n'roll hits boomed out like a gospel through the centre of town as the car cruised around with open windows. Behind the wheel sat the young dandy, fashionably dressed and with *that* haircut. Most people thought he was an American – there weren't any Icelanders who looked like that! And Baddi played up to this a little; he would go into crowded kiosks and ask for cigarettes in English and hear the young ladies whispering about him in the language of their forefathers as they stood sucking malt ale through a straw. On the way out he would turn, give the girls a meaningful look, and say in Icelandic: 'See you in the war!'

But he couldn't play the American for ever; after a couple of weeks all the young folk in the town knew who he was. Everyone wanted to be friends with him; Baddi from Thule could make the thermometer rise from well below zero to room temperature just by being there. Friends flocked around him. The car had gone only a few yards before it was packed with people; and if he made a tour of the town, the entire traffic system turned into an orderly motorcade led by Baddi, with a whole procession tailing along behind him. 'It looks like a goddam funeral,' said Höskuldur the taxi-driver. Baddi picked up this remark; he took Grettir's hearse without asking, and that evening the black 'Plymount' led the motorcade.

Among the new friends there were also some old acquaintances from the district and the football club. Stína Begga's Lúddi, the formidable goalkeeper from Kári's first team who had been taken out of circulation and sent to the country by the lofty Children's Panel, had returned from his year-long exile and was now busy earning himself a dubious reputation in the capital. 'Well, so Louie Louie's back again,' said Baddi when they met for the first time, and from then on he was always called 'Louie Louie'. Big Maggi from Camp Thule had become a rather colourful character in the town's night life, a great trawler rowdy and brawler. Maggi was not exactly good-looking; his face was swollen and coarse-featured, he had hardly any teeth, and his fiery red pug nose had once been broken in a fight and now spread over one cheek. No matter what he wore, all his clothes seemed too tight for him, even his seaman's oilskins. His breathing sounded like the wind in an old castle. Baddi named him 'Maggi Beauty'. Then Deaf Grjóni came to town after doing his six months in prison. How he had aged in recent years! Although his body was as strong as an ox, his face was thin and pale, his eyes watery and dull, his eyebrows the same colour as his skin. His shock of red hair had receded to a pale pink down on the crown of his head. But he was in a terrific mood and the shouts of delight came straight from the heart as he and Baddi met again. They must now toast their reunion, the friends felt as they sat in Lína's kitchen and wolfed down the thick meat soup you could almost stand a spoon in; a bottle of the old poison would not go amiss. Old Tommi was at home, sick, that day; it was the first time in years he had felt ill. He lay there in bed, unable to keep his food down, tormented by pains in the stomach and ashamed at being off work. There was no question of calling a doctor, of course.

The old man cheered up despite his sufferings when he saw

Grjóni. He shook the lad's hand and said he had always known that Grjóni would make it. Money? You bet, lads, hand me my trousers from the back of the chair there, Baddi; and out of the shabby old wallet in the back pocket he fished out some banknotes, which half an hour later were in the till of the state monopoly liquor shop. Tommi was left lying in bed; his sickness got worse, not better, but now and again the pain eased and then he thought of the lads out enjoying themselves over a glass or two, perhaps with a hand of cards or having a dance – they were at that age.

One thing is quite certain: the friends went nowhere near any games of cards or dancing that night. What they actually did is harder to establish, but there was something of an uproar that night, some sort of riot which was remembered long afterwards but never really talked about. It was Baddi's first drinking spree in the Old House. 'Remember the bloody racket there was that night?' people would sometimes say, but that was all.

'Or when Tommi got appendicitis?' others would say a bit later. And then there was no need to say more.

What actually happened? The noise could be heard from far away as the motorcade approached and tore through the district with headlights blazing and horns blaring. Much of the damage in the Old House could be traced back to the night the crowd came barging in. The fortune-teller thought that her little ray of sunshine was bringing some friends back for a coffee, and she called Dollí down to do some serious baking. When Baddi appeared in the kitchen doorway she began to tick him off in a friendly way – he should have told her beforehand that his friends were coming, she could have been ready with cakes and hot chocolate. But now it was not Granny's darling boy who glared from Baddi's eyes, just ice-cold savagery and fury. Dollí took the brunt of it: 'Fucking bitch!' She was frightened and confused and fled upstairs to her room in floods of tears. There was to be no baking for the old woman that night because in an instant the kitchen was full of people. Two men started fighting over a bottle although there was plenty to drink; crockery was

crunched underfoot, and the Kenwood Mixmaster from Gógó
went flying through the window. What was happening? Tommi
had a relapse upstairs; he was trying to mumble something above
the racket but of course nothing could be heard; people could
scarcely hear themselves shout, and the music, which was turned
up so loud that the windows in the nearby barracks-huts rattled
in their frames, drowned in the din.

More people arrived and the party spread to the whole district.
In the course of the evening someone set fire to the outside privy
of Hreggviður's barracks-hut; and the smell which arose when the
drum caught fire was not exactly pleasant! It was said that Louie
Louie and someone else had locked themselves in the scullery with
a girl who had been brought along to the party, and from the
scullery could be heard screaming and weeping and sobbing. Later
in the evening she was seen, bruised and half-naked, stumbling
about in the dark. She came back a little later with her father,
who was a burly man with murder in his eyes, but unfortunately
the first people he met were Baddi and Grjóni who stood there
spoiling for a fight and quick to defend themselves. It was a
mercy that the girl managed to drag her father away, battered
and bloodstained.

This was full-scale war! A resident in the basement of the
Artists' Block called the police when Maggi Beauty, all fifteen
stone of him, came crashing through the window and on to the
parlour floor. He lay there crying his eyes out, mumbling some
incoherent nonsense which the artist did not understand. Sobbing
loudly, Maggi Beauty was carted out to the Black Maria waiting
outside. This episode was never fully explained.

There was a kind of motor-rally going on through the streets,
and it must have been the police who crashed into Baddi's car from
behind to avoid a worse accident; these were probably the same
policemen who for much of the evening had been trapped in the
Old House where they lost their caps, whistles and gold uniform
buttons. But no one knows for certain when the police went into
action; perhaps they turned up with the fire brigade which arrived
because of the fire in Hreggviður's privy.

Somehow the rumour arose that there was a mortally ill man

lying in the midst of all the chaos; perhaps it was Lína who reported it, but more probably it was Dollí, because Lína for the first time in living memory was completely at a loss for words as the two women trudged aimlessly about the district in their slippers with the children. After midnight an ambulance arrived. The party was at its height. The ambulance men hurried into the Old House but got no further than the hallway, where they ran into problems; at any rate it was Deaf Grjóni and Louie Louie who re-emerged in uniform caps with the stretcher, on which Baddi himself sat upright, blowing kisses in all directions. Hot on their heels came the ambulance men, seething with fury; they called for help from the policemen, who had enough trouble on their hands already. Soon afterwards, powerful reinforcements arrived in two cars, and a real effort was now made to put a stop to this game. The three with the stretcher were arrested, Baddi and Grjóni were thrown into the car, but Louie Louie went on the counter-attack against the mass of police, and during the ensuing mayhem the other two managed to escape into the darkness. The stretcher was taken back into the house, this time for Tommi, who turned out to have acute appendicitis and had to be operated on immediately. After that the noise began to die down and by three or four in the morning Dollí and Lína dared to go back into the Old House, into the battlefield.

It really got on Dollí's nerves that so little was made of all the commotion, of which she had been the main victim: the boy had threatened her with every evil, he had assaulted her and even her children. But Lína had forgotten all about it as soon as most of the mess was cleared up next day. 'He called me such horrible names,' Dollí whimpered in the kitchen. 'He said he was going to kill me,' she went on, when Lína seemed not to hear. 'What have I ever done to him?' she shrieked at last, but Lína put a finger to her mouth, for her darling boy lay snoring on the sofa. Dollí seethed. As if to show agreement with her over something, at least, Lína said that Baddi would have to learn to choose some proper friends, but that was as far as she would go. Dollí then ran around the district looking for someone who could confirm how her brother had persecuted her, but when the neighbours realised that Lína wasn't bothering about it, no more was said. People just got irritable and silent when it was mentioned. Dollí was left with palpitations, in tears of rage; but the culprit himself was right there and when he woke up in the evening, hoarse and hung-over, he certainly got to hear the story of the night's events.

'And what was it all about?'

Baddi merely rubbed his eyes wearily and held out his cup, which Lína filled with coffee without a word.

'So what was it all about, Bjarni Heinrich Kreutzhage, tell me that?' Dollí repeated.

Baddi looked her up and down, in his worldly way. 'Is something the matter with you?' he asked. In the midst of the haranguing he rose to his feet and strolled out to the yard. All the same, he seemed to have a twinge of conscience; he came straight back in, pained and angered at all those goddam sons of bitches who had been at the house. 'And poor Tommi there, mortally ill, wow! I must go and visit him at . . . Mount Sinai Hospital or wherever. My God, someone's dented my car, too!'

Feeling sore and angry he sat down in the parlour, then lay down on the sofa and listened to soulful ballads by his friend Elvis on the gramophone. Lína had been taught how to turn over the records for him; she sent some children from the district to the kiosk to buy a pack of Camels and a bottle of Sinalco, and then at last the lad began to feel better.

In the evening, to everyone's surprise, the hearse drove into the yard and Grettir emerged, silent and downcast. Dollí cheered up a lot. Grettir clearly had a lot on his mind, though it was hard to get a word out of him.

'I've given up working for the Americans,' he said at last. 'It's no good, that job! The Americans aren't so bad, it's the bloody Icelanders who are so stuck up – it seems that being an Icelander isn't good enough for them. They've always got to be talking American!'

Next day, Grettir got a job in a sports shop which imported rifles and shotguns. Baddi got hold of Grjóni, and together they went and visited Tommi at the hospital.

Tommi had little to say to begin with. He remembered the lads' wild behaviour during his suffering in the Old House – had he really deserved that of them? But the lads were so friendly and chummy during the visit that he forgave them for the time being; he even began to think it had all been just a bad dream. Baddi did everything he could for him – he fetched a glass of water, he lent the old man a handkerchief: 'Just keep it, Dad!' The two friends shook out the grocer's duvet, in spite of his vigorous protests, and it was as he had feared – they couldn't do it properly: the down feathers bunched into a clump and the cover ripped. But Tommi decided to look on the bright side and was pleased with this short visit; it was only some time later that it occurred to him that Baddi had perhaps only come in order to ask him for money to have his car repaired.

America may well have lost some of its zest after the friends Baddi and Elvis went into exile; most of the glamour went from that continent. A month later a huge young man came striding in out of the winter twilight with Tommi's big sea-chest on his back. Without a word he opened the front door of the Old House; the floorboards protested under his weight as he walked slowly towards the kitchen. At the kitchen table, the heart of the house, Lína sat telling the fortune of a respectable young lady. They both looked up and stared curiously at the giant who appeared in the doorway. He was wearing laced leather boots, a light-coloured army shirt, and jeans held up by a pair of black braces. His hair was combed back over his ears, but one lock fell in a curl over his forehead, shading his dark eyes.

'Hello, Granny.'

'Is that you, child? Good Lord, how you've grown!'

'Yes.'

'This is Daniel, my grandson,' Lína explained to the young lady. 'He must have got bored in America.'

Danni blushed. He stepped back and straightened up, so that his forehead and eyes disappeared behind the upper door frame. Then he turned and walked up the stairs with his trunk, his steps making the stairs creak as though they were about to break.

In the Old House people didn't talk in low voices. Mumbling and muttering were considered bad manners; the tradition was for people not to moderate their voices: they either talked to everyone or to no one. But after Danni arrived home from America, he and Tommi sat every evening talking together in lowered voices in a corner far from the others. My God, it was irritating! Lína and Dollí, least of all, could understand what this conspiratorial whispering was about. What secrets and underhand dealings were afoot? Were they perhaps talking about people behind their backs? Lína began to listen on one occasion, and heard that Tommi was telling boastful stories about his affairs with women.

'. . . to see the world and have a few adventures. I went to Norway and took a berth on a trawler. Fine chaps, the Norwegians; but then the First World War came and the British commandeered the boat; they paid for it, of course, the Charlies are gentlemen, after all, they needed boats for troop transport and suchlike while they were fighting the Austrian Kaiser and . . . yes, that's how it was. So there I was, stuck in that Brit business for more than three years! Of course, one got around a helluva lot, you know, all the way to the Arab countries . . . they're a lot of shitheads those Arabs, ugh! You'd better watch out for them, Danni, if you ever end up . . . among them. Yep. Why? Because they're thieving devils, you can never trust them; always pulling their daggers, ready to kill a man like nobody's business. I landed among them . . . No, they didn't kill me, luckily, but they tried to saddle me with some stolen goods, but I just told them, "Go to hell with your rubbish! I don't want to buy anything! Go away!" Yes! In Norwegian! There were several of us, the Norwegians and I, brisk fellows, all of us ready to beat up those guys if they wanted a taste of our fists. We'd had a nip or two . . . eh? Oh yes, we lads sometimes had a drink if we wanted to have a good time, no shouting or nonsense like . . . Well, anyway, they were circling round us, but didn't dare do anything because there were so many of us. Then I got separated from the other lads, I met this very attractive dancing girl who was dead keen on me' (Tommi lowered his voice, leant forward and glanced over at the kitchen), 'and she insisted on introducing me to her parents, although we didn't . . . Well, anyway, when I got back to the ship again, those Arab dogs were waiting for me. I could see their knives gleaming under those bedsheets they wear.

'But I was young in those days and pretty well built, so I laid them flat with a good Icelandic back-heel! Yes! heh heh! And they just lay there gasping and groaning on the quay in those . . . er . . . er . . . bedclothes of theirs. But I hopped on board and said "Farewell France! *Bisquit*! Heh heh heh!"'

'What do you think you're up to, Tómas, filling the lad's head with such lies and nonsense? He's up in the clouds enough as it is. He'd do better to think a bit more about his family!' said Lína, suddenly looming over them so that they fell quiet and looked down and then got up, looking a bit piqued.

Grettir sometimes sat with them during their men's talk, and for the most part they just let him sit there while they carried on their conversation; but if Grettir said anything, it always seemed out of place and the thread was broken, and silence descended on the corner where they sat.

When Grettir had been with them, Dollí would question him when they went to bed.

'What were they going on about?'

'They were just chatting. Talking.'

'What about?'

'Dunno. Flying lessons, mostly.'

'Flying lessons?'

'Yes. Learning to fly.'

'Who's going to learn to fly? Danni could fly with his ears, I suppose!'

'Dunno. Didn't ask them.'

Sometimes Baddi sat with them, too, if he were at home. He would then take the lead in the conversation; he didn't talk in an undertone like them, and soon Elvis and Jerry Lee would be on the record-player. Tommi would not stay long after that, as he liked only accordion music, nothing else. The brothers stayed on, usually lying on the sofas with their hands clasped behind their necks, listening in reverent silence to the heavy beat of the music; at such moments the brothers seemed to get along well, even though they didn't talk. Indeed, they almost never talked together and had little to do with one another except at weekends, when Baddi would hold boisterous drinking parties at the house which usually ended with Tommi trying to put a stop to it and Danni helping him. After everyone else had gone, the brothers would fight like cat and dog.

An old man telephoned the Old House and asked for Sigurjón Traustason. This was Grjóni's grandfather and namesake who had been in an old folk's home for many years, ever since his daughter Thórgunnur had moved away with Grjóni and the others to Camp Thule.

Poor old Sigurjón. Thórgunnur was his only daughter, and the break had not been painless, anything but; but people had their pride, and this printer who could remember the old days and had taken part in the struggle for Iceland's independence and workers' rights could not begin to kiss the rod in his old age by moving into an American military barracks: it was shameful enough that his daughter should have sunk so low, and after it happened he tried to blot out all memory of her. But it wasn't easy; father and daughter had lived together after he had become a widower and she a widow. They had been very close; but she was her own worst enemy, not to mention the blessed children who, old Sigurjón knew, would never recover from growing up in such a place. His prediction came true more tragically than he had allowed himself to fear, when little Diddi took his own life. And when the newspapers wrote avidly about Grjóni and the events in Siglufjörður, the old man began to have second thoughts. It occurred to him that he had let his grandchildren down, and when his grandson was cleared of the murder charge, Sigurjón decided to swallow his pride and get in touch with him as soon as possible. He finally managed to do this through the police, and Deaf Grjóni decided to invite the old man for a drive: he understood from Karolína that this was the best way of pleasing old folk. Baddi offered the use of the car, with himself as chauffeur.

The two of them drove around the city a few times, and Grjóni was sunk in thought. Baddi knew that men sometimes need to be alone with their thoughts, and said nothing. He was at the wheel in short sleeves although the weather was cold, and had his left elbow out of the window. A cigarette hung from the corner of his mouth, and when biting gusts of wind came in, glowing ash blew over the dashboard. The speedometer wore sunglasses.

'I think the old guy has money,' Grjóni said at last. 'Otherwise I wouldn't be bothering to visit him.'

'He's *your* granddad.'

'What would you do?'

'I would visit my granddad in this, er, funny farm, if he had money.'

Grjóni was pensive again. 'Your granddad?' he then asked.

'Yes, don't you think I have a granddad? The birds and the bees, Grjóni boy.'

'Who is your granddad?'

'Who's my granddad? He's, er . . . the Devil's daddy.'

'Okay, let's go!' said Grjóni. He gave the directions, and a few minutes later Baddi's noisy car turned into the courtyard in front of the old folk's home. Grjóni sat for a moment, plucking up the courage to go in. They gazed at the gloomy building and met the guilty looks of the old people at the windows.

'Heartbreak Hotel,' was Baddi's verdict.

Old Sigurjón received them in his room. He tried to be dignified, although he was unsteady on his feet; he had blacked his galoshes in the places where the canvas backing showed through the rubber. It wasn't that he couldn't afford to buy new galoshes – he had just drawn his old-age pension; he was just one of those men who are loyal to their old belongings – especially galoshes. He had a pocket watch on a gilt chain, and he looked at it now with a trace of annoyance when the two lads appeared in the doorway – like a schoolmaster when pupils arrive late for lessons.

Granddad had been waiting in some excitement for several days; he saw himself embracing Sigurjón, his eldest grandchild and namesake. But the barriers went up around him when those casual young men sauntered in with their jackets slung from their

index fingers over one shoulder. Baddi rolled his chewing-gum so
that his cigarette jiggled at the corner of his mouth. Grjóni went in
hesitantly, rubbing his right hand on his trousers like a mechanic
wiping the grease off before writing a receipt. He reached out and
shook his grandfather by the hand. 'Hi.'

They stood there for a moment, a little embarrassed. Then
Grjóni let his hand go and pointed to Baddi. 'My pal.'

Granddad looked at Baddi suspiciously. 'Are you a friend of
Sigurjón's?'

'Aye-aye, sir,' Baddi replied. He was courteous and deferential,
like an ordinary seaman towards the captain in a war film.

'Smoking's not allowed in this part of the building,' said
Granddad, and with a lightning flick of the hand and a click of
the heels Baddi threw the reeking cigarette into the washstand in
the corner of the room.

The old man winced. 'The same goes for cud-gum.'

'What?'

'He means chewing-gum,' explained Grjóni, who had been to
sea with men from up country.

Baddi took a crumpled packet of gum from his trouser pocket
and offered old Granddad a piece of Wrigley's. 'I usually keep it
for the ladies,' he said, giving the old man a dig in the ribs which
doubled him up.

In the car the old fellow was seething with rage, nearly beside
himself. He told Baddi for God's sake to turn off the caterwauling
of the American radio station. Baddi did so, and put a record on
the record-player instead. Grjóni asked Granddad if he liked the
car, but the old man didn't answer; he just thought that it smelled
and he could hardly breathe. And Baddi was driving much too
fast, like a road-hog, the old man said, and Baddi responded
by accelerating and taking the next corner on two wheels. He
crooned tunelessly along with the music from the record-player,
and pretended not to notice when Granddad was thrown about
in the back seat. Grjóni sat in front and wrinkled his colourless
eyebrows when the old man gripped his shoulder and said he
wanted to get out. Baddi stopped the car and looked questioningly
at his friend. Grjóni was quiet for a moment, then glanced

into the back of the car and said: 'We'll drop him off back at the home.'

If anyone knew when not to hesitate or delay but to carry out an order quickly and decisively, it was Baddi. He made a U-turn and drove the most direct route back. When the old man realised what was happening, his eyes grew large and sad; the schoolmasterly expression was wiped away like chalk from a blackboard. Grjóni avoided his gaze and tried to look stern, staring out of the windscreen. When they arrived, Baddi leaned back without a word and opened the rear door the moment the car stopped. Granddad, stooping, got out into the slush, which dissolved the shoe polish on the canvas of his galoshes, leaving a trail of black in his footprints. Then he turned round and looked at the car as it disappeared with its large red rear lights and a snarl as the wheels churned up the gravel.

It isn't easy to be angry with old people, especially if they want to make peace over something and walk stooping and lonely up the steps of an old folk's home. Sigurjón the elder rang the Old House and got Baddi to give Deaf Grjóni a message that he would like to have another visit from him. This time Grjóni went there alone. The friends agreed to do without the car on this occasion. They had a bottle which Grjóni had already sampled, and Baddi was to wait with the remainder down at the Coffee Waggon.

When grandfather and grandson arrived there in a trice by taxi, there was scarcely time to exchange greetings. The old man now wanted to do all he could to be friends with the young lads, and made no protest when they poured from the bottle into his cup of coffee at the same time as into their own. The bottle was soon empty and all three had begun to feel rosy, the young men loud-voiced and in good form, while Granddad was beginning to go on about times so distant that no one wanted to hear about them. So they had to buy more booze and Sigurjón the elder had some money and paid the taxi-fare down to the State Monopoly shop and went inside himself to make the purchases. He had to stand in a queue and listen to comments about what old folk in galoshes wanted with three whole bottles of the hard stuff,

then a scolding in the taxi where his friends had been waiting
far too long. To make up for it, Granddad had to be sociable
and drink with them in the taxi, where the driver turned up the
radio so as not to hear the flood of confessions the old man kept
pouring out, and said it was okay for them to drink as long as
they didn't make a mess and paid up with no nonsense.

The old man showed him the money he had in his pocket, the
latest instalment of his pension. He began to count it with trembling
hands, scrutinising the money with short-sighted, doubtful eyes as
if he expected the banknotes to be forged. He dropped the bundle
of notes on the floor as the taxi accelerated from a green light, and
at that the youngsters laughed in the back seat in a grown-up sort of
way. Otherwise they paid little attention to the old man, who sat in
the front with his own bottle between his knees.

'Just drive anywhere,' the boys told the driver; they were away
in a world of their own. Grjóni asked Baddi about America – the
big houses, the rich men, the gangsters and the Indians: Baddi
knew it all.

'The Indians? Real crazy. They just cut a hole in a carpet, stick their heads through it and go around like that,
they're never cold. Then they dance in circles, all very impressive. Oohoohoohoohoohoo! And all sorts of monkey business.
Actually, I think that Granny is an Indian, man, she dances just
like that, oohoohoohoo, when she's crazy and on the warpath.'

Baddi told story after story, and Grjóni had to put his oar in
too: there was a thing or two to see in Siglufjörður, as well –
endless drinking and madness, endless fighting, man, they're all
off their heads! Little twerps in specs, all thinking themselves
boxing champions the moment they come to Siglufjörður, and
the screwing in the sheds every night, all the girls crazy – even the
country girls, too, you know, really stupid! They all became part
of it after only two or three days in town.

In the midst of their discussions there was no chance that the
friends would take much notice of the old man in the front seat,
and a lot more would happen before they came to their senses.
Old Sigurjón disregarded the taxi-driver's warnings and made an
awful mess – he vomited all over the dashboard. The driver didn't

waste any time; he stopped the car, leaned over to the door on the right-hand side and sent Sigurjón senior rolling out into the dark-brown slush at the side of the road. The young men didn't notice he was gone until the car started moving again, and then they just thought it was funny – until they realised that the old man had all the money, and the driver twigged he wouldn't get paid anything for the trip unless the old man were retrieved. This was done, but the driver had had enough of the goings-on in his car and wanted rid of all three, and since the lads were now ravenously hungry they decided not to make a fuss but just to go to a hotel like toffs and order the dish of the day.

The old man was covered in mud and the doorman at the hotel refused to let him in. The lads stood with the old man and protested: 'Wha-a-a-t's this, man?' But it had turned cold and the boys didn't feel like hanging around on the pavement any longer, so they went inside after Grjóni had grabbed a wad of notes from the old man.

They acted like lords in the restaurant, smoking cigars and lounging in their chairs as they waited for the food. After a long delay, a fine roast was brought to the table, and the plate was cleared in a flash with much smacking of lips. Grjóni crunched the bones with his teeth and washed his meal down with *brennivín*. They took their time about the meal, and two well-fed young men emerged almost two hours later.

They had forgotten all about the old man, of course, but he had not forgotten them. He had been waiting outside on the pavement all this time and was beginning to look like a snowman in the sleet as they came out. He was becoming a nuisance, the bloody old man – they were all broke now, and it was no longer any fun having him trailing at their heels. The friends set off into the sleet and the old man followed them. They turned and told him to clear off back to the old folk's home, but he begged them to wait; he was tearful and confused, and whined that he didn't want to go back to the old folk's home. 'Wait for me, Sigurjón!' But they couldn't be bothered waiting, and walked quickly through the darkness to Camp Thule; and although the old man was weak in the legs and stumbling, he managed to keep up with them remarkably well. When they arrived at the outskirts of the district he was still in tow. They could make out this rolling shape in the foggy darkness and could hear his muted half-frozen shouts. Perhaps the galoshes made the difference; the young men found it hard to keep their footing on their smooth-soled patent shoes. Grjóni stopped and looked at the shape approaching them. Baddi was impatient and wanted to get back to the Old House, but Grjóni seemed to have other ideas, and waited until his grandfather had almost drawn level with them. Then Grjóni calmly led the way into the camp, and Granddad followed at their heels, babbling incoherently. Grjóni had a hard, determined look, and the friends walked past the door of the Old House which awaited them, warm, lit up and vibrant. They went right past the Old House, over the charred remains of Hreggviður's outside privy and on to Grjóni's former home, Thórgunnur's barracks-hut, which stood there, dark and cold and about as enticing as a derelict salt-fish shed. Grjóni shoved the door open and slammed it in the face of old Sigurjón, who was trudging along behind them.

'Let him knock!' hissed Grjóni. He was sitting on the bunk while Baddi stood shuffling his feet on the unsteady floor and rubbing his hands, which were blue with cold. Outside it was dark and snowing heavily, and through the gusts of wind the old man's feeble knocking at the door could be heard. Thórgunnur was not at home. The two of them sat there in the barracks-hut, and although Baddi wanted to get home to his grandmother's warm kitchen he didn't say anything; he just shrugged his shoulders, lit a cigarette and sat down on a chair beside the stove. Sometimes men have to be alone with their thoughts; so it was with Grjóni now. He stretched out on the bunk, put both hands over his face, pulled at what was left of his tuft of hair and uttered a peal of loud but not very convincing laughter whenever there was knocking at the door. He got up and paced the floor, cursing, muttering and half-laughing. Baddi sat in his chair pretending nothing was amiss, smoking one cigarette after another and glancing at Grjóni.

Grjóni now stood by the door as if he were contemplating opening it. The knocking from outside was becoming feebler and more irregular.

Then Grjóni clutched his head in both hands and screamed at the door: 'Go and shit your trousers out there! What do you want here, eh? Eh? Haven't you got a tongue in your head? Why can't you answer? Are you scared? Just go!! You're not my grandfather! I only have one grandfather, and that's Tommi over in the Old House! You're crazy! Why are you here now? Mum hoped you would come for Diddi's funeral! And I hoped so too, for otherwise she would cry all the time. And did you come? NO! And so you can just shit your trousers out there! Fool, idiot!'

The knocking from outside had stopped, but as if to make up for it, Grjóni began to bang on the door from the inside. He banged so hard that the barracks-hut quivered and shook at every blow. His voice seemed about to break, and the door would doubtless have been shattered if a key had not been put in the keyhole from the outside; the door opened and in came daughter and father, Thórgunnur and old Sigurjón, sobbing loudly as they supported one another. Their weeping filled the barracks-hut, and Grjóni was taken aback at the sight. He stood there open-mouthed, dishevelled and motionless by the open door, as the snowflakes blew into the barracks-hut over Granddad and Thórgunnur, sitting there in the middle of the floor . . .

9

Summertime blues

*The doctor told me: Man, you don't need no pills, just a
handful of nickels and a jukebox to cure your ills.*
(Carl Perkins)

When the sun shone in the district it blazed brilliantly, baking
the curved roofs of the barracks which some people said looked
like serpents or punctured tyres. From the sun's point of view
they looked like pieces of dirty yellow plaster on the ground.
On the stones. On the porous gravel.

But in the Old House, in among the pieces of plaster, life
blossomed on sunny days like this. The creaking door was pushed
open early in the morning. The first to come out was Tommi
in his deerstalker. It was so early that the sun was still hiding
behind the peak of the mountain, and a shred of mist wisped
between the old man's boots as he set off, wheezing like a
steam-engine in the clouds of smoke vented by his morning cough.

Tommi had already been weighing, sorting and pricing goods
for hours when the door of the old House was once more
pushed open on its squeaking hinges. First a long sunburned
arm appeared through the opening with a small light-blue
folding chair half hidden in its fist. The chair was set up against
the wall, then the rest of Danni appeared, with an enormous
sandwich in one hand, a glass of milk in the other, a rug under
his arm and a book between his teeth. He pitched camp on the
small piece of lawn which had decided to grow in the corner
where the scullery joined the east gable. The family called it the
Patch. Danni sat in the sun with a blissful expression. First he
enjoyed his snack, then he flicked through the book in between

doing some relaxing yoga exercises – breathing and meditation – while the sunbeams created bright, strange rainbows behind his eyelids. He was at peace.

The next to rise was Grettir. He slipped out, short-legged and whistling in his suit on his way to work, and went over to the big black hearse which never wanted to start but then got going, coughing and spluttering, just as Danni put his book down and rose with a sigh to give it a push. The car was enveloped in a cloud of exhaust fumes as Grettir revved the engine to warm it up; there was the sound of movement as the car set off; when the fog lifted, the children of the barracks appeared, dirty, ragged and waif-like.

The greasy kitchen windows of the Old House gleamed like a pool of oil in the sunshine; behind them Lína and Dollí were having their morning cup of coffee. Dollí, in her dressing-gown and with curlers in her hair, was smoking a cigarette in a holder, pale and listless, while Lína was buttering rye bread with her thumb and pouring out cold milk for Dollí's children, who drooped, tired and sleepy, over the stained wax cloth on the kitchen table. When Gillí finished his glass and asked for more, Lína said it was bad to drink too much ice-cold milk – a man she knew had downed so many glasses of ice-cold milk one morning that he had simply gone rigid and fallen down dead.

Dollí lifted the tattered curtain from the window and frowned as she looked out. It was just as she had feared – the suntanned muscle-mountain lay immobile on the Patch, turning his face towards the sun as though all the world's problems which lay on her shoulders were none of his concern.

'Look at that!' she said to Lína, pointing out of the window. 'There's that swine enjoying himself! He'll soon be eighteen and doesn't do a stroke of work! I'm fed up slaving for that conceited arsehole.'

Dollí's voice was tearful, and with a shaking hand she stubbed out her cigarette in the ashtray while the twins hurried to put on their rubber boots, for they knew it was fun being with Danni when he was sunbathing on the Patch; he would usually tell sunbathing-stories, fairy-tales he made up. They took place in the jungles of Africa, or among pirates in the Pacific Ocean or in big cities abroad. The children themselves were the main characters, fighting against natural disasters, criminals and wild animals, abseiling into steep chasms and climbing high cliffs, flying in hot-air balloons and driving speedboats. The fat, the ungainly and the misfits who would otherwise never have had a chance were always the heroes of the sunbathing-stories; they always saved the situation with cunning and skill while the big shots in the group, the strong boys and the pretty girls, the leaders of the pack, usually suffered defeat in Danni's stories: they wet their pants with fear, or were unable to flee fast enough because Granny had to accompany them, and so on.

Then Tommi came home at lunch time and he and Danni went into the kitchen to eat the boiled cod and curds which Lína served up. They all ate like horses, except for Dollí, who stood at the kitchen window, inhaling smoke and sipping steaming coffee from a cracked cup, not saying a word although quite a few words hovered on the tip of her tongue which she would like to say to Danni. But she kept silent because Tommi was at home; for some reason he always took that crazy boy's side.

As the meal was ending, Grettir came clattering into the yard and rushed in to swallow a bite of food. He was in a hurry as always and set off again at once after giving Dollí a peck on the cheek. Dollí stayed behind and wondered why he was always in such a hurry. Was it really because there was so much polishing of rifles to be done down at that sports shop in the town centre? Or was he whoring around?

The sun had moved, and Danni moved his position; he lay down under the parlour windows on the south side of the house and enjoyed the warm sunshine. He was sheltered from the northerly breeze there; he had nothing on except a pair of shorts, and stayed there motionless all afternoon except when he waved the book to fan his face.

'You're just a piece of shit!' yelled Dollí, who had brought some washing out to the line. She hung around putting up the pegs and shouting abuse at Danni at regular intervals. He was resolved not to let her tantrums trouble his thoughts, and he didn't say anything, pretending not to hear her.

Even so, after one of the outbursts he was heard muttering softly: 'Yakkety yakkety yakkety yak . . .'

She flung the pegs down and stormed into the kitchen to Lína. 'I can't stand it, I can't sta-a-nd it, something has to be done about that boy!'

Lína was now frying a steak for Baddi, who had just woken up. He was in the toilet clearing his throat, then he came out and ate his meal quietly, with a glass of milk. Lína warned him, too, against drinking too much milk – that fellow Snæbjorn she once knew had drunk too much ice-cold milk one morning . . .

Baddi made no reply, although he looked as if he had slept well and was in a good mood. He merely poured another glass of milk, stood up in front of the women and gulped it down so that his throat gurgled, then handed the glass to the old woman with a smile, bowed, and went out.

'You ought to listen to my advice, Baddi dear,' she yelled after him. He farted with a flourish, opened the front door and looked up at the sky, then went into the telephone room to clean his patent shoes with the pointed toes.

On these few sunny days of the year not many people came to have their fortunes told; but in the afternoon two girls from the fish factory arrived and Lína spread the cards for them with a brooding air. It was quiet in the house and they sat undisturbed at the kitchen table. Baddi could be heard humming Elvis songs as always when he brushed his shoes. The parlour window was thrown open on one occasion and Dollí bawled: 'Why don't you put matchsticks between your toes so you get a tan there as well?'

The girls from the fish factory giggled; a little later they walked down to the bus station in a good mood and bought tickets to Thingvellir: Lína had predicted that they would be going on a journey.

It was six o'clock that Friday afternoon when Danni finally left off sunbathing: Lína had joined Dollí in a noisy chorus of complaint. Danni jumped to his feet with a start and rushed off

to his room, slamming the door with all the world's disappoint-
ments and suffering on his broad shoulders.

Baddi didn't speak to anyone; he just carried on brushing his
shoes, crooning in his throaty Elvis voice:

> '. . . who cares for fa-a-a-me
> and fortune . . .'

Lína, who was still in the kitchen and had begun to prepare
supper, admired her sunshine boy and his diligence with the
shoe brush; now and again she glanced into the telephone room
and knew that some day this lad would grow into a real man.
What's more, he sang so nicely, he really ought to be a priest:

> 'Fame and fortune!
> (Doo-wappa-doo!)
> how empty they can be
> but when I hold you in my arms
> That's heaven to me!'

Then he carried on with the shoes. Brushing. Polishing. The
toecaps shone like the mirrors of Versailles.

Then the shops closed and Tommi suddenly appeared in his
galoshes like a silhouette against the sun-haze outside; his face
was gloomy, but he was puffing contentedly on a Roy cigarette.
By then Danni had already stormed out of the house in a huff.
Lína shouted that supper was ready, and the sea-breeze began
to drift up from the shore with its mist mingled with ghosts and
the restless souls of Lína's ancestors whom she dreamt about at
night, playing a game of poker. The sun blessed the quiet as it
glowed red in the western sky.

As they sat at table in the Old House, a wine-red chrome-plated
Chevrolet Bel Air sedan with tail-fins drove through the centre of
town, zoomed up Hverfisgata like thunder, with sparks shooting
out of its exhaust. If a pretty young girl on the pavement wiggled
her hips, the car horn blared: 'Shave and a haircut, two bits!'

At the same time several brilliantined heads poked out of

the windows. On the back window-ledge there was a green sheepskin. The steering-wheel had a leather cover. Under the dashboard there was an air freshener with a picture of a blonde who put her pink bathing costume on and off as she winked. A pair of small football boots dangled from the mirror. The car had a record-player, and from it reverberated the sound of a guitar playing 'Summertime Blues'. Then the car accelerated and four leather-clad elbows stuck out of the side windows and the car leapt off in the direction of the barracks district.

Inside the Old House the car wasn't heard until it went speeding past the barracks-huts. It made a half-turn around the house and the gravel thrown up by its tyres sprayed in the direction of the Artists' Block and the nearest barracks-huts. The doors opened upwards like wings and the passengers spilled out: Deaf Grjóni, Louie Louie and Maggi Beauty. With them was a very slim young fellow who did not quite seem to fit in with the group. Deaf Grjóni leapt up the steps to the front door and knocked so hard that the house shook. Baddi appeared in the doorway at once and he and Grjóni greeted each other by striking their hands together.

'Who's this Bony Morony?'

'Hey Baddi, he's a dead cool guy,' Grjóni replied, adding softly: 'He's loaded.'

'Okay, Okay.'

Lína had also come out to the doorway as she always did when the lads were having a get-together with Baddi; she stood in the hallway sizing them up like a bouncer at a bar. 'Welcome, Sigurjón dear,' she said with a cackle. 'Come in, come in, you are always welcome in my house!'

'Thank you, Lína dear,' Grjóni replied in a husky, polite voice. 'We understand one another!' With a bow he went inside, slipping a tin of snuff into the old woman's hand.

'Yes, you're a proper man, Sigurjón, I've always said that!'

Lína folded her arms across her chest and turned down the corners of her mouth as Maggi Beauty came up the steps. He looked a bit embarrassed. He was combing his hair and looking down at his feet, which were cautiously feeling their way up the steps.

'I don't want to see that man inside my house!' said Lína.

'Hey! Granny . . .'

'He caused nothing but trouble the last time he was here.'

Maggi was still combing his hair, standing on the steps with an anxious expression. He looked across at Baddi; Baddi put his arm round Maggi's shoulders. 'Hey, Granny, dear . . .'

'I simply don't understand, Baddi, why you have such dreadful friends. As far as I know, that fellow walloped you the last time he was here.'

'We were just fooling around, Granny.'

'A damned funny kind of fooling around, if you ask me. He knocked one of your teeth out and was so rough with you . . .'

Baddi tried to stop the old woman, who had begun to wave her arms about and was approaching the stage in her fury when the Indian war dance would begin.

'Hey, Maggi, have you got any money? Give her a twenty-five-*króna* note,' Baddi whispered. Maggi fished a crumpled, squashed note out of his back pocket and gave it to Lína.

She said nothing when she saw the note, looked doubtfully at Maggi, then smiled warmly and said: 'Yes, perhaps there is some good in you after all, my lad, it's nice of you to think of us old folk and give an old woman twenty-five *krónur!*'

So Maggi got in, but Lína said in a loud voice: 'I must ask you not to do any fighting, boys, you'll only hurt yourselves!'

Louie Louie was admitted without objection. At last it was the thin fellow's turn. He walked right up to the old woman, formally offered his hand, and looked her straight in the eye with the expression and bearing of a man who knew his manners.

'Good day, my name is Jakob Tryggvason.'

Lína was almost speechless. 'Oh really, sir?'

'You must be the lady of the house.'

'Ehhh? Yes, I am!'

'Pleased to meet you, ma'am.'

Baddi stood in front of the mirror, snapped his fingers and pointed: he was a weird guy, this Jakob Bony Morony! When Bony came into the hallway Baddi pushed him ahead of him and said: 'Walk right in!'

'Don't crowd me, man,' Bony replied, and Baddi was taken aback at how tough this strange young guy talked. Louie Louie and Maggi Beauty each had a bottle of *brennivín* in their belts, and Bony Morony conjured a litre bottle of Bols gin out of his waistcoat. Baddi's mood improved as soon as he sat beside Grjóni on the sofa. He got up and put a record on. 'Whole Lotta Shakin' Goin' On' reverberated through the house as deafeningly as the mono loudspeaker could manage. Then he shouted through into the kitchen and ordered his grandmother to bring some Sinalco and some glasses.

She appeared in the doorway and said: 'Yes, but Baddi, dear, we haven't any Sinalco!'

'What, we haven't any? . . . Damn it, didn't I tell you I wanted some Sinalco?'

'I didn't hear it – perhaps it was your sister Dollí you told.'

'That damn cow Dollí, I'll kill her . . . okay, bring some water then. Can't you tell Dad to go and buy some Sinalco?'

'I'll send someone!' Lína had to shout in order to be heard above the din from the record-player.

Through in the kitchen Lína wanted to send Gillí, Dollí's daughter, for twenty bottles of soft drinks, but Tommi would not hear of it – he would rather go himself than make a small child have to slog back with all that. He put down his fork and went out to the shop to fetch soft drinks for the party guests. As he set off, stiff and tired, he wondered why he was doing it, but could not come to any conclusion.

When he got back there was tumult in the parlour. Baddi had started yelling rock'n'roll slogans at the furniture, and Dollí had fled up to her room with the children; when Baddi was in this kind of mood he always had some home truths to tell her. Bony had started dancing in the parlour and Grjóni and Louie followed suit, grinning and looking at one another – they weren't used to dancing in this sort of company. Old Tommi did not want to stay in the doorway, although the lads tried to get him to talk about the football training he had organised in the old days. 'Hey, Tommi, old guy! Do you remember "Long live Kári's heroes in adversity, victory and every kind of

endeavour!"? Just get the ball, man! And the trumpet! Hahaha!
Don't you remember the trumpet, Tommi?'

Oh yes, Tommi remembered it: 'I remember the trumpet,
Ludwig dear,' he said, and smiled sadly and went, reflecting
on how silly it sounded. He had no time for these lads when
they were as drunk as this; he really ought to throw them out
– they'd never thought of him and his trumpet when he'd had
appendicitis that time.

In the kitchen Lína was talking about the new fellow: he might
not be much to look at, he was so weedy and thin about the
cheeks, 'But he's also very polite and proper, even called me
ma'm! He's obviously a gentleman. Baddi ought to get some
more friends like him, instead of crazy criminals like Maggi!'

'I don't think he's any better or worse than the rest,' Tommi
murmured.

'What?'

'The new lad – as far as I know he's been turning the whole
parlour upside down with some kind of cannibal dance.'

'I don't think there's anything wrong with them dancing. I
seem to remember that you were the best dancer in town when
you were young.'

Tommi smiled into his coffee cup and said nothing.

Maggi and Louie had begun to pocket everything in the parlour they considered to be of value: small glass candle-holders,
a miniature replica of the Statue of Liberty, an Eiffel Tower
thermometer and the Little Mermaid all vanished into their
pockets.

Grjóni told them to stop it and to put the things back double-
bloody-quick, but they paid no heed until Grjóni knocked Maggi
to the floor. During the brawl something fell over and the
sound of it breaking could be heard in the kitchen, where Lína
jumped to her feet and Tommi buried his nose even deeper in
his coffee cup.

Baddi came out: 'Hey, Dad, haven't you any money-honey
for me?'

'I haven't got much left now, Baddi dear, these have been . . .'

'Dad, give me a hundred-*króna* note!'

'. . . these have been hard times,' Tommi said, pulling the worn wallet out of his back pocket. 'A hundred *krónur*, can't you manage with a little less . . . ?'

'Oh, go on, give the boy a hundred,' shrilled Lína, 'or two hundred . . .'

Baddi waited at the ready with outstretched hand and had begun to snap his fingers impatiently. Tommi hastily shoved a hundred-*króna* note into his hand before Lína worked herself up to telling him to give Baddi the whole wallet.

'Now out you go and enjoy yourself with it,' Tommi said hopefully.

'Thanks, Dad.'

Lína did not reply when Tommi asked about Danni. She ranted and cursed about the meanness of grudging a paltry hundred *krónur* for the blessed boy who wanted to have a good time now and again. The old man buried his face in his hands in the hope that the woman would shut up and that Danni would come home soon to give him some support if everything boiled up; but his most ardent wish was that the drunks would clear off so that he could get some peace to sleep that night.

At around eleven a shrill car horn sounded outside the house. It was Tóti the Ponce in a gigantic old Chrysler. The five friends lurched, drunken and bawling, out of the house. Shoving and pushing, they got into the car, Baddi and Grjóni in front beside Tóti, and Bony in the back between Maggi and Louie. Although Bony seemed self-assured enough, he had been silent all evening and was clearly feeling a bit nervous between these ruffians in the back seat.

It was hot in the car and there was a smell of petrol; the exhaust system was broken and the floor was not sealed; but the thunder of the engine was drowned out by the chatter and music from the hissing, crackling radio.

They drove around the town. Among the scattered and low-built timber houses of the town centre, people's faces gleamed amid the red rear lights of the cars doing the rounds. In Austurstræti an American-style snack-bar had just opened, with a shiny floor, mirrors, a jukebox and girls on rollerskates serving milkshakes and soft drinks from a high bar-counter. It was packed with people waiting to get at the jukebox and the bar, but when Baddi came in with these five leather-clad champions, walking through the place as though he had two revolvers slung round his waist, the other customers drew back. Baddi selected Elvis on the jukebox and then parked one buttock on a high bar-stool and ordered Coca-Cola in English. But there wasn't much action there, so they went back out to the car, and its tyres screeched on the asphalt as they sped away.

At the restaurant of the Hotel Borg the ornate doors opened to men in dinner jackets and girls in party dresses. The Chrysler stopped at the pavement there and the engine boomed and the car horn hooted as the friends discussed their chances of getting in to the bar; but those chances were rather small, as all of them but Bony were on the doorman's blacklist because of improper dress and a remarkable propensity for causing trouble.

So instead they headed for the Winter Garden club in Vatnsmýri. There was rock'n'roll there every weekend. A fleet of cars stood outside. The sound of a heavy beat and bass rhythms pulsated from the building. Outside, and all the way round, there was a kind of country-hop atmosphere: boys fighting, girls screaming, unconscious bodies everywhere and bottles going the rounds.

When the Chrysler appeared it was greeted with shouting and whistling and cheering; it was obvious that the people who got out of the car were no strangers at that place.

Grjóni and Baddi were the leaders. A large group formed around them. 'Hey, man, Baddi boy! Rock'n'roll! Come on in. Here, have a swig, Grjóni!'

Baddi and Grjóni laughed shortly and snapped their fingers, kicked an imaginary ball with a back-heel, jabbed people lightly in the stomach and felt good.

A pack of Camel cigarettes was passed around and one fawning creep was knocked into the gutter with threats of being beaten up if he didn't go to hell; then most of the gang went inside the dance hall.

First they entered a large corridor with a cloakroom, which held no interest for the friends. They turned right into a hall which was divided into two by a partition: on one side there was dancing and on the other side people sat at tables. Hidden under most of the tables were bottles of *brennivín*.

The dance-floor was a teeming mass. The whole building was a teeming mass. 'Steingrímur Ásgeirsson's Dance Band' played on the stage. The band consisted of some jazz and dixieland musicians of various ages. They had been popular for many years, as the bandleader had the sense to change the lead singer at regular intervals to match the latest musical fashion. At present the vocalist was an eighteen-year-old guy from Baddi's circle, Buddy Billó: 'Steingrímur Ásgeirsson's Dance Band with vocalist Böðvar Billó plays for you this evening.'

Buddy was a sensitive singer with a big voice. He had the blues in his veins. He sang 'Love Me Tender' and 'Only You' with such feeling that only the coolest of the toughs could hold back the tears.

When the guys came in, the band was playing 'Blueberry Hill'. The booming rhythm vibrated through the floor and Baddi got in the mood at once. He had to stop and close his eyes for a moment, half-intoxicated with the music. When he opened them again he had a girl on each arm. On one side was his girlfriend Gerða – she was from Hveragerði and was always called HveraGerður; the other was Linda, Maggi Beauty's sister. He led them through the room, across the dance-floor where all the well-groomed dancing partners in white shirts and patent shoes moved aside and greeted Baddi with apprehensive respect. He was about to buy a Coke at the soft-drinks counter, but as he turned round in order to have a quick word with an acquaintance, someone bought the drinks for him and the girls.

When Baddi saw this he raised his eyebrows in surprise. 'Hey! Who did that?'

'A very good-looking boy I've never seen before,' said HveraGerður, putting a cigarette between her red-painted lips. She tried to point out to Baddi the man who was disappearing into the crowd, but failed.

They walked to the nearest table where three plump lads got

up for them at once. Baddi fired off some joke at them, and they fell about laughing.

Baddi fished cigarettes out of the pocket of his leather jacket, turned his Zippo-lighter thoughtfully in his hands, and looked out over the dance hall. He exchanged a thumbs-up greeting with Buddy Billó who was having a quick smoke up on the stage. Then Grjóni and Bony Morony came over to the table. When Gerða saw them approaching, she pointed to Bony with her cigarette, which was smeared with red lipstick, and said that was the guy who had paid for the drinks.

Bony pulled the bottle of gin, which was still half full, out of his jacket and placed it discreetly beneath the table and nodded to Baddi. Baddi looked him up and down and decided he liked the young guy. Grjóni and Bony sat down at the table. Baddi raised his glass to Bony. 'Thanks, boy.'

'That's okay.'

'Hey, listen, do you mind me calling you Bony Morony?'

'No, that's just fine, man.'

'Call me Baddi.'

'Okay, Baddi.'

Baddi's lighter was out of fuel. He leaned over to Linda with the cigarette between his lips and said: 'Match me handsome.'

She held a burning match to his cigarette and he inhaled, then blew a light cloud of smoke in her face and winked. Then he turned back to face Bony. 'You dance great,' he said, and grinned.

'Yeah?'

'Do you like Jerry Lee Lewis?'

'He's real good, man, but actually I think Chuck Berry is the best.'

'Long-distance information/give me Memphis Tennessee.'

'Ahaha.'

HveraGerður had been following the conversation. 'Baddi never wants to dance,' she butted in.

'Hey! Cut the crap, baby! Didn't we dance all night at Maggi and Linda's the other night . . .'

'Yes, but . . .'

'A-reelin' and a-rockin' till the break of dawn!'

'Yes, but I mean, never at dances.'

'Among all these creeps!' Baddi snorted, nodding towards the men on the dance-floor. Then he and Grjóni laughed, very grown-up.

Maggi and Louie stood at the other end of the hall with some young leather-clad giants; they were trying to start a fight by shoving, and thrusting with their elbows, swearing at one another and trying to grab hold of girls who had boyfriends. There were too many of them for anyone to do anything about it. Two louts from this group went over to some girls who were sitting at a table listening to the band; the girls were barely fourteen years old, and one of them was Veiga, the girlfriend of Buddy Billó who was at present singing 'A fool such as I'. The other was her sister. The louts sat down at the table with the girls and passed a few comments, but the girls looked away in annoyance. The louts began to pull at them and push at them to try to get them to react, but the girls seemed to be half-frightened.

These rowdies were called Viðar and Tryggvi, trawler-hands from a small village up-country, fat, puffed-up and muscular. At last Tryggvi grabbed hold of Veiga's wrist. She winced, and he dragged her on to the dance-floor. She looked terrified, but Tryggvi held her tightly round the waist and moved in time to the music.

Baddi saw what was going on and gave Buddy a signal. Buddy stopped abruptly in the middle of the verse 'Pardon me/if I'm sentimental/when we say goodbye'. He climbed off the stage, ran to the middle of the hall and felled Tryggvi with a single punch. Then he took the girls over to Baddi and Grjóni's table and quickly jumped back up on the stage again. It all happened so fast that the band even managed to fill in with the melody, and then Buddy was back at the microphone, continuing a little breathlessly: 'Now and then/there's a fool/such as I.'

The atmosphere was hostile. Thick-headed giants were forming alliances. Maggi and Louie were in the lead, their arms folded across their chests. Baddi, Grjóni and Bony had run out of *brennivín* and had gone to the back door, where they knew they could usually get a bottle from the restaurant manager at blackmarket prices. They found someone who stopped them with a wink and a gesture and brought something out from under his jacket and slipped it to Bony, in exchange for some blue banknotes. The friends lost no time in taking the top off the bottle.

They were all drunk now. They quarrelled and wanted to fight. 'Your mother's a whore!' They went outside. Tóti was staggering and bellowing as usual. A bottle was circulating. A big, well-built lad of about twenty was getting worked up. He stood leaning against a black Opel, shouting abuse. 'Relax, Thórir,' said his friends, as Thórir began to threaten Baddi and Grjóni. 'Stop it, Thórir, come along with us.' But Thórir was drunk, full of divine anger. He talked about his sisters and his daddy with a lump in his throat and pointed at Grjóni. 'It was you! You jerk! And you, too, Baddi! What shits!' 'Stop it, Thórir,' said his friends as Baddi and Grjóni went over to him with their fists clenched. Thórir wanted a fight. 'I'll pulp you!' He looked as though he came from a good family, with a wholesome expression and neatly cut hair, clear and fluent in speech, tall and broad-shouldered – he looked like Cary Grant. Against him were the devils themselves. They let Thórir strike first and then gave him the usual treatment, five or ten seconds of punches and smothered shouts until he lay huddled in the gravel, holding his stomach and trying to catch his breath as the blood seeped into his fair hair; as a parting gift Baddi gave him a full-blooded kick in the backside with his pointed patent shoe.

Back at the main entrance, Bony was getting to work on HveraGerður – hugs and kisses. She was leaning against the wall and had her leg up on a car-bumper. Then they looked inside again. Two hundred men at the door thought it wasn't fair that Baddi and his clique should be allowed to waltz in and out like that. The bouncers said they were friends of the band – they were in there having a chat with the singer and a quick drink. They weren't used to conversing, these giants, and they were so drunk that they gave their vocabulary a rest for the most part. Gestures, snapping fingers, shouts of 'Hey!' and laughter – quick, dry laughter – that was how they communicated for a while, but not a single word was misunderstood.

'Now look here, boy, don't step on my blue suede shoes!'

'Hahaha!'

When the band had finished playing 'Red River Rock' and 'Rebel Rouser', Buddy had to go on stage and sing again. As they parted, Baddi said: 'Hey, that was real tough, man, just jumping down, "A fool such as I" . . . and that's it, bang . . .' He gave up trying to talk, and mimed the rest of the scene when Buddy leapt down from the stage and punched Tryggvi; he was also acting the scene because it was quite certain that Tryggvi and Louie and the other giants who stood there dejectedly watching the conversation from a safe distance knew they were being laughed at.

Later on they all went back to the Old House, Baddi and Grjóni and Bony and HveraGerður and Buddy and Tóti, who was dead drunk, and the giants, in two big cars, shouting and roaring; the police turned a blind eye, even though everyone knew that the drunkest ones were usually behind the wheel. Besides, they were careering along as if they were driving racing cars; they nearly drove through some of the barracks-huts, and one of the old wrecked cars outside Hlynur's place turned ninety degrees as the hot-rods tore past.

They didn't tiptoe into the Old House, even though they knew everyone was asleep. The door was hurled open and the heels of their cowboy boots clattered on the wooden floors. There was much shouting, and Elvis boomed from the loudspeaker. Everything was cleared from the tables, to be replaced by feet and bottles. Bony and Gerða danced, Grjóni looked as if he were falling asleep, the giants ground out their cigarettes on the carpet and clenched their fists; two of them went out to the yard and got up on to the roof of a car and waved their bottles and bellowed until Hreggviður emerged furiously from his barracks-hut doorway and told them to shut up and be quiet in a voice so thunderous that the lights in the bedroom windows of the tower blocks almost all went on at the same time. Hreggviður, black and hairy, had come out in his vest, though his stubble was turning grey and the old shoulder and biceps muscles were sagging. He went on shouting abuse but was calmed down by swigs he was given, and had become quite cheerful by the time he joined the group and went inside the house and into the hubbub in the parlour.

When he saw the shot-putter, Grjóni perked up. 'Hreggi boy, hahaha!' Hreggi smiled and nodded his head and pretended to pay heed to what was said to him, but in reality all his attention was focused on getting as much as possible from as many bottles as possible. His eyes were everywhere as he sneaked around and stretched and gulped down the neat spirit until it trickled from the corners of his mouth.

Everyone in the house was awake. Old Tommi put his trousers on and slipped his braces over his singlet. The old woman got up and Dollí began to chain-smoke cigarettes at her dressing-table, cursing and swearing. She was upset and her hands were shaking and she seemed on the point of bursting into tears because her children couldn't get any sleep. She quarrelled with Grettir who lay in bed half-asleep, trying to get her to put the light out and lie down and relax. But she was so upset that she began to screech at him that she couldn't stand this, she couldn't sta-a-a-and it! Something had to be done about all this, her nerves were in shreds because of this endless commotion in the house and she told Grettir that he had better get up and throw that rabble out. With that he realised that it was wiser to agree with her before she began to turn her words into actions. 'Yup!' said Grettir, 'yup! What a hellish noise! Yup! A person can't get a wink of sleep at night because of them! Drunken idiots!'

Baddi prowled about the house like a prairie wolf, muttering to himself; he tramped up the stairs to have a few words with his sister Dollí, but he didn't dare to go into her room while Grettir was at home: Grettir had rifles and shotguns, and it was best not to fall foul of those. As he went into the kitchen in search of money or food, old Lína came downstairs in her dressing-gown and began to read the cards, and Baddi informed her that she was nothing but a hounddog. 'Jesus!' she exclaimed and crossed herself as she always did when the blessed boy began to speak in tongues.

'Hey, Baddi, do you remember when Hreggviður set the world record? Baddi, come and talk to us,' said a voice from the parlour.

Baddi sat down with Grjóni and Hreggviður.

'Man, do you remember it – Hreggviður Barðason, world champion shot-putter! Ahaha,' they said, slapping Hreggviður on the back and laughing and poking his flab and telling him his stomach muscles were like Floyd Patterson's; Hreggviður just agreed with everything and laughed too and played along with them, for he knew that as long as he said yes he had an unrestricted right to drink all he could lay his hands on – which was a lot. Suddenly his head sagged on to the back of the sofa and he was out for the count. The old champion. Snoring.

The giants were trying to get Buddy Billó into a corner, to teach him some manners, but he escaped from their grasp and got cheeky and told them they were ugly and boring. The giant Viðar was stupid enough to start arguing with Buddy about it, ruining the silent atmosphere of battle there had been in the air.

'Do you think you're any better?'

'Get back to the byre, mutton-head! Go back to the smell of your own shit!' said Buddy. He got byres on the brain along with cunts and arseholes, and Deaf Grjóni started to laugh and the giants were well and truly put down.

Upstairs in the bedroom Baddi stood in the doorway and the old man sat unshaven and low-voiced on the edge of the bed, fingering his watch. 'Do you think you could get some of those people out of here, Baddi dear, it's already . . .'

'Hey big man, hey big daddy . . .' Baddi was so drunk that he had lost all control of speech; he just stood swaying in the doorway, and the glowing cigarette ash fell off the stub and on to the floor.

'Take care with that ash, this is just a timber house,' said Tommi, and as he spoke the words the door opposite flew open and Dollí appeared, shouting and ranting, in the doorway.

'Yes, it would be just like it if the bloody fool were to set fire to the roof over our heads; there's no attempt to show consideration to women and children, he just thinks of himself. You ought to be ashamed of yourself, Baddi, and have the sense to go away, you're causing nothing but trouble and driving people mad, it was so nice and quiet here when you're in America and –'

'Okay, hey! Dollí, relax, woman! Are you crazy? Is there something wrong with your damned cunt or something? You want me to clear off? And where should you go?'

'Where should I go?'

'You should go to the loony bin.'

Baddi had come to the doorway of her room, and he gave a loud dry laugh when she began to wipe the tears from her face. She slammed the door so hard that the house shook; she could be heard screaming at Grettir, who doubtless still lay there indifferent and lazy under the warm duvet.

From downstairs there was the sound of shouting and of things breaking. Out in the hallway Louie and Tryggvi and another lout had got Bony Morony in a corner; he fought and kicked and struggled and the hallway mirror and table got smashed. The giants had Bony in a head-lock and beat him half-unconscious and snatched his wallet which was full of money. Then Baddi and Grjóni jumped in to help Bony.

Old Tommi watched the wild fighting from the stairhead. Bony was on his back but otherwise the giants were in retreat before the kicks and blows administered by Baddi and Grjóni. In the end Tommi had had enough and came down to put a stop to it all; the children in the Old House and the nearby barracks-huts had started to cry, but a clenched fist soon put a stop to the old grocer's attempts to bring peace as he slumped in a dazed heap to the floor.

Now Lína boiled over with fury. She let out a long-drawn-out wail and rushed out of the house. First she went hopping round the yard, yelling and at a gallop, then she set off on an obstacle course around the house, round and round; her hopping became wilder and wilder until she began to dance, beating her palms against her mouth so that her whoops sounded like Red Indians praying for rain. The children howled. Argument raged in the parlour. Hreggviður was on his feet, bouncing off the walls. Dollí yelled from the top of the stairs that they ought to call the police, and Tommi managed to drag himself to his feet and over to the phone. Then Buddy and Grjóni decided to make their getaway, and disappeared in different directions into the darkness.

The telephone had been knocked out of action and Tommi was trying to catch Lína's attention in the middle of her Indian war-dance, but it was hopeless: she just stormed past the door, whooping and galloping, so he decided to go and look for a phone to make a call. He went over to Fía and Tóti's where the housewife was depressed, apparently because her eldest son Gummi had gone out that evening and had not yet come back.

When she saw how Tommi looked she let out a cry of 'Jesus!', but while he was making the phone call she began to complain about how expensive it was to have a telephone nowadays and how high the cost of a call was. When Tommi had finished he bade her a curt goodbye and gave the woman a five-*króna* note in payment, muttering to himself as he went down the stairs that he didn't want a skinflint like that to get the idea that he owed her anything.

When the police arrived only Baddi and Bony and Louie were left, along with Tóti, who lay stretched out on the parlour floor, and Hreggviður the shot-putter who was still ferreting around for some alcohol. He was in such a stupor that he didn't even have the wit to protest when he was hauled out to the police car with the others; they were going to lock all five of them up. At that moment Lína stopped her Indian war-dance and came storming over to the car, and told the guardians of the law to let Baddi go: he hadn't done anything wrong, the blessed boy: he had been so relaxed and content and singing so nicely before those madmen arrived, and just you leave my Baddi alone!

Eventually only three of them were arrested. Gréta, Hreggviður's little wife, came stumbling out of her barracks-hut in her night-dress, took hold of her giant and whacked him and scolded him roundly, and the big policemen watched the woman drag her victim away, pushing him ahead of her through the narrow opening and slamming the door so hard behind her that the barracks-hut rippled as if an earthquake had struck it.

Baddi was the only one left at the party. Then he, too, lost his head completely. He was like a raging bull, breaking things and overturning the furniture; he even took a swing at the old woman, but luckily Danni came in through the door just at that moment after a night out and took Baddi by the scruff of the neck and told him to calm down.

But Baddi didn't want to calm down. He fought and struggled, and Danni had to hoist him up and throw him flat on his back, and put his knee on Baddi's chest. 'Do you give up?'

Baddi wriggled and writhed but couldn't break free, and in the end he had to say that he gave up.

Big Danni probably thought that people always kept their word, and released his grip; but as soon as Baddi was free he jumped to his feet and grabbed a chair and smashed it over his brother's head. Danni sank to the floor, half-stunned.

So Tommi went back to Fía and Tóti's house and rang the police. Again.

When the police arrived Baddi was so out of his mind that he tried to fight them, too, but there were five of them. They put him in handcuffs, and all the neighbours leaned out of their windows and watched as the hero was led out. Dollí walked round the car, chain-smoking in her dressing-gown, and told the police they should put the man straight into the State Prison because he was violent and dangerous to everything around him, and women and children and old people were in dire peril when he was about. Lína was too beside herself to protest; she was utterly distraught, with laddered stockings and her hair sticking out like the bristles of an old tom cat.

The police took Baddi away and the others went back into the house. Grettir had got up at last and was standing in his blue-spotted pyjamas at the head of the stairs, asking what was going on. No one was listening. Dollí and Lína went into the parlour and threw up their hands in horror at the terrible damage which had been done, and then sank into their chairs, utterly exhausted.

*　　*　　*

Tommi and Danni sat at the kitchen table over a cup of coffee.
Tommi looked tired. 'Where have you been, Danni, dear?'

'Just out walking.'

'That's a horribly big bump you've got on your head.'

'It's nothing, Dad.'

'Oh well, then.'

Silence.

'Damn it all,' said the old man, 'this is beginning to happen
every weekend. Maybe not always as bad as this, but this isn't
the first time either . . . bloody hell . . .'

'Yes.'

'You know, it would help me a hell of a lot if you were at home
when things like this happen, I can't manage on my own . . .'

'No, Dad.'

'We ought to know by now that when he starts polishing his
shoes, this kind of thing is brewing up.'

Silence.

'I simply don't understand it. After all, you've never been a
drinker, Danni, no indeed. Perhaps you think everyone goes
completely crazy if he takes a drop; but believe it or not, it
wasn't like that in the old days. I often had a good glass or
two with friends and acquaintances when I was at sea and . . .
well, people were cheerful and laughed and sang and danced and
enjoyed themselves in a civilised way. But now! I mean, it's not
just Baddi and his friends . . . Listen, I can tell you something'
(and here Tommi lowered his voice), 'I went over to the block
where Fía lives to use the telephone, twice I went, and the first
time she told me that her son Gummi was out and that she was
waiting up for him. Well, when I went the second time I noticed
a strange unpleasant smell somewhere when I opened the door
to the hallway downstairs, next to the entry-phone. I turned on
the lights, and would you believe it, that damned fool Gummi
was lying there snoring under the mailboxes, with shit in his
pants! The bloody fool had shit his pants! Don't you think that's
abominable? The damned fellow is in his thirties now and had
brown crap in his pants!'

* * *

In the lockup in the police station there had been fun and games far into the evening, but then the prisoners fell asleep, one after the other. Bony, Louie and Tóti were all fast asleep when Baddi was brought in, but Baddi didn't feel like sleeping. He rattled the bars of the cell and shouted obscenities at the guards and demanded to see a lawyer, the way it always happened on TV shows like *Perry Mason*. Somehow he managed to cajole them into letting him have some cigarettes; with that he calmed down and sat on the bunk and piled the cigarette-ends and half-spent matches on the floor between his feet. Then he got tired of this and lay down on his back, straight and stiff, his feet crossed and his hands behind his neck.

He had drifted off to sleep when he suddenly felt a shove. He looked up and it took him a moment to get his bearings when he saw Deaf Grjóni's grinning face on the bunk next to him.

'Hey, Grjóni boy, what . . . bloody hell!'

They lightly knocked hands together.

'I saw all the cigarette ends there and was wondering if you had a fag.'

Baddi fished out the half-empty packet and showed it to him. 'I'd walk a mile for a Camel!'

Grjóni lit a cigarette, sucked a big mouthful of smoke into his lungs and muttered as he blew it out: 'I had ten cartons just now, but those damned cops stole them from me and put me inside.'

'Oh? What was the trouble, man, why couldn't they leave you alone?'

'They claimed I'd broken into Árni's Store and stolen ten cartons of cigarettes.'

'Well? And what did you say?'

'They talked so damn quiet, those guys, that I couldn't make out a word of what they were saying.'

'Ahaha!'

They talked a bit more and then each lay down on his bunk with feet crossed and hands behind his neck. Silence. Then Baddi called out: 'Grjóni! GRJÓNI! SIGURJÓN, WHAT

THE HELL IS THE MATTER WITH YOU, MAN, ARE YOU DEAF?'

Then they both laughed quietly.

As soon as Lína had recovered from her exertions she began to worry about Baddi. They mustn't lock him up, he was so sensitive and had such delicate nerves. He wouldn't get anything to eat or drink in that dungeon. Those damned policemen were probably beating him up. Danni had fixed the telephone and the old woman rang the police station.

She had the amazing good fortune to get through to her cousin, Inspector Guðlaugur, who was on duty that night. He laughed nervously when she ordered him to release Baddi at once.

'Is that advisable, my dear Lína?'

But as the night wore on he became bored and irritated by the old woman's phone calls. Besides, her threats made him nervous, as he was convinced she had some very close connections with various powers of darkness, so he gave his men orders to let Baddi go. The boy was roused with great difficulty, sleepy and hung-over, and was kicked out into the chill of the morning. He was surly, and hammered for a long time on the door, shouting abuse and demanding to be driven home; he threatened to file a complaint with the United Nations, but they told him to shit his pants and said they would sort him out if he didn't shut up. So the hero had to set off on foot and walk all the way home.

When Baddi finally got there, Tommi was up and ready to go to work after just three hours' sleep. He was having some coffee in the kitchen when the hero came in, exhausted after his walk. They did not exchange a word, for Baddi trudged straight up to his room and threw himself on his bed.

Later that day Bony Morony came to fetch his car, which had been standing in the yard all night; it was the dark red Chevrolet in which they had arrived the day before. Lína thought very highly of this lad and invited him in for coffee at the kitchen table; he told her that the fighting during the night had started when Maggi and some other thugs had tried to steal his wallet, but Sigurjón and Baddi had stopped them.

Old Lína threw up her hands and said she had suspected it all along – those damned policemen were persecuting Baddi without cause. When Bony had left she sent someone down to the shop for a pack of Camels and some Sinalco and specially baked Danish pastries so that the boy would have something to eat and drink when he woke up. Then she put the morning paper in his room: no one was allowed to touch it until he had finished reading it, even if he didn't wake up until suppertime and only skimmed the cinema adverts and said: 'Poof, I saw all those in America when I was staying with Mum!'

Epilogue

There were other sunny days. There was rain. The good years continued. Life went on drawing breath in the camp. Life went on treading its dance in the Old House. Winters came, and the district was like a glossy photograph when the freshly fallen snow lay on the convex lines of the camps. Many felt that snow like this suited the district well, and something like a country idyll took shape there in the barren wilderness: the cars and the wrecks turned into hayricks, and you could almost persuade yourself that the barracks-huts were pretty turf cottages under the snowdrifts. A bit of bah-ing and moo-ing would have completed the picture, and some clanking of milk pails. But sometimes there was silence. You might hear nothing but singing and drunken clamour from Hreggviður's barracks-hut, or long-drawn-out laughter from Sæunn's barracks-hut. Perhaps sobbing. Perhaps laughter. Baddi's rock'n'roll music. Coughing. Or snoring.

There were spring rains which melted the snow, and autumn frosts which froze the slush. And so it went on, over and over again, like the generations which came and went in the story of the family, a story whose beginning no one knew and which perhaps would never end.

Now and then you heard voices from the tower blocks – loud voices complaining about coal-smoke and strife; most people knew that it was the artists who had led the way in sending a petition to the city council, which was asked to rid honest taxpayers of the barracks rabble. These complaints aroused much sympathy in the council chambers.

The last days of Camp Thule seemed to be fast approaching.

But if this narrative began with Karolína the fortune-teller, it does not really end here.

A long, long time later the author of Icelandic patriotic plays came knocking at her door; it was the man who had once gone to the Old House along with the treasurer of the National Theatre to complain about coal-smoke and vandalism. He hadn't forgotten Lína. Year after year she materialised before him, sleeping or waking, not least during difficult hangover depressions or when his plays, which the newspapers said were becoming ever thinner concoctions, were booed off the stage by the dinner-jacketed first-night audiences. He knew all too well why he was failing: he lacked courage, he always squandered his best opportunities through cowardice. Like now: having an ancient, oracular undiscovered sibyl in a nearby house, without interviewing her about everything she knew. 'If I talk to the old woman,' thought the playwright, 'I'll have enough material to set the whole of Scandinavia by its ears.'

But there was always something which held him back. The district wasn't exactly welcoming; there was also the fact that the police often came to that house – sometimes a fleet of cars with a posse of policemen to combat drunken delinquents driving thundering cars to the accompaniment of blaring music.

All the same, he went there at last; he plucked up the courage a quarter of a century after he had first gone to the Old House to complain. A lot of water had flowed under the bridge by then: one of the playwright's deadly serious tragedies had just been laughed off the stage, the Old House had been torn down and light and easily portable tape-recorders had become commonplace. With one of these in a brown school satchel, he went off to meet the old woman in the New Cottage.

There were to be many visits. The playwright never succeeded in setting Scandinavia by its ears, but the tapes still exist, and on one of them there is the following conversation:

Q: Did your parents have premonitory dreams?

Lína: Eh?

Q: Can you remember if your parents had premonitory dreams?

Lína: Premo– what?

Q: Pre-mon-it-ory.

Lína: I don't know anything about that. What sort of monitory might that be?

Q: Premonitory dreams . . . er . . . that . . .

Lína: Of course, people dreamed a lot in the old days.

Q: Well, did your parents have prophetic dreams?

Lína: Yes, they dreamed. My late father was damn . . . was quite psychic, but he kept it a secret, more or less. For example, when he used to take us children out for walks – because there was no village then, nothing really, we lived at Gufunes, tut-tut-tut, now that was something – anyway, he would be out for a walk with us children and he would say: 'There will be changes here, something big and powerful, a factory and smoke and something to make the grass grow but all around there will be dirt and pollution.' We children, or girls – we would laugh, heh-heh! What on earth could it be? . . . 'Oh yes!' he'd say, 'mark my words: although I won't be alive then – mark my words.' We just laughed at it, but how did it turn out? Isn't there a fertiliser plant there now? And rubbish dumps across the whole area? And now they even want to bury people there! I wouldn't fancy that, tut-tut-tut, in that muckheap, no thank you! Yes, there were a lot of things like that. Eh? Don't you think it's strange?

Q: Er, yes . . .

Lína: *Eh?*

Q: Yes, very . . .

Lína: *What d'you say?*

Q: Extremely . . .

Lína: Yes.

Q: I'd like to ask you if there were any ghosts in the area where you grew up at Gufunes?

Lína: *Wha-a-a-t?*

Q: Were you much aware of inexplicable things at Gufunes?

Lína: Now, look, it's all that Gufunes business which the character-assassins are trying to pin on me now, I've never liked that. The fact is that Dad was not a poor man; on the contrary, he owned a shipyard, but Éggvan the Faroese cheated him out of his property. Éggvan the Faroese swindled him of everything. Nothing was put down in writing in those days, your word was your bond. I wasn't born then, but I think they'd been playing poker and Éggvan swindled my dear late father of everything, and he had no choice but to end up in Gufunes. Yes! That's how it was, you see. But then I got out of the place with my dear late mother, but she had gangrene in her gut by then, tut-tut-tut, and well . . . Well, for example, we never ate anything but fish-boilings. Do you know what fish-boilings are? No, you're too young . . .

Q: Yes . . . I . . .

Lína: Fish-boilings, see, you take the bones and the fins and the tail and all the inedible parts of the fish, and then it's all ground up and mixed together and that's all we had to eat . . .

Q: I imagine it must have been rather unappetising, er . . .

Lína: It was revolting! Anyway, what was I saying? Yes, well, then there was an outbreak of typhoid and the Chief Medical Officer ordered our house be burned down, so then we had nowhere to live except in a mound which had been hollowed out as a cave and was used for storing potatoes; but it was a fairy mound and there were Hidden Folk* living in it.

Q: Really?

Lína: Sometimes we heard someone shouting 'Borg!' and the shout would echo and then someone also shouted for my late mother, but when we rushed outside, no no no, there was no one there shouting. Don't you think that rather strange? Don't you think it rather peculiar?

That was what everything was like there. There were cockroaches and millipedes and all kinds of creepy-crawlies living in the cave

---

* The 'Hidden Folk' (*huldufólk*) were the elves in Icelandic folklore. They lived in rocks and mounds, and looked and behaved just like ordinary mortals – they farmed and fished, and had their own churches. They were usually invisible to human beings, but could manifest themselves whenever they wished.

in the mound and swarming over us at night, and the whole place was filthy!

Q: Doesn't Icelandic folklore say that a dirty man is always rich?

Lína: Eh? Do you think so? Well, my late father was an awful slob and always looked like he lived on a dungheap, and what was he? Was he rich? Perhaps you think so, but Éggvan the Faroese stole everything he owned and my late father didn't even have enough to cover his arse. And then my grandson there, over there, the one in the picture, Baddi, every so often he would get together with Siggi the Faroese, but I said *no*! No Faroese are coming into my house, they . . .

Q: Er, about the Hidden Folk – were you much aware of them? . . .

Lína: Ye-e-e-s! Those dear Hidden Folk. I hope there are lots of them all around me now; but later, when I went to the cave again, to the side where no digging had been done and the Hidden Folk lived – this was after I and my late mother and my late sisters had moved away and were living in Urðarstigur – I dreamed then that I was in the hallway, it seemed to be all trodden down, like the hallway here, tut-tut, oh, I knew that cave all right! It so happened that my daughter, Gógó, whom I had with Arnkell, the damned wretch, then it was put to the test, ha! . . . That stupid boy, he's dead now, I don't know whether it's because I put a curse on him or because Brynjólfur and his wife Kristín sent him to England to make a tailor of him, but then the war came and I couldn't follow him abroad and he went off on the *Flora*, I think, the ship was the *Flora*, I think, and it was sunk, but he survived, he a-a-always landed on his feet, the damned blabbermouth, tut-tut. But I'd done nothing about getting maintenance from the bloody fool for the girl, Gógó. Then I dreamt, just before Christmas, the last year Mother was alive – I dreamt that I'd gone into the Hidden Folk's mound. I just seemed to go there on foot, and walked straight in, and then I came to a room, there were beams and rafters on the ceiling like there were in the old days, and there was a parlour and the window turned like this, and there was a girl, and I began to ask her if she knew anything of Arnkell. She had just come from abroad, and no-o-o, she hadn't come across him. And then she asked me, 'Would you like me to make him come?' I said yes. So she went over to the cupboard which stood in the corner, not a very high cupboard, and she took two eggs out of it, shaped like Easter eggs. She tapped them together (tap, tap), and said he would be coming soon. Hmm, I thought, well, no way. I hadn't left anything at the door when I went in, although I had heard, when awake, that if you go to see the Hidden Folk you should always leave something at the door so that you can get out. But I got straight out, and what happened then? My late mother said I should take notice of the dream. And what happened? Mother died, and I would take the girls out to the cemetery, for she lies buried in the cemetery here, not out at that rubbish tip – and then I bumped into Arnkell in the street! Yes! I ignored him, of course, but then I pulled myself together, I can tell you, and went to the police and put in a claim for maintenance.

And so you see, it was all very strange, wasn't it? Eh? Don't you think it strange? He hadn't been meaning to come to Iceland, he said – he was on his way to Holland, he said, but he couldn't get any peace of mind, and felt driven to go to Iceland, but it was only so that I could get him into my power.

But he's dead now. He ended up in Istanbul. He has to answer for himself now – like everyone else. Ahahaha!

Q: Quite!

Lína: Don't you think it strange?

Q: Very peculiar.

Lína: Don't you find it mysterious?

Q: Absolutely! Certainly!

Silence.

Q: But, um, I wanted to ask you in a little more detail, since you've mentioned that you had put the 'fluence on Arnkell, somehow or other – was there much of that sort of thing among people in your family . . . any runesters, for example?

Lína: *Whaaaat?*

Q: Runesters.

Lína: Rhymesters?

Q: Yes . . . whatever they might have been called.

Lína: No one ever wrote rhymes in my family, except perhaps for him over there in the picture, my grandson. I brought him up, he was an airman but he's dead now, bless him . . . he wrote a few very sad verses, the poor darling. And now and again I've cobbled a few lines together against individuals, like that president of ours – that damned fool, he should never have been . . . But I've stopped all that now, I'm not in the habit any more, no no no. I don't need it any more.

Q: Yes. Hmm. Yes. Karolína, I assume there have been many changes in your lifetime?

Lína: Since the old days?

Q: Er . . . yes.

Lína: Yes, you can say that, thank goodness. For example I can tell you that in the old days there was never any money! Haaa! Life wasn't much fun, I can tell you! Tut!

Q: Mmm – a lot of hard times . . .

Lína: Yes, there was never any money, not what I'd call money. But I don't want to say any more about that, it's just ghosts from the past.

Q: But were . . . ?

Lína: I can tell you, for example, that my late father could hardly ever afford tobacco, proper tobacco that is, and just had to go without and make do with chewing tarred rope and creosoted sail cord; he also had to use rotten wood dust and all kinds of rubbish instead of snuff, and we children sometimes had to make it for him. The damned man . . . The way he treated Mother. Tut-tut-tut.

Q: But, er, Karolína, you said, or it actually became clear earlier, that you could be 'spiritually hot', as it were.

Lína: *Wha-a-at?*

Q: Yes, there were indications that you could be 'spiritually hot'.

Lína: That I could be prayerfully hot?

Q: No, spiritually hot!

Lína: Well, what do you mean by that?

Q: Well, that . . . that, er, that you could make things happen.

Lína: Yes.

Q: Was it a family thing?

Lína: Well, my family were pretty steeped in occult matters, heh heh heh! But, of course, people believed in a lot of nonsense and rubbish in the old days. Take doctors, for example – people didn't always have money for a doctor when they needed one, and then things were done under the counter by people who didn't know anything . . . and there were . . . well, for example, when my late mother got gangrene in the stomach and I ended up having to move here with her and my sisters – although my brother Gummi and that idiot of a father didn't come, may they never be forgiven! We had no house to go to, but out there in the country there were no doctors and no pills, we were just told to take live rove-beatles and put them on the sore place, as they would eat all the infected parts. In Mother's case, she was given ash from burnt excrement and dust from dried excrement, and pepper, and ash from burnt human hair, and they killed Mother [*choking sound*]. Damned . . . tut-tut.

Q: But, er . . .

Lína: Yes, those were the remedies. One also had to clean wounds with human urine and tobacco ash and warm sheep's bile. And they gave her – a mortally ill woman – chewing-tobacco boiled with pepper in *brennivín*; in fact she was always deathly pale, also when she was being given sulphur . . . the damned pack of shits . . .

Silence.

Q: But when you came to the city, had you begun to tell people's fortunes?

Lína: No no no, I was just a teenager then, and all I wanted was to get a job, but there was such a housing shortage and Mother was so ill and I had the little girl . . .

Q: And . . .

Lína: . . . and something had to be done. Well, there were us three sisters; and dear dead Hugrún, the eldest, she could do practically anything, and she saw a lot of things other people never see. But she moved to Norway, and she's very well known there. She could borrow something from you, and then she could speak through you! Don't you think that's strange? Isn't it remarkable, what I'm telling you? There were a lot of things like that, really . . . I've told you already how I dreamed about a house I could get, and that can be verified, but then dear Mummy died and my dear dead sister Gíslína left four children and I had to look after them . . .

Q: And how many children of your own did you have?

Lína: Well, I had my daughter Gógó and that was all. But I and my late husband, Tómas, such a proper and lovable man . . . we brought up all those children and then Gógó's kids, and then I had Dollí's children, there in the picture, with that undersized little . . . I just call her Dollí, though her real name is Dóróthea. So as you can see, I always had plenty of children around me. Yes, don't you find that . . . ?

Q: Mmm, I haven't much time left, but finally for now I want to ask you if there was much religion in your childhood?

Lína: W-e-e-ll, not really, there was no church there then, but nowadays I often go to funerals conducted by Óli Óla, and others around here.

Q: But what about prayers, can you remember any prayers which . . .

Lína: Yes, there was the Lord's Prayer, of course, and my late father sometimes chanted:

An angel met me on my way to school,
He had horns in his cheeks and gored me like a bull.
May God's guardians watch over me well.
Amen